A
STORM
OF SMOKE
AND
FLAME

ALSO BY MARION BLACKWOOD

Marion Blackwood has written lots of books across multiple series, and new books are constantly added to her catalogue. To see the most recently updated list of books, please visit: www.marionblackwood.com

CONTENT WARNINGS

The Oncoming Storm series contains quite a lot of violence and morally questionable actions. If you have specific triggers, you can find the full list of content warnings at: www.marionblackwood.com/content-warnings

A STORM OF
SMOKE AND FLAME

THE ONCOMING STORM: BOOK THREE

MARION BLACKWOOD

First edition

ISBN 978-91-986386-4-6 (hardcover)
ISBN 978-91-986386-3-9 (paperback)
ISBN 978-91-986386-2-2 (ebook)

Editing by Julia Gibbs
Book cover design by ebooklaunch.com

www.marionblackwood.com

For family, by blood and by choice

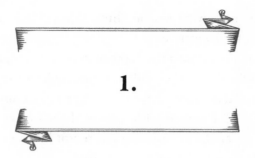

1.

A sharp blade pressed against my neck. I froze. Blood pounded in my veins beneath the cold kiss of steel.

"If I hadn't turned down the contract offered by the Builders' Guild, you'd be dead right now." The sword left my throat. "Lucky you."

"Shade." I blew out an exasperated chuckle. "Always a pleasure."

A late summer wind blew its warm breeze across the rooftops as I rose and turned to face the Master of the Assassins' Guild. Red and orange streaks from the setting sun painted the city in colorful hues all around us. I let my stiletto blade disappear back into my sleeve as I studied the assassin through narrowed eyes.

"The Builders' Guild wanted to put a hit on me?" I frowned. "Why?"

Shade tilted his head slightly to the right. "You did assassinate their Guild Master, remember?"

"Well, yeah, but no one's supposed to know that. How the hell did they find out?"

"Don't know. But when I turned down the contract I told them it was because I knew you hadn't done it so there'd be no point in carrying it out." He offered me a light shrug. "They seemed to take my word for it."

I lifted my eyebrows at him. Huh. That had been uncharacteristically generous.

When Shade noticed the expression on my face, he cracked a lopsided grin. "Also, they didn't pay enough. If they'd offered more money, I'd definitely have taken the contract anyway."

"Obviously," I replied with a short shake of my head. "So, what do you want? I'm assuming you're not just here to tell me the Builders' Guild is stingy with money."

For a moment, the Master Assassin just leaned his shoulder against the brick face of the chimney and regarded me with that soul-penetrating gaze of his. Below us, the chatter of people moving around the Merchants' Quarter mingled with the distant squawk of seagulls. After he had let the silence stretch a while longer, Shade uncrossed his arms and straightened.

"I am here to offer you your deepest desire."

Surprised laughter erupted from my chest before I managed to slap a hand over my mouth. Well, hadn't that been an unexpected statement? Especially coming from him.

"That right?" I replied once I'd let my arm drop back down. "And what would that be?"

He gave me a quick rise and fall of his eyebrows. "Come with me and you'll find out."

"As a matter of fact, I can actually tell when I'm being set up for a sales pitch, you know."

Shade's black eyes glittered in the golden light. "Fair enough. But aren't you curious what I'm selling?"

I was. Very curious, in fact. Usually when he wanted something from me, he blackmailed me or manipulated me into doing it for him, but not this time. This time, it seemed as though he wanted me to agree to it willingly. How odd. I wondered what had changed.

However, before I could open my mouth to voice any of that out loud, he simply cracked another lopsided smile, turned, and strode away while leaving me there to decide what my next move would be. Blowing out a noisy breath, I threw my hands in the air and stalked after him. Curiosity hadn't killed anyone. Well, maybe some people. But not me, I hoped.

We jogged along the Thieves' Highway in comfortable silence before climbing down the side of a dressmaker's shop at the expensive end of the Merchants' Quarter. People from all steps of the social ladder bustled past us, trying to finish their afternoon activities before darkness blanketed the city.

"You have a lot of enemies," Shade suddenly stated.

A group of seamstresses carrying bundles of colorful fabric blocked the way so I had to weave through them before I could turn back towards the assassin. "Well, yeah, so do you." I frowned at him. "What's your point?"

"Yeah, I have enemies too," Shade confirmed before leveling piercing eyes on me. "But very few of them dare come at me. The point is, *you* are not powerful enough to make your enemies leave you alone."

Not powerful enough, huh? And yet, here I was. Still alive after everything they'd tried to bring me down. A smirk spread across my face. "Let them come."

Shade released a pleasant chuckle and shook his head just as the hulking shape of the Silver Keep became visible in the distance. Its white marble walls gleamed in the afternoon light. A sense of déjà vu flashed through me. Now that I thought about it, I realized that all my most recent adventures had begun with a meeting at the royal palace. Goosebumps prickled my skin. *This is how it starts.*

Not wanting to show the Master Assassin just how curious I was about this deepest desire of mine that was apparently located in the Silver Keep, I simply continued following him through the silver-speckled passageways in silence. The doors to King Edward's study had been left gaping so we both slid through the opening without knocking.

"Ah, you're back." The young king looked up from his messy desk and gave us a bright smile. "Perfect."

"Good to see you," I said with a nod.

It felt a bit inadequate after everything we'd survived together at the beginning of summer, but making conversation wasn't exactly my strong suit, so it was the best I could do.

"And you," he replied before motioning at the two chairs in front of the desk. "Please, have a seat." After I'd dropped into the empty one next to Shade, King Edward continued. "I, well, *we*, have a proposition for you."

"Yes, I was promised my deepest desire," I said with a glance at the assassin next to me.

King Edward chuckled. "Yes, Shade seems to think so at least." He cleared his throat. "At the end of the week, that tall ship in the harbor will leave for Pernula. How would you like to be on it?"

I sat back and blinked at him. How would I like to be on it? I knew they'd been getting ready all summer to send a ship across the wild sea and I had spent many a night trying to figure out how to manipulate events so that I would be on it as well. But my scheming had been quite unsuccessful. Or so I'd thought.

A wide grin threatened to appear on my face so I ran a hand across my chin to wipe it off. "What's in it for me?" I said instead.

Shade whipped his head towards me and drew his eyebrows down. "Oh, shut up. Of course she's in," he said and cast a quick look at King Edward before turning back to me. "Being on the first ship to the continent? There's no way you'd pass that up. And as if that wasn't enough, the Fahr brothers vowed to come back and kill you, so going after them first is in your self-interest." He looked me up and down. "And if there's one thing I know about you, it's that you do whatever it takes to survive."

My mouth was left open without producing any sound. After William and Eric Fahr had left with the Pernulans a few months ago, I'd been getting ready to go after them so I could end the threat to me and those I care about before it got started again. I'd even started learning Pernish. Hmmph. Shade had calculated the situation exactly right. Damn him for seeing right through me.

The excited smile I'd tried to hide earlier settled on my lips. "Yeah, alright." I let out a small sigh and shook my head at the Master Assassin before turning to the black-eyed king. "I would love to be on that ship."

King Edward matched my smile and gave me a nod. "It's decided then." He leaned back in his chair. "For the operation we have in mind, we need a small team with a very specific skillset and Shade suggested that you would be a perfect addition to it."

"Did he now?" I said and raised my eyebrows at the suddenly very flustered-looking assassin.

The young king suppressed a chuckle. "Can I assume Liam will be joining as well?"

I nodded. "Yeah, there's no way I'll be able to talk him out of it."

"Good. From what I've been told, he possesses charm that..." He cleared his throat. "...*other people* in our elite team lack. And it saves me from having to send an unknown to fill that position. I need people I can trust for this mission."

My eyebrows shot up. "You trust *me*?"

Edward cocked his head slightly to the right. "Oddly enough, yes, I think I do."

The King of Keutunan trusted me? Huh. Did so not see that coming. I wasn't even sure *I* trusted me.

A metallic ringing echoed through the room. King Edward whipped his head towards the large clock by the wall. Scrolls sailed through the air and landed on the floor in a rustle of paper as he flew up from the chair. We both stared at him in surprise.

"By all the gods, the Council of Lords!" He rounded the desk and marched towards the doors. "I forgot about the special meeting I called. Shade, fill her in on the rest and then see if you can find us that last recruit."

"Will do," Shade replied but Edward was already gone.

Turning my head, I looked between the assassin and the empty doorway. Shade pushed off from the chair and smirked at me.

"Told you you'd get your heart's deepest desire."

I snorted. "Uh-huh."

"Come on, your first assignment as a member of this team starts now." Without waiting for a reply, he strode towards the door.

After an irritated shake of my head, I followed. Well, to be fair, I might've been annoyed that he was once again ordering me around, but nothing could dim the excitement sparkling in my chest. I would be on the first boat to Pernula. There was no telling what extraordinary wonders we might find there. This was what I'd been waiting for. I grinned to myself as I caught up with Shade in the corridor. Adventure lay waiting for me in the land beyond the horizon – and I was so ready to meet it.

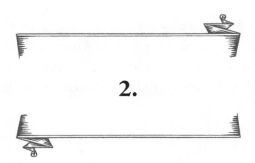

2.

"Should I be worried?"

Shade's face was an unreadable mask. "Always."

The dark door leading down to the dungeons loomed before us. I watched it warily as the Assassins' Guild Master pulled it open and motioned for me to step through. He wouldn't lock me in there, I was almost certain of that. Almost. Blowing out an exasperated breath, I stalked across the threshold. He might not have manipulated me this time but these mind games he played weren't much better.

Cold air met me as I descended the stairs but it wasn't the chill that made me shiver. I'd been in these cells below the Silver Keep before, when King Adrian had imprisoned me here. Drawing a lungful of stale air, I pushed out the memory.

"What are we doing here?" I asked as we got to the bottom of the staircase.

"We're finishing up our recruitment." He reached for the torch on the wall. "I already know what I think but a second opinion can't hurt."

"A second opinion on what?"

Shade passed the burning stick to me. "Pick out the most desperate person in here. The man who will do just about anything to get his freedom back."

I raised my eyebrows at him for a moment but then gave him a slow nod and started towards the first cell. Shade remained by the stairwell. The dungeon was as damp and miserable as I remembered but it was nothing compared to its occupants. Moving the torch closer to the iron bars, I studied the first prisoner. A Pernulan man hunkered against the back wall. His pale eyes flicked up before squinting against the sudden light. I watched him for a few more seconds before continuing to the next one.

When I had analyzed each person locked behind the bars in the narrow corridor, I turned back to Shade. "They're all Pernulans," I stated.

"Yes, they are," the assassin replied from the other side of the hall. "They're the ones who survived the battle but didn't make it onto the ships. So, which one?"

I moved back to the third cell from the stairs. The torch hissed beside me as I raised it and angled it so that the fire illuminated the space inside the bars. "This one."

Shade pushed off from the wall and joined me. He nodded at the figure in the corner. "Him?"

The prisoner's dark eyes darted between us. I blew out a soft chuckle and shook my head. "*Her.*"

The tall assassin raised his eyebrows at me, but when I nodded in confirmation, he let them fall back down and inclined his head. "Come with me." He started back up the stairs.

After one last look at the woman in the damp cell, I followed him. A Silver Cloak met us as we emerged from the dungeon and snapped to attention when he saw Shade.

"The prisoner in cell three, bring her to the battlements on the south side."

"Her?" the guard asked, surprise coloring his voice. When Shade only nodded, he went on. "Right away."

We started in the other direction as the guard made for the stairs. Shade led us through a series of empty hallways until I couldn't keep my curiosity in check any longer.

"Why are we still hiding in back corridors?" I asked as we climbed a narrow staircase. "After that stunt in the throne room with the Pernulans, all the nobles already know that you and King Edward work together."

"True," he said as we reached the top. "But getting them to accept that their king has an assassin as his advisor has been difficult enough without adding more shady people to the mix." He pushed down the handle of a metal door. Afternoon sunlight spilled through. "*I* am not hiding in servants' corridors, *you* are."

"Hmmph," I muttered and followed him out on the parapet.

Dark red and purple shadows fell across the city. Night was only a few moments out. I put a hand to the stone wall and gazed towards the distant harbor and the tall ship the Pernulans had left behind. Abandoning that boat and all the navigation charts and tools it contained would cost them dearly. I had no doubt Shade had already made one of the unfortunate souls trapped below sing like a bird until he knew exactly how to use them, which made me wonder what we needed this final recruit for.

"So, did we pick the same one?" I asked and nodded towards the approaching Silver Cloak and his prisoner.

"We did."

"But you didn't know she was a woman?"

Shade glanced at me from the corner of his eye. "No."

Ha! Beating the arrogant Master Assassin at his own game never got old. However, I refrained from pointing that out to said assassin because the royal guard had arrived with the Pernulan. He let go of her arm and retreated a respectful distance away, his silver cloak billowing behind him.

"What's your name?" Shade asked.

She cast suspicious looks between us while her shackled hands stayed in front of her.

"You do know how to speak the tongue of the elves, don't you?" the assassin pressed on.

Watching her, I could understand why Shade had assumed she was a man. In a way, at least. She wore her dark hair tied back in a bun the way men did and her clothes hid her figure well. However, as someone who had masqueraded as a member of the opposite sex on more than one occasion, I could see past that. Beneath the dirt and grim, I had a feeling that she might even be rather striking. Her dark eyes were filled with distrust as she moved them between me and the now very impatient-looking assassin.

Shade produced a knife from somewhere in his sleeve. "It's in your best interest to answer."

It was so nice to watch someone other than me be on the receiving end of his thinly veiled threats for once.

"Zaina," the woman said at last.

"Zaina?" the Assassins' Guild Master repeated. "Do you see that ship in the harbor, Zaina?"

Turning her head, she squinted at the horizon before nodding. "It's one of ours."

"Do you know how to sail it?" Shade asked and we both watched her nod in reply again. "Would you be able to find your way back to your country if you had that ship and the equipment in it?"

She paused for a moment and furrowed her brows at the black-eyed assassin. Mistrust swirled around in her own dark eyes. "Yes," she finally said.

A calculating smile spread across Shade's lips. "Excellent. How would you like to get your freedom back?"

"In exchange for what?"

"Assistance. We want you to get us to Pernula without anyone noticing, help us with our mission, and then sail us back."

Zaina narrowed her eyes at us. "What mission?"

"We're going to force a peace treaty between our countries." Shade shrugged. "And kill a couple of our lords who fled there. Help us with that and you're free to continue your life doing... whatever it is that you do."

The Pernish prisoner fell silent as she considered the proposition. Wind whipped across the walkway, loosening strands of matted hair from her bun. She turned calculating eyes on us. "What's to stop me from just leading you into a deserted alley and slitting your throats once we get there?"

I snorted. "Come try it. I promise, it won't end well for you."

Shade arched an eyebrow at me but then just motioned lazily in my direction as if to say: *what she said*.

It was a real risk, of course. But between the Master of the Assassins' Guild, me, and whoever else they'd recruited for this mission, she would have a hard time accomplishing something like that.

Zaina cocked her head and studied us until a mask of blazing conviction slammed onto her face. "I'll do it. I'll get you there, help you out, and get you back again. And then, you leave me alone."

"Done." Shade nodded at the determined woman before motioning for the Silver Cloak to approach again. "Get her settled in a room, a real room, where she can clean up and get ready," he said to the guard before turning back to Zaina. "I'll come by later so we can hash out the details."

Both the royal guard and the Pernish prisoner nodded before disappearing back the way they had come. That had gone well. As expected. Leave it to a thief and an assassin to recognize the truly desperate. When I saw her in that cell, Zaina's eyes had screamed of it. She would do what we wanted.

"So, who else is coming on this little trip?" I asked and turned to the deadly Guild Master.

He flashed a knowing grin. "You'll see." I opened my mouth to protest his unsatisfactory answer but before I could do that, he held up a hand. "I'm sure you have lots to attend to before we leave. I do too. So, I'll leave you to it." He started towards the door. "See you at the end of the week. First light. Don't be late!" he called just before the door swung shut behind him.

Crossing my arms, I shook my head at the now closed door. Damn assassin and his damn secrets. Why couldn't he just tell me who else was coming? I turned towards the harbor. Candles flickered in the windows across the city. Tiny pools of light breaking up the darkness that had fallen. If I strained my eyes, I could still make out the tall ship in the bay.

What a turn this day had taken. In only a few days' time, I would be on that boat, riding the waves towards an entirely new land. I couldn't wait to tell Liam about this. And then I'd have to talk to the Guild Masters. And the elves. And get everything ready. Shade had been right; I did have a lot to do.

An excited grin stole across my mouth once more while giddy excitement thrummed through my body. I started towards the stairs. The time had come for another adventure.

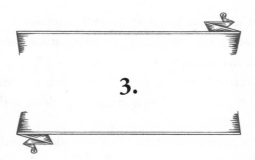

3.

Brisk winds snatched at my clothes as Liam and I walked across the pier in the gray morning light. I took a deep breath of salty sea air.

"I can't believe we're actually doing this," Liam said.

I chuckled. "Yeah, me neither."

Shade stood in front of a rowboat at the edge of the dock. Gusts ruffled his black hair. "Storm. Liam," he said once we'd arrived. "You can drop your packs in here." He motioned at the small boat where his own backpack lay waiting.

After we'd placed ours next to his, I glanced around the empty harbor. "So, where's the rest of this elite team?"

"On their way."

Wood creaked under my feet as I paced restlessly back and forth across the planks. Saying goodbye to Bones and the elves had been rough, so my excitement was now mingled with sadness. But I would see them again. Soon. Or at least, I hoped so. When living the kind of life I did, nothing was ever certain.

"Wait, is that...?" I began as I noticed three tall figures striding towards us.

"Yep."

I stared in open-mouthed shock as some people I knew very well joined us by the rowboat. Liam beamed next to me.

"What the hell are you doing here?" I exclaimed.

"Shut up, it's not up to you," Elaran muttered and dumped his backpack in the rowboat.

"Hey, Storm! Surprised to see us?" Haela grinned at me as she grabbed her brother's bag and threw it, along with her own, on top of the others.

Haemir clapped a hand on Liam's shoulder. "Did you really think we'd let you leave without us?"

Confusion mixed with a lot of relief swirled around inside me. I hadn't realized how glad I was that they were coming until I'd seen them march across that pier.

"Why didn't you tell me you were coming too?" I gave Haela's shoulder a push. "I said goodbye to you just the other day, for Nemanan's sake!"

Mischief sparkled in her yellow eyes. "I know. And it was so sweet to see how teary you got." She grinned at the curse I grumbled in response to that. "But we wanted to keep it a secret."

"Why is everyone so fond of these bloody secrets?" I muttered and cast an annoyed glance at Shade. "Who else is coming? Any more surprises I should know about?"

The Master Assassin shook his head. "Nope, this is it."

I drew back and frowned at him. "What do you mean *this is it*? The six of us are gonna take on an entire nation on our own? Why aren't you bringing like half of your assassins? Won't we need them?"

"No, we won't." He stopped my protest with a raised hand. "Because we can't send an entire army. This whole mission depends on stealth. And besides, we need different kinds of people. Everything my assassins can do, I can also do." A smirk spread across his lips. "I can do it better too."

Elaran studied Shade through narrowed eyes but before he could interrupt, I pressed on. "So, what do we represent then? If we're supposed to be different kinds of people."

"King Edward and Queen Faye had a meeting about this a while back and they decided that the six of us would complement each other pretty nicely. Meet killing," he said and motioned at himself before pointing to me and then Liam in turn, "stealing, and charming." His hand moved to Elaran. "And here you have strategizing," he said before continuing towards Haela and then Haemir, "spontaneous improvising, and last but not least, careful consideration."

My eyebrows almost reached my hairline. "I'm sorry, what?" I whipped my head from person to person. "Tell me I'm not the only one who finds this weird."

"It's weird," Haemir confirmed while Liam backed me up with a nod.

I threw my arms out. "See!"

Elaran pushed past me and started towards the rowboat. "It doesn't matter if we like it or not, the Queen said to go, so we're going. Now, let's get a move on."

Shade studied the grumpy elf while that unreadable mask of his settled on his face. Haela offered a shrug and pulled her brother towards the boat as well. Liam gave me an encouraging smile.

While I watched them all climb into the rowboat, I shook my head with an incredulous look on my face. What were they thinking? I didn't care that two monarchs had decided that this was the best plan. It would never work. I understood that we couldn't exactly send an army because that would contradict the whole point of a peace treaty. But six people? And *these* six people? I shook my head again.

"Right, okay, let's send six misfits to take down a nation. Sure. Piece of cake," I muttered.

"Seven," Shade said. When I only frowned at him, he clarified. "There are seven of us. Don't forget Zaina. She's going to do a lot more than just sail the ship. Can't set out on a mission in a foreign land without someone who can navigate the language and culture."

"Good point." I blew out something between a sigh and a chuckle. "Still, seven people against an empire?"

The Master Assassin gave me a lopsided smile. "Aren't you glad you came?"

He jumped into the boat, leaving me the only person still standing on the pier. I shook my head at him. This was insane. We would surely get ourselves killed on this mission. I glanced between the auburn-haired ranger and the black-clad assassin who seemed to be hitting it off about as well as flame and gunpowder. Or maybe we'd kill each other first. But then again, we had survived crazy shit before. What was one more dance with Lady Luck?

After sending a quick prayer to Cadentia the Goddess of Luck herself, I stepped into the waiting rowboat. Fire and doom might await us in the land across the sea, and though I had a very healthy sense of self-preservation, I was also way too curious to pass it up. I would just have to see what else life had in store for me. A grin spread across my face as we moved out. This was going to be fun.

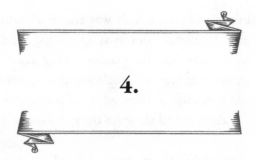

4.

F un was not the word I should have used. At all. Apparently, getting seasick is a thing. I didn't know that, but I had found out pretty quickly and then spent most of the journey emptying the contents of my stomach over the railing. Not quite the glorious way of riding the waves to adventure that I had imagined.

"Land ho!" a sailor suddenly called from the mast above me.

Land? A bubbling sensation spread through my stomach, and this time I was pretty sure it wasn't because of the rolling ship. I squinted at the horizon. If he said we were close to the coast then we probably were, but in the dark of night, I couldn't see anything.

Zaina had been briefed on our need for secrecy and had suggested making port at a hidden smugglers' dock a bit down the coast from the city of Pernula. How she happened to know about said clandestine and no doubt illegal harbor, we didn't ask. It made me like her, though.

In the time we'd spent on the boat, I'd gotten to know her a bit better and had come to the conclusion that Zaina was a rather impressive woman. And I'm not easily impressed. At first, the sailors from Keutunan we'd recruited for this mission had been uncomfortable with a female captain but she'd won them over.

Not by flirting, mind you, which was the way women usually won men over in Keutunan. But by simply being excellent at her job. I don't really know anything about sailing but even I could tell that Zaina knew exactly what she was doing. After that, the sailors' attitude had shifted. Now, some of them even looked at her like they'd take a sword through the gut for her. Like I said, impressive.

"Did he say land?" an excited voice called to my right as Liam skidded to a halt next to me and peered over the railing.

"Yep, but it's too dark to see it," I replied.

"No, it's not," Haela said and leaned over the balustrade. She lifted a graceful arm to point. "It's right over there, can't you see it?"

I heaved an exasperated sigh. "No, we don't have your super senses, remember?"

The energetic twin grinned sheepishly. "Oh, right."

Liam turned back from staring at the dark horizon and looked me up and down. "How are you feeling?"

"Like someone threw me out of a window. And then ran me over with a horse cart." I plastered a smile dripping with irony on my mouth. "But other than that? Splendid."

My friend nodded with a satisfied look on his face. "Sarcasm. That's a good sign."

Letting out a chuckle, I bumped his shoulder with mine. "Moron."

"Says the woman who throws up because of a boat."

With Haela giggling on my left, and Liam on my right, all I could do was shake my head. Idiots.

While the three of us watched the dark smudge in the distance grow larger, the rest of our group appeared. Shade and

Elaran had both kept to themselves most of the journey, but given everything I knew about those two grumps, that wasn't exactly a surprise. However, now we all clustered together against the railing, watching a new world rise from the sea.

DARKNESS BLANKETED the hidden cove. With my pack slung over my shoulder, I climbed over the side of the rowboat. All around me, the others did the same.

"Everyone, grab a box," Shade instructed, keeping his voice low.

Elaran threw him an irritated look but we all did as he said and picked up a lid-covered wooden crate each. Zaina waved us forward from further up the beach. The contents inside clanked as I hoisted my box and followed Zaina. Sand stuck to my boots as our group of seven left the waterline and trudged towards the lone house atop the bank.

"Why are we even bringing this many pistols?" Elaran muttered and turned to Shade. "You do know that we don't use pistols, right?"

"Of course I know you elves don't like guns," the Master Assassin snapped back. "They're not for us. According to Zaina, pistols are illegal on the continent so they're for bribes and black market trading." He shot the auburn-haired elf a hard stare. "Which you would've known if you hadn't spent the whole journey hiding from the humans."

Elaran stopped dead in his tracks. Anger flashed in his eyes. "I do not hide."

"Zaina!"

A man's voice stopped the increasingly heated argument as both fighters dropped their boxes and whipped towards the sound with weapons drawn. The thin man who had emerged from the house dashed forward until he was right in front of Zaina. He seemed completely oblivious to the arrows and swords pointed at him from across the sand. Torrents of rapid Pernish spilled from his mouth. I wasn't anywhere near fluent in that language yet but I swore I picked up the words *see you*, *dead*, and *how*.

Zaina put a hand on his arm and replied something I didn't understand before turning back to us. "This is Redor. He's a friend." She stared pointedly at Shade and Elaran until they lowered their weapons. "I'm gonna catch him up on the situation and make arrangements so that the crew will be taken care of. Don't worry, this isn't the first time a ship with a crew has had to stay hidden here for long periods of time."

Shade gave her a nod.

"If you go around the back," Zaina continued and motioned at the tall, two-story house, "there's a wagon back there. You can put the boxes in there while I get Redor up to speed. That's what we'll use to get to the city."

"Alright, let's get going then," Haela announced with a bright smile, and took the lead.

Elaran and Shade exchange a look but no one dared argue with Haela's excitement so we all fell in behind her.

"She's nice," Liam said once I caught up with him at the house. "I like her."

"Zaina? Yeah, she's alright, I guess. I think she might be one of us."

Liam furrowed his brows at me. "One of us? You mean an underworlder?"

"Yeah. Or whatever they call it over here." I shrugged. "If she knows about this place, she has to be some kind of smuggler."

The horse cart creaked as Liam heaved his box of pistols onto the flat, empty space behind the driver's seat. "True." He took the crate from my hands and pushed it in beside his own.

After we'd loaded our boxes and backpacks into the wagon, we leaned back against its wooden side and waited for Zaina to return. I took a deep breath through my nose.

The air smelled different here. Kind of like spices. And warmth. If warm air actually had a distinctive smell, that is. I knew it didn't make sense but I was going more on feeling than actual catalogued scents. There was no other way to describe it. Keutunan's air had a crisp and cold scent while Pernula smelled like spices on a warm summer day.

"It's so warm," Haemir commented, echoing my thoughts. "It's nighttime and it's almost fall but it feels like we're in the middle of summer."

"I know, right?" his sister filled in.

"It's because we're further south," Zaina supplied as she rounded the cover with a large black horse in tow. She strapped the majestic animal to the long, open wagon. "Redor is gonna ride ahead to the city and get things sorted for the crew."

Just as she finished her sentence, another dark horse flew from behind the house and tore across the dirt road. Redor and his horse disappeared quickly in a cloud of dust.

"Hop on," the female captain said and motioned at the cart. She patted the horse before climbing into the driver's seat.

To no one's surprise, Haela jumped into the wagon first. Anticipation sparkled in her eyes. I released a soft chuckle and followed her while Liam and the others did the same. Zaina clicked her tongue and flicked the reins. The cart jerked as we began our journey.

While the horse brought us closer to our destination, I studied Zaina. She looked a lot better than she had the first time I'd seen her in the dungeons. Since then, she had scrubbed off the dirt and grime and ditched her disguise. Now, her curly, black hair was pulled back in a ponytail and she wore clothes that complemented her figure. Courtesy of His Majesty King Edward, no doubt. In addition to an athletic body, her face was all high cheekbones and her jawline was as sharp as her eyes. I had been right earlier. She was a striking woman.

"Are you sure elves are a common sight in Pernula?" Haemir asked, interrupting my assessment of Zaina's physical appearance.

The striking Pernulan barked a laugh. "You do know that this is the fifth time you've asked me that, don't you?"

"I know," the black-haired twin said. "But where we're from, elves and humans don't really mingle. Not until recently, anyway."

He was right. Our civilizations had been extremely divided for hundreds of years. It was only in these last few months that the elves of Tkeideru had started visiting Keutunan. Their help saving the city from the Pernulans had truly begun the process of washing away the centuries of mistrust between our people. But after such a long period of separation, I understood Haemir's caution.

"Don't worry, as I've said before, elves are a normal sight in my city." Zaina ran a hand over her jaw and lifted one shoulder in a shrug. "Your kind, anyway. If you'd been star elves, that would've been a different matter. But you're wood elves, so you're fine."

Shocked silence filled the wagon. That was news to me. Based on the stunned looks of everyone around me, it was news to them too. Well, maybe not Shade. It was difficult to tell because that cool impassive mask was back on his face.

Elaran was the one who finally broke the silence. "What do you mean?"

"Mean by what?" Zaina threw a confused glance over her shoulder before turning back to the road ahead.

"What do you mean star elves and wood elves?"

The curly-haired Pernulan opened her mouth but didn't say anything. She turned around again, her brow now thoroughly furrowed. "I... Do you not...?" She blew out a sigh. "By Saiwa, you really have been isolated on that island, haven't you?"

"Stop with the rambling," Elaran snapped. "Are you telling me there are elves, other kinds of elves, here?"

Zaina had turned back to the road but she gave him a firm nod. "Correct. You have a lot to get caught up on, it seems. But let's save that for when we're inside. I have a safe house in the city we can use."

The elves looked like they were about to argue, but before they could do that, Shade cut in. "She's right. Establishing a base of operation comes first. After that, we can deal with everything else."

The auburn-haired archer watched the assassin through narrowed eyes but didn't press the matter. Only the sound of cicadas disturbed the silence after that. I watched the landscape roll past as the warm night wind caressed my face.

We moved along the dirt road next to the coast, so on one side the vast dark sea spanned the area all the way to the horizon. On the other sides of the wagon lay wide grasslands. Trees and bushes dotted the greenery but I had no idea what kind, so I was back to establishing that they were brown at the bottom and green at the top.

After a while, I leaned back, rested my head against the side of the cart, and closed my eyes.

"We're almost here," Zaina said after what felt like a very long ride.

I jerked up and whipped my head forward. A gigantic city rose in the distance. And I'd thought Keutunan was huge. I mean, Keutunan *was* big, but this monstrosity made it look like a fishing village.

Liam shook my shoulder and pointed at the enormous walls ahead. "Are you seeing this?"

"Yeah." I continued staring, dumbfounded, at it. "Yeah, I see it."

"We're approaching the back gate," Zaina said and nodded ahead. "The guards on this side know me, so there shouldn't be a problem. But don't say anything until we're past the gate. I'll get us through."

She watched us nod in agreement before turning her attention back to the road. In a few moments, I would be inside the city of Pernula. *Me.* I was already one of the first Keutunians to ever set foot on another continent and now I would also be one of the first to see another human city. It was rather insane, when you thought about it. Who was I? Just a thief from the

Underworld. Fate sure had dealt me a strange hand. My heart pattered against my ribcage. This was it. It was time to meet the Pernulans on their home ground.

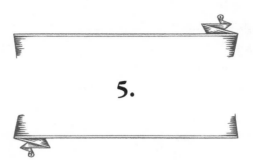

5.

Trying to act normal had never been as hard as it was at that moment. Not that I'd ever been normal, by any sort of standard, but I'd always been good at pretending. Until now. All I wanted to do was gawk at the scene around me but I forced myself to stare at the bottom of the wagon instead, as if I'd seen a city like this a million times before.

The rhythmic sound of the Pernish language drifted from the driver's seat as Zaina convinced the guards to let us through. I had no idea what kind of arrangement she had with them but after a few moments, leather creaked and steel clanked as they stepped out of the way. Our driver clicked her tongue and drove the cart through the gateway.

No one dared say anything since we were in unknown territory, so we continued further into the city in silence. Only the horse's hooves hitting the stones echoed between the walls as the rest of the area lay deserted at this time of night. I studied our surroundings. The streets here at the edge of the city were just barely wide enough to get our wagon through. A strange sense of familiarity filled me until I finally realized that it looked surprisingly similar to Worker's End.

"Damn," Zaina swore and pulled on the reins until the horse stopped. She jumped down from the driver's seat and strode to the back wheel on the right-hand side. After inspecting it, she straightened and beckoned a finger at Haemir. "A little help, please."

"What's going on?" the male half of the twins asked as he landed on the stone street.

"Something's stuck in the wheel." She pointed to the middle of it. "See there?"

Shutters and doors banged open along the whole road. I shot to my feet. Men and women poured onto the street and surrounded the wagon while others popped up in every window. Crossbow bolts pointed at us from every direction. Right as Shade, the elves, and I started towards our weapons, Zaina's voice cut through the night.

"If you go for your weapons, he dies," she said from next to the wagon.

We all whipped our heads towards her. Haemir crouched in front of the cart's supposedly broken wheel with Zaina behind him. A curved knife gleamed at his throat.

"If you dare hurt him I swear I will–" Haela growled before Elaran's hand on her shoulder shut her up.

My eyes darted around the area. Some of the people on the street held swords but most of them brandished crossbows. And there were a lot of them. By my calculations, we were outnumbered five to one. They wouldn't even need the swords; we would all die by the crossbow bolts alone. This was bad.

"What the hell is going on, Zaina?" Shade said, his voice filled with cold fury.

She raised her chin and grinned at him. "Oh, come now, Shade. It's not like I didn't tell you. I did say that I would lead you into a deserted alley and slit your throats once we got here, remember?" The Pernish captain turned towards a thin man with brown hair who had just appeared from a nearby doorway. "Good job setting up the ambush, Redor."

The man from the house at the hidden cove smiled. "When everyone heard you were alive, they were more than eager to help set it up."

Zaina drew the blade further up Haemir's throat and then turned back to us. "Now, we'll take all those pistols, thank you."

Shade stared at her with steel in his eyes. "And after that?"

"After that?" She tapped her sharp jawline with her free hand. "Let's just say after that, your stay in this city will be a lot shorter than you planned."

This was not happening. After everything I'd survived, I'd be damned if I died in some foreign alley right on the cusp of a great adventure. Anger built in my chest and flooded through my whole body. For Nemanan's sake, I had not spent a whole damn journey vomiting over the side of a ship only to die once I finally set foot on dry land again! It was ridiculous. I would not allow it.

My fingers twitched and my eyes threatened to turn black. I wanted desperately to start throwing knives at them but I couldn't. I flicked my gaze to the dark-haired elf on the street. If I attacked, Haemir would die. The darkness pulled at my soul, screaming at me to release it. I forced it down. If I let it out, I would get us all killed. Maybe we could talk our way out of this.

"Killing us would be a mistake," Shade said.

Zaina swung her ponytail back behind her shoulder. "Really? Why is that?"

"Because it would start a war between our nations."

"Uh-huh." She smacked her lips. "I've seen your city. And now you've seen ours. If our nation decided to go to war, *really* go to war, they'd wipe you out in a week and you know it. Besides, do I seem like someone who is particularly loyal to our rulers?" Zaina shook her head. "No, I didn't think so." When she noticed the fury building in the foreign eyes around her, she lifted her toned shoulders in an apologetic shrug. "Sorry, it's nothing personal. Just business. Now, let's see those guns."

Gods damn it. Why had I even bothered to come on this stupid journey if it was going to end like this? What a colossal waste of time. Pure rage–against Zaina, the fickle gods, myself–bubbled through me. The man closest to me lifted his crossbow.

No. The darkness ripped from my soul. Black tendrils whipped around me while lightning crackled over my skin. My eyes filled with death and insanity. I locked them on Zaina. She stared back at me with wide eyes as the darkness built around me like storm clouds.

"*Ashaana*," she whispered, still holding my gaze. She withdrew the blade from Haemir's throat before snapping her fingers and motioning for her people to lower their weapons. "You're one of them."

I had absolutely no idea what Ashaana meant or who the 'them' she was talking about were, but I figured it was in my best interest not to reveal that. All around us, the men and women lowered their swords and crossbows. Surprise and apprehension danced across their features when I swept my gaze over them. My companions glanced at me but said nothing. I closed my eyes briefly and, since the immediate threat was gone, managed to force the darkness back into the deep pits of my soul.

An apologetic grin flashed across Zaina's mouth. "Perhaps we got off on the wrong foot. If I'd known that your people..." Looking at me, she trailed off and spread her hands instead. "Maybe we could come to some sort of arrangement instead."

My people? Countless questions exploded like fireworks in my mind. What had she meant by *my people*? I opened my mouth to demand an answer to that exact question but before I could articulate it, a strong hand encircled my wrist. I scowled at the man attached to it but Shade just gave me an almost imperceptible shake of his head before releasing me. He put a hand to the side of the wagon and leaped off it.

"Yes, I think some kind of arrangement could be made," the Assassins' Guild Master said as he drew up in front of Zaina. "I can see now that simply offering you your freedom wasn't enough." He locked eyes with her. "You want more. My only question is, why didn't you just say that from the beginning?"

The Pernish captain studied the assassin through narrowed eyes. "Maybe because I don't trust people who've held me prisoner."

"Distrusting." Shade let out a soft chuckle. "Smart. But now that we've gotten all this double-crossing out of the way, let's talk business. We want a peace treaty and we need help with language, connections, culture stuff, and maybe another trip or two across the sea."

"And in return?" Zaina said.

"Once we're sure Pernula won't attack Keutunan you can have..." He cocked his head to the right. "You can have that ship we arrived on. Plus, you can ask the crew on it to join you. Given how they looked at you there towards the end, most of them'll probably say yes."

An excited murmur rippled through the crowd around us. Zaina raised her eyebrows. Beside me on the wagon bed, Elaran was fuming but he didn't say anything.

Shade gave a lazy shrug. "I'll even throw in a couple of crates of pistols that you can get when you return us to our island."

Redor blurted out a couple of sentences in Pernish that flew by too fast for me to comprehend but Zaina nodded at him. Maybe we would survive this after all. Zaina lifted her knife. I gave myself an internal eye roll. *Or not.*

She drew the blade across her palm. "Deal." Blood dripped from her hand when she held it out towards Shade.

For a moment, we all just studied her with mirrored expressions of confusion on our faces.

When no one moved, she barked a short laugh. "Alright, first culture lesson. All important deals concerning really valuable or high-risk stuff are sealed in blood. That way, you make certain no one betrays the other."

Huh. What an odd custom. Why in Nemanan's name would drawing a little blood stop someone from double-crossing the other? I could almost hear Shade thinking the same thing but in the end, he just pulled a blade and drew a shallow cut as well. Their hands met over the sand-covered stones.

"Deal," the Master Assassin confirmed.

"Alright then, let's get off the streets." After snapping some orders in Pernish to the rest of the ambushers, she turned to Haemir. Another apologetic smile settled on her lips as she waved the blade in the air. "Sorry about the knife."

Both twins watched her with wary eyes but then nodded in unison. She nodded back. Rustling clothing filled the night as the gathered men and women withdrew from the alley.

"Get on," Zaina called to Shade and Haemir while she climbed into the driver seat. "We've got to get somewhere safe."

As soon as all the wagon's previous occupants were back on board, she clicked her tongue and urged the horse on. Wood creaked as the cart rattled over the stones. Liam cast a quick glance towards Zaina before leaning closer to me.

"Why did you attack?" he whispered.

It was meant for my ears but I could tell that the rest of our companions were listening in as well. I shifted uncomfortably in my seat.

"Please, Storm, you have to be careful," he continued in a soft tone. His dark blue eyes were filled with worry. "If that hadn't worked, she would've killed Haemir."

Guilt twisted like a hot knife in my gut. "I know."

Haemir wasn't the only one who would've died. If Zaina hadn't believed that I was part of some unknown group of people, they would all have died. And it would've been my fault. All because I couldn't control the darkness.

"It's also the reason we're all still alive right now." Shade raised one shoulder in a shrug. "I'm just saying."

I lifted my eyebrows. That had been an unexpected comment coming from him. But the person who worried me the most was Haela. Because of my actions, I had put her brother in danger. I barely dared meet her eyes. Warm night winds tickled my face as I braced myself for looks of anger and disappointment on the twins' faces. There weren't any.

You did the right thing, Haela mouthed over her brother's shoulder.

Relief flooded my chest. I'd never cared what people thought of me before, but as much as I hated it, I did care about these particular people's opinion of me. Damn. Feelings were so inconvenient.

The horse snorted and whinnied as Zaina pulled the wagon to a stop outside a large building. It was long and rectangular with a courtyard far larger than any of the surrounding houses. I studied the grand double doors located at the middle of the long wall. Whoever lived here had to be filthy rich.

"Wait here," our driver said and jumped down from the seat.

She snuck across the stones and approached a small door at the edge of the house. Three soft knocks drifted through the air. Candles flickered in the windows until the door was pushed open and light spilled onto the ground outside. A cry rang out.

We all tensed up, ready for trouble, as the young woman in the doorway flew across the threshold and into the arms of the Pernish captain outside. Zaina patted the dark hair of the woman clinging to her neck. After a few moments, the stranger pulled back. She stared at Zaina for a second before giving her a hard shove and launching an assault. The athletic captain just stood there and let the young woman pound delicate fists on her chest until she wore herself out. Muted sobbing floated across the courtyard as the unidentified woman broke down and leaned into Zaina's embrace. Zaina pulled her arms tightly around the woman.

"Another person who loves her and who believed she was dead," Liam stated, sadness washing over his features.

"Yeah, and it looks like we'll get to stay here so we don't have much time before she comes back," Shade said and swept his gaze over our group. "We need to get some things straight."

"Listen here, *Deadly Nightshade*," Elaran said in a mocking tone and narrowed his eyes at the assassin.

"Shade," the Assassins' Guild Master cut him off.

The grumpy archer furrowed his brows. "What?"

"Yeah, it comes from deadly nightshade but that's not my name. My name is Shade."

"Whatever," Elaran replied with an irritated shake of his head. "You're not the boss here. Who gave you the authority to just give away our ship without consulting us first?"

The Master of the Assassins' Guild locked hard eyes on the ranger. "I don't need anyone's permission. And besides, we need her. Without someone with local contacts and culture knowledge we'll never pull this off." He blew out a frustrated breath. "Look, we don't have time for this right now. We have more pressing matters." Shade turned towards me. "What the hell is Ashaana?"

All eyes turned to me as they waited for me to explain something I didn't have a clue about either. I threw out my arms. "Fuck if I know. But I'm gonna find out. As soon as we're indoors, I'm gonna ask her."

"The hell you are," Shade said.

"Yeah, I am. She said *one of them* and *your people*. That has to mean there are others like me." I flicked my eyes between my companions. "I need to know."

The Master Assassin leveled eyes dripping with authority on me. "Until we have what we came for, you are not going to breathe a word about this. Not a single word."

I snorted. "Or what? We're a long way from your Assassins' Guild now."

"I don't need my guild for that." He ran his eyes up and down my body. "We both know how our last fight would've ended if that horde of Pernulans hadn't interrupted us."

"Yeah, we do. Because we both remember who took out that whole room of attackers *single-handedly*."

Shade's mouth dropped open but only a disgruntled huff escaped. He was about to try again when he was interrupted by a voice filled with exasperation and anxiety.

"Enough, both of you," Haemir hissed before turning to Shade. "You said it yourself, we don't have time to argue right now." He looked at me. "And you, Shade is right. The only reason we're alive is because she thinks you're one of those people. If you start asking questions, that falls apart. And not just asking her questions. The same goes for everyone in this city. No one can find out that we don't know what Ashaana is."

Liam nodded. "He's right."

And now they were ganging up on me. Fantastic. But, yeah, they did have a point. I threw my arms up.

"Alright, I won't ask any questions until we have what we came for."

Shade watched me with an unreadable mask on his face. "Swear it by Nemanan."

I crossed my arms. Damn him for knowing I'd never break a vow to the God of Thieves. Releasing a slow sigh, I conceded. "Fine. I swear by Nemanan that I won't ask questions about it until we've accomplished our mission."

"Guys, she's coming back," Haela whispered.

When Zaina arrived at the wagon, we were all acting like our hurried argument had never occurred. She looked from one face to the next before offering a shrug.

"We're sleeping in here. Grab all your stuff, the pistols too, and follow me." Zaina flashed a smile. "We have a lot to discuss but right now, we all need some sleep. I'll get you settled in and then we'll talk in the morning."

Without waiting for an answer, she turned and strode back towards the house. The six of us scrambled to follow her. I swung my backpack over my shoulder and picked up the closest box of pistols.

Well, would you look at that? We'd made it to the continent, and in only a few hours, we had infiltrated the capital, survived an ambush, made a somewhat dependable ally, and gotten a safe house. Maybe the seven of us would actually manage to take on an entire empire. Excitement bounced around inside me as I slipped in through the door and into the lit hallway beyond. I couldn't wait to see what tomorrow would bring.

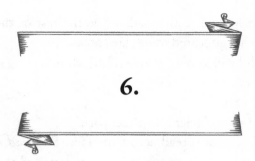

6.

Thin rays of sunlight filtered through the windows and made the soft layer of sand in the air sparkle. I ran my hand across the closest tabletop.

"What is this place?" I murmured as my eyes glided over the mass of desks and chairs. "Is this a...?"

"School," a voice finished behind me.

Whirling around, I found Zaina leaning against the doorframe. I furrowed my brows. "Let me get this straight: you're a smuggler, a wannabe pirate... and a teacher?"

"Me? A teacher?" She threw her head back and released a hearty laugh. "Wouldn't that be something? No, I'd probably throw myself, or them, out the window before the first day was over." Pushing off the painted frame, she flashed me a smile and jerked her chin. "Come on, and I'll introduce you to the real teacher."

Time had not been on our side when we arrived last night, so I'd only been able to map my own room and a route to the exit before I had to cram in a few hours of sleep. As soon as I was up, I'd started a sweep of the building. If we were staying here, I needed to know the layout so that I could create contingencies in case shit hit the fan. The far corner we'd entered at held a cluster of bedrooms, a kitchen, and a living room—all of which

I assumed belonged to the staff—while the rest of the building contained what appeared to be classrooms.

"How did you know?" Zaina asked while leading me down a flight of stairs.

"Know what?"

"About the smuggler and pirate part."

A satisfied grin spread across my face. *So I had been right.* "The way your face lit up when Shade mentioned the ship and crew." I released a short chuckle. "What else were you gonna use it for? You don't exactly strike me as a friendly neighborhood merchant."

Zaina arched a well-manicured eyebrow at me as we drew closer to the living room. "You're saying I'm not friendly?"

"I'm saying you're like us." I lifted my shoulders in a shrug. "Take it however you want."

Her lips quirked upwards in a smile but she didn't say anything. Instead, she put her hand on a metal handle and swung open the door to a large room. Two elves and a human were sprawled on the couches in the middle while the room's remaining two occupants both leaned against the far wall with their arms crossed. I strode towards the unadorned wall and took up position between Elaran and Shade.

"Been scouting the building, have we?" the assassin commented.

I snorted. "As if you haven't."

Elaran turned to scowl at us both. "There are other walls. We don't all have to be standing in the exact same spot."

"Yeah, there are. But this is the best spot because it both keeps your back protected and gives you a clear view of the whole room." I gave him a knowing look. "Which is why you picked it too. And why he picked it." I tipped my head to the assassin on my other side before giving Elaran a lazy wave of my hand. "You can move if you want."

The discontented elf muttered but didn't have time to fully form a reply before Zaina's voice cut through the room.

"We have a lot of topics to cover but I think we should start with some introductions," she said just as a young woman walked through the door.

The twins sat up straighter on the couch and Liam actually stood up. I frowned at him but he didn't notice because his eyes were glued to the woman's face. When I shifted my gaze to her, I understood why. She had the same high cheekbones and intelligent black eyes as Zaina but her face bore a softer expression. Glossy black curls cascaded down her back and long lashes framed her eyes. She was gorgeous. And very obviously related to Zaina.

"Alright," Zaina said and started moving her hand from one person to the next. "This is Shade, Storm, Elaran, Haemir, Liam, and Haela." She dropped her hand and then nodded towards the beautiful woman in the doorway. "Everybody, say hello to our hostess and my little sister, Norah."

Polite greetings rose from the twins on the couch while the three of us by the wall nodded in acknowledgement. The window of casual replies had just closed when Liam finally got his mouth working.

"Hello," he blurted out after that slight delay.

I had to bite my tongue to keep from chuckling. Between the two of us, the socially awkward one had always been me, so seeing his conversational skills flounder for once was deeply satisfying. Norah gave Liam a kind smile before moving towards the dark brown sofa. Her sister followed suit while Liam sat back down.

"Are the three of you just gonna stand there like sentries? No one's gonna attack you in here," Zaina complained while motioning in our direction. "You're stressing me out! Come sit down, for Saiwa's sake!"

After a quick huff, I peeled myself off the wall and stalked towards a blue and green armchair between two of the couches. Shade and Elaran did the same but settled for the last unoccupied sofa in the circle around the low rectangular table.

"Saiwa is the Goddess of the Sea," I said as I plopped down on the soft cushion and folded one leg underneath me. "You worship the same gods we do."

"Yeah, I noticed that too," Zaina said from her spot in the armchair across the large table. "I'm assuming your ancestors were from this continent too and that they brought their gods with them."

We all nodded in agreement. Religion was a tricky part of a nation's culture and very easy to mess up. Luckily, we already had a firm grasp on this one. At least that was one thing less to worry about.

Shade was just about to start the line of inquiry but Norah got there first. "Before you get into any lengthy discussions, I have a few things to say because I have to leave soon." She waved a hand at the building around us. "I do have a school to run."

How in Nemanan's name was she responsible for running a school? She looked no older than Liam. However, I decided not to voice that and instead gave the young teacher a brief nod.

"Zaina told me that you are here because you want peace between our nations," Norah said. "That is certainly something

I can support, which is why I'm allowing you to stay here until you've completed your mission. However..." She swept her gaze around the room of foreigners. "This is a school. This is *my* school. So whatever trouble you might get yourselves into, you leave my students and my school out of it."

"Of course," Liam said and leaned forward until he met her eyes.

"Got it," Haela filled in.

The rest of us settled for nods of acknowledgement. Once Norah had seen us all agree, she stood up and gave us a sparkling smile. "Fantastic! When I'm free, I could also help teach you Pernish, if you want?"

"That would be very beneficial, thank you," Shade said.

"Are you sure we're not in the way?" Haemir glanced around the room. "With occupying all those bedrooms, I mean."

The beautiful teacher was already halfway to the door when she replied. "Oh no, not at all. The other teachers all have their own houses in the city so it's really only me here." She stopped briefly before the door. "I'm sorry, I really have to go so I can get everything ready for the day but it was lovely meeting you all." And with that, she was out the door.

Soft creaks escaped from the couch as Liam tore his eyes from the doorway and shifted back to the circle of Keutunians and the Pernish smuggler. Steel filled Zaina's eyes as she watched the six of us.

"If you ever hurt my sister, the deal's off and you will find your corpses floating in the harbor. Blood oath or not."

Protective, that one, wasn't she? I couldn't blame her, though. She'd let a group of shady underworlders and fierce elves into her home and that would make most people nervous. I expected Liam to be the one to assure her that we wouldn't harm her sister but to my surprise, it was Haela who spoke up.

"No one will hurt your sister." The black-haired twin gave the pirate an approving smile. "Where we're from, we protect our siblings too."

Zaina's eyes swirled with understanding as she gave Haela a slow nod. Despite their rocky start with the ambush mishap, it seemed as though those two might be on their way to becoming friends.

"Good," the smuggler said. "Now, you want to force a peace treaty between our nations. What's the plan for making that happen?"

We all looked to Shade since he and Edward had been the driving force behind this mission. The Master Assassin leaned forward on the couch and rested his elbows on his knees.

"Actually, that's what we need your help figuring out," he said.

Facial expressions around the room varied from mild surprise to utter bewilderment.

"Are you serious?" Elaran spat out while staring daggers at the assassin. "You dragged us on a journey across an entire sea to infiltrate a foreign nation... *and we don't even have a plan?*"

Shade drew his eyebrows down and leveled hard eyes on the auburn-haired elf. "How were we supposed to make a plan? Huh? We knew nothing about this nation. We had no idea what it looked like, how the power structure was set up, what their strengths and weaknesses were."

"You didn't think to... I don't know? Ask one of the prisoners?" the elf muttered.

"Torture can only get you so far because you can never be sure if they're telling the truth or just saying what they think you want to hear so that you'll stop." Ignoring the horrified expressions around him, Shade gave an irritated flick of his wrist. "We needed to scout it out for ourselves before we could make a real plan. It's the same as with any other mission." He lifted his eyebrows at Elaran. "I mean, how do you assassinate someone?"

Elaran sent him an annoyed look. "I don't know. I don't assassinate people."

The expert killer let out a loud groan and threw his arms in the air. "Fine. You," he said and locked eyes with me. "How did you plan your assassination of the Masters of the Scribes' and Builders' Guild?"

I jerked back in my armchair. *Shit. Why did he need to bring that up? I hadn't told...*

"Wait, what?" Liam said from the couch to my right. "You're the one who killed them?"

"I... uhm..." I began.

Confused dark blue eyes met me from across the room. "Why?"

"I, well..." I stammered again while racking my brain for an explanation that didn't involve the real reason for my little murder spree.

The room around us had gone dead silent while everyone watched our exchange. Unfortunately, I didn't have time to formulate a proper answer to my friend's question because the look in his eyes told me he had already figured it out.

"You did it because Makar threatened to kill me if you didn't," he stated flatly.

"Yeah."

A range of emotions flashed across Liam's face. Some of them I wished I hadn't seen.

"The Builders' Guild Master had a family!" He raised his voice to match the devastation in his tone. "He had a kid, for Nemanan's sake! What were you thinking?"

I picked at a stray thread sticking up from the armrest while painful feelings burrowed into my chest like maggots in a corpse. How was I supposed to reply to that? Upon seeing the expression on my face, Liam wiped both hands up and down his face a couple of times. He took a deep breath.

"I didn't mean that. It's just..." His gaze drifted to Elaran. "People keep dying so that I can live. And I don't want that."

Still not knowing how to respond, I averted my eyes and pretended to study the bookcases along the walls instead. From the corner of my eye, I noticed Shade watching me intently.

What was I supposed to say? I wasn't going to apologize for saving my best friend's life. Shoving the uncomfortable feelings out of my chest, I slammed my mental armor back in place. Life was complicated and messy and I would always do whatever it took to protect the people I love.

"Wow, you really are a bunch of dysfunctional misfits if I ever saw one," Zaina announced. Her humorous comment drew a few snorts and broke the heavy mood that had settled. "So, you need help getting the lay of the land so you can make a plan?" A grin spread across her striking features. "I have just the thing. Come with me. It's time to meet the marvel that is Pernula."

The Pernish smuggler jumped out of her armchair and strode towards the door. After a collective shrug, the rest of us followed suit.

Exploring a whole new city was exactly what I needed to stave off the weeds taking root in my heart after this conversation. No time to feel bad about the kind of person I was. Checking my knives, I made my way towards the door. The city of Pernula was waiting for me.

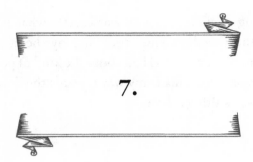

7.

Color was everywhere. Men and women bustled past wearing garments of every shade. Slick black suits and crisp white dresses mixed with loose-fitting pants and shirts ranging from bright yellow, to forest green, to pale blue like the sky on a sunny day. Flowers in full bloom decorated the city in artistic patterns while awnings in rich hues rustled in the soft wind. It was mesmerizing. I'm not usually one to get all excited about some plants and pretty fabric but even I was having trouble keeping my jaw from falling to the ground.

"It's gorgeous!" Haela exclaimed and spun around in a graceful twirl.

"Yeah, for a city, this is actually kind of beautiful," her brother filled in.

Probably pretending not to hear the 'for a city' part of that comment, Zaina broke into a wide smile. "Oh, you haven't seen anything yet."

As we continued moving deeper into the capital of Pernula, another thought struck me. Weapons. I was fully armed because, well, I'm always armed, but so were my companions. Shade wore his twin swords and the elves had their well-crafted bows strapped to their backs, but no one looked at us twice. In fact, quite a lot of the people we passed sported weapons of one kind or another as well.

"Is it normal for people to walk around like this?" I turned to Zaina. "With lots of visible weapons, I mean."

"Yeah." She released a short chuckle. "I noticed in Keutunan, there in the beginning, that when we walked around with our swords, we drew lots of attention. But yeah, here, strolling to the market fully armed is completely normal."

Huh. How odd. But very convenient. Not having to hide my knives in public all the time was going to be quite useful.

"Oh, crap!" Zaina drew up short and slapped a hand to her forehead as if she had just realized something. Her dark eyes flicked from one elf to the next. "You're wood elves. You have that weird thing about people not touching your bows, right?"

"That's right." Elaran narrowed his eyes. "Why?"

The Pernish smuggler grimaced. "Things are gonna get a bit crowded so people might accidentally end up touching them." She scratched her temple. "Okay, I'll see if I can get us there without using the busiest roads. But next time, maybe leave the bows back at the school?"

The grumpy archer frowned at her. "Are you saying we're supposed to walk around *unarmed*?" He crossed his arms over his chest. "I don't think so."

A broad grin spread across Zaina's lips. "I do have swords. Quite a lot of them, actually, if my stash from before is untouched. And of great quality. If you throw in a few extra pistols in those crates you'll give me afterwards, I can give you some."

The three elves pondered in silence for a few moments before Elaran spoke up. "Okay. That will work."

I raised my eyebrows at him while surprise colored my voice. "You know how to use a sword?"

He scowled at me. "Of course we do."

Haela jabbed an elbow in my arm. "Come on, Storm. What do you think we do with all the time we've got on our hands?"

"Practice with your bows?"

"Yeah, alright, that too. We do prefer bows whenever possible but we're also pretty competent with swords. Though, we haven't had much use for them in Tkeideru."

I studied her through narrowed eyes. "Something tells me you're a bit more than simply *competent* with a sword."

Haela chuckled in a satisfied manner while her yellow eyes sparkled. "What can I say, I seem to have a natural talent for using weapons."

"As we all well know, thank you very much," Haemir muttered.

We all laughed at the sibling rivalry constantly present between those two.

"Alright, that settles it. I'll see about getting you some swords as soon as possible then," Zaina announced and started out again. "Come on, let's keep moving."

Our group of six fell in behind the smuggler. Just as Zaina had promised, the crowd thickened the deeper into the city we got. Shops selling different kinds of food lined the wide road we followed, filling the air with heavenly scents of spices and baking bread.

Two tall figures suddenly appeared in front of us. They nodded at our group while continuing down the street in the other direction. All three of my elven companions stopped dead in the middle of the road and stared at the strangers.

"Those were elves," Haemir blurted out. "Exactly like us. But not... from... us."

"Yeah," Zaina confirmed with a shrug. "Like I said, wood elves are pretty common here."

Elaran locked eyes with the pirate. "One day, very soon, you are going to explain that whole thing about wood elves and star elves."

"I know. There's so much I need to catch you up on." She blew out a deep sigh. "One thing at a time."

"Zaina," Liam began. He was staring at something above the rooftops. "What are those black things sticking up?"

"That," she replied and swept her arms theatrically to the sides, "is our destination."

The black spikes in the distance grew bigger the deeper into the city we moved. Zaina kept her promise and steered us through streets that were crowded but not fully packed with people until a sharp turn finally dumped us in a large square.

"Whoa!" Haela and I exclaimed in unison as we took in the gigantic building in front of us.

"Welcome to Blackspire," Zaina said with a wide smile.

While the Silver Keep back at home was a sturdy fortress made of brilliant white marble, this thing was the exact opposite. A castle of polished black obsidian soared into the sky. High walls surrounded what I assumed to be gardens or maybe stone courtyards because the actual building was situated further in from the defense fortifications. The actual palace was breathtaking. Graceful domes and twisting spires reached for the heavens while red stained glass windows accentuated the shiny black surface.

"It's stunning," I said.

"Right?" The Pernish smuggler led us towards an unadorned wall at the back of the square so that we wouldn't be standing in the middle of the busy crowd. "This is where the rulers of Pernula... well, rule."

Haemir raised his eyebrows at her. "*Rulers*? There is more than one?"

"Yep. Three, to be precise." Zaina held up three fingers and ticked them off as she talked. "The High Priest, the Master of Knowledge, and the General. The current High Priest is called Sorah, the Master of Knowledge is Herodotos, and the General you've already met, of course."

"Marcellus," Shade said.

"Exactly." Zaina waved a hand towards the castle again. "They all have different areas of responsibility but all the decisions about war and stuff like that rests with the General. Including peace treaties."

"Which means that the person we need to convince to sign a peace treaty is the same person who tried to kill us, and who we tried to kill too, only a few months ago," I summarized. "Fantastic."

Our group of seven fell silent as we all no doubt tried to come up with ideas for how to make that happen. While we pondered, a very round man climbed onto a small box by the castle wall. His double chin flapped as he bellowed sentences in Pernish across the square. I frowned at him. It was difficult to understand everything he said but I was pretty sure he shouted something about hurrying.

Haemir nodded in the direction of the large man. "What's going on? What's he saying?"

"Oh, uhm, he's telling people to hurry if they want to register for the election because the sign-up closes in a week," Zaina supplied.

"What does that mean?" Elaran demanded. "What election?"

She released a short chuckle. "Right, another thing you of course don't know about. Every three years, we vote for who should be our three rulers. Mostly it's just the same people who win several years in a row but if people are unhappy with any of them, they kick them out by voting for someone else."

"So, the leaders have to actually be good rulers or they get replaced?" Liam added. "Cool!"

"Well," Zaina began, drawing out the word into one very long syllable. "It's not a perfect system. People are pretty easy to mislead too. Rulers who are actually good for the city can get voted out because people don't understand that what they're doing actually benefits the city in the long run." She lifted her shoulders in a shrug. "Or some new power-hungry person launches a smear campaign against them so that they *look* bad and get voted out because of that."

"Huh." Shade studied Zaina with analytic eyes. "Who can register as a candidate for this election?"

"Anyone."

"Anyone?" Haemir cut in. "That sounds very risky. What if the queen of another country or something decides to join? Then they could just take over the city."

"In theory, yeah." Zaina shrugged. "But just because anyone can register doesn't mean anyone can win. A majority still gotta vote for you."

The black-haired elf tipped his head to the side in thought but then nodded. Zaina did have a point. Next to us, only scattered conversations from strangers filled the area until a certain Master Assassin spoke up.

"I know how to get our peace treaty." Schemes filled his black eyes. "I'm going to run for General."

I whipped my head towards Shade. All around me, the rest of our group did the same. The chatter of people bustling past our corner of the square seemed to disappear as we all stared at him in shocked silence. At last, Elaran broke the stillness.

"Are you out of your mind?" The auburn-haired archer scowled and threw his arms out. "We can't win an election in a foreign country!"

"He's right," Liam added. "Didn't you hear what Zaina just said? A majority of the people here need to vote for you if we're going to win."

A smirk settled on Shade's handsome face. "We don't have to win. We just need to create enough trouble for Marcellus so that he's afraid he'll lose, to us or someone else running, unless he signs the peace treaty."

"So, mess with his election campaign until he's so desperate for us to stop that he gives us what we want?" A malicious chuckle slipped my lips. "I like it."

"Yeah, it's a solid plan," Haela said.

Her brother nodded his agreement. Liam scrunched up his face in consideration but then replicated the gesture. We all turned to Elaran. After another few seconds of deep scowling, he gave a curt nod as well.

"You people really are crazy." Zaina barked a laugh. "But that's also why this might actually work." She pushed off the wall she'd been leaning against. "Alright, no time like the present. Do you know how to find your way back to the school?"

The six of us glanced at each other before reluctantly shaking our heads. I'm usually pretty good at mapping out routes in my head but we had taken so many twisting turns and back streets to avoid the worst crowds that I'd lost my sense of direction after a while.

"Figured as much. Okay, I'll guide you back to the school so that you can start planning this insane mission and I'll also send someone to get swords for you three." She nodded at the elves before turning to Shade. "And then, you and I will go and get you registered for the election. No time like the present, indeed."

Zaina gave us a short jerk of her head, suggesting that we should get moving. The sun had climbed high in the sky while we'd been busy navigating the city and plotting mayhem. Sweat trickled down my back as we pushed our way through rows of people. I wondered how many people lived here. And how many of them we'd need to fool in order to scare Marcellus into a peace treaty. Elaran was right, but so was Zaina. We were out of our minds thinking we could manipulate an election in a foreign country, but we were also crazy enough that we might actually pull it off. I shook my head and released a chuckle as we left Blackspire behind. After all, crazy was kind of my natural state.

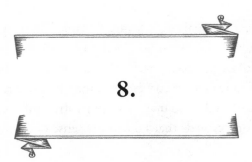

8.

"How can we even trust her?"

Liam frowned at the grumpy elf. "What do you mean?"

"I mean," Elaran said and leaned forward on the couch, "she betrayed us. She set up an ambush and was ready to kill us just yesterday and now we're trusting her with all our plans."

I threw a quick glance at the door to the living room to make sure Zaina or her sister weren't standing there lurking. Only the long rows of bookshelves watched us like silent sentries but I kept my voice low anyway. "It's *because* she betrayed us that we know we can trust her."

Elaran sat back and turned an irritated frown on me. "That doesn't make any sense. At all."

Liam opened his mouth, then furrowed his brows and closed it again. My attempt to get support from the twins fell flat too as they only stared at me with mirrored looks of confusion on their faces. I let out a loud groan.

"Okay, look, the problem with trusting new people is that you never know if or when they will betray you. Or why they'll do it." I shrugged. "But Zaina has already betrayed us and we know why she did it so we upped our offer and became the highest bidder. So now, we don't have to constantly worry whether she'll double-cross us or not, because she already has, and we don't have to worry about her doing it again because we're already the ones offering what she wants most of all."

Silence fell across the room. The dark brown sofas creaked slightly as both Liam and Haela adjusted their positions. I swept my gaze over my human friend and the three elves.

"That actually makes sense," Haemir said with a thoughtful expression on his face.

His sister raised her eyebrows and gave an impressed nod. "Yeah, in a strange sort of way."

I only had time to hear Elaran mutter something about sneaky underworlders before footsteps in the corridor outside drew my attention. Two black-haired humans stepped through the door.

"It's done, your boy Shade here is now officially a candidate for the election," Zaina said and jerked her head towards the assassin entering behind her. "And your swords are on their way."

The Master Assassin took a seat in the blue and green armchair across from mine while the smuggler plopped down on the couch next to Liam and swung her feet onto the low table.

"Alright, come up with any great ideas while we've been gone?" she asked.

"Yeah, I've been thinking," Haela began, "if we boost Shade's campaign so people like him at the same time as we ruin Marcellus' then that'd double the effect and we should have him desperate enough in no time."

"An attack on two fronts," Elaran commented while drumming his fingers on the couch's armrest. "Smart."

"Yeah, that is smart," Shade said. "It would make it much more difficult for him to protect himself. How could anyone defend themselves against someone else's popularity?"

"That's what I just said," Elaran muttered and crossed his arms.

The assassin sent him a scorching look before turning to the rest of us. "Then we should probably split into two teams to cover more ground and work more efficiently."

Haela stretched her arms above her head and leaned back on the sofa. "Sounds good. So, who should cover what?" A grin spread across her face. "I'd be up for creating some mischief."

Shade ran a hand along his jaw. "Actually, I think it's probably best if the three of you," he pointed at Haela, Haemir, and Liam, "cover the Upperworld and try to boost our campaign while the three of us," he motioned at himself, me, and Elaran, "cover the Underworld and do the sabotaging."

"Why?" Haemir asked.

"Because your skill set is better suited for it."

I released a snort followed by low chuckle. The room turned to look at me with eyebrows raised, waiting for an explanation of my strange reaction.

"What he means is that you," I waved a hand at Liam and the twins, "are actually nice people who make friends easily, while we are not."

Elaran shot me a dirty look. "Speak for yourself."

The rest of the room, however, seemed to see the logic in my statement. Shade studied me with barely concealed amusement on his face while Liam giggled and the others outright laughed.

"You know what," Haela said after one final snort. "That's actually a great point. We'll do the wooing and the charming."

She released another brief chuckle. "I mean, could you imagine Storm trying to sweet-talk someone?"

"Oh, shut up," I said and threw a pillow at her. When she caught it and winked at me, I just shook my head. "But yeah, you do that and we'll handle the threatening, blackmailing, and sabotaging."

"Is that feet? *On my table*?" a voice rang out from the doorway.

Zaina whipped her legs off the table and grimaced. "Sorry, sis."

Norah stood just inside the door with her hands on her hips. "Uh-huh. Incorrigible as always," she muttered. "I was going to make some chili. Do you want some? Or have you already eaten?"

Several stomachs seemed to have heard her because they rumbled in reply. Zaina twisted on the couch until she faced the door.

"We'd love some." She gave her sister a thankful smile.

Norah's stern mask from the feet-on-the-table episode melted and she smiled back. She really was pretty.

"Yeah, and Liam will help you," I announced and nodded towards my friend.

He blinked at me. "I will?" His eyes darted from me in the armchair next to him to the beautiful teacher in the doorway. "I mean, yes, I will."

Norah raised her eyebrows in surprise but then a bright smile lit up her whole face. "Lovely. Come find me in the kitchen when you're ready." She disappeared back into the corridor.

"Go on then," I said and gave Liam's shoulder a push.

"Why did you do that?" he hissed under his breath so that only I would hear.

I wiggled my eyebrows at him. "Just you and her, alone in the kitchen. Who knows what'll happen?"

Liam's face flushed beet red. "What do I even talk about?"

"I don't know. You're the socially competent one. Figure it out." I gave his shoulder another shove. "Now go."

He stood up and gave me his best imitation of an angry stare but between his mop of curly brown hair and sweet-looking face, he failed miserably. "I hate you," he announced matter-of-factly.

I grinned at him. "I hate you too."

After releasing something between a laugh and a sigh, he wandered off towards the kitchen. Right as he vanished from view, a thin man I recognized and a very muscular man I didn't recognize appeared in the doorway. They lugged a heavy-looking chest across the threshold.

"Ah, Redor, Samuel," Zaina said and jumped up from the couch. "Perfect timing."

The smuggler's two companions sat the chest down in front of the desk by the wall. It hit the floor with a thud. Redor unlocked the lid and threw it open, revealing glints of steel.

Zaina beckoned at the three elves while a wide smile spread across her face. "Come choose your swords."

Haela practically leaped from the couch and bounded over to the stack of weapons. Excitement gleamed in her eyes as she rubbed her hands and peered into the wooden chest. Her brother rolled his eyes but wasn't far behind while Elaran rose from the sofa and made his way over in a few graceful steps. I chuckled. Elves.

The three of them lifted sword after sword from the stash, weighing them in their hands. Swishing sounds filled the air as they tried them out. After a while, I shifted my eyes from the weapon-wielding elves to the assassin in the armchair and found him studying me with a curious look on his face.

"So," I said. "Time for some excessive threatening and blackmailing again, I suppose."

Shade's mouth drew into a lopsided smile. "Yeah, I suppose so."

"How refreshing to not be doing it to each other, for once."

"Hmm." His black eyes glittered. "There'll be plenty of time for that too."

"You're right. We wouldn't wanna get out of practice, now would we?"

His lips drew into another lopsided smile but his reply was cut short by an announcement from the elves.

"These are elven made," Elaran stated, holding up two gleaming swords. Genuine surprise colored his face.

"Yep," Zaina said. "Told you I had great quality weapons."

The long, beautifully decorated twin swords whooshed through the air as Elaran danced across the room in a flurry of steel. The auburn-haired elf moved with effortless grace before coming to a halt by the bookshelves on the other side. He gave an impressed nod in the direction of the swords.

I stared at him. Damn. He was most definitely a lot more than simply *competent* with a sword as well. Drawing my eyebrows down, I swatted at the feelings of inadequacy sneaking up behind my shoulder.

Haela looked like a child receiving a present as she hoisted her own two swords in the air. "I love them!" she exclaimed.

"I like the weight of these," Haemir added and nodded at the long weapons in his hands. "They fit me nicely."

Zaina chuckled knowingly. "You all picked elven swords. No surprise there." Her intelligent eyes flicked to Shade. "They're quite expensive so I expect to be generously compensated for them in pistols."

The Master Assassin nodded at her. "You will. You have my word."

"Fantastic!"

Right as the satisfied smuggler uttered her exclamation, Liam stuck a head through the doorway. "Norah says dinner will be ready in ten minutes." He looked at the swords occupying the whole room. "And she says no weapons at the dinner table."

The smuggler threw her head back and barked a laugh. "That's Norah for you. Alright, let's get the rest of these packed up."

While the three elves helped Redor and Samuel return the discarded swords to the wooden chest, I stood up and moved towards the door. If no weapons were allowed at the table, I'd better head back to my room and remove the army of knives currently strapped to my body. Well, the visible ones, anyway. I released a soft chuckle. This was going to be an interesting stay.

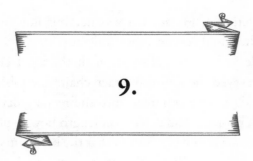

9.

Darkness enveloped me as I stood outside a shabby-looking tavern. I brushed a hand over the leather pouch full of pearls secured at my hip before checking all my knives. This was just an Underworld tavern like any other. How many of those had I visited in my life? The only difference was that this one was in a different city. On another continent. Where people didn't know my reputation. And spoke a language I still didn't fully understand. Yeah, nothing to be anxious about at all. I pushed down the door's metal handle.

In the days since we arrived, our shady team had come up with our first act of sabotage. While our friendly and socially skilled team, with a little help from Norah, had started making connections in the city's upstanding circles, the rest of us had gotten acquainted with the Pernulan Underworld. Zaina had introduced us to a fence who we'd used to sell a couple of pistols in exchange for several bags of pearls. Then she'd taken us on a tour of the city's sketchy areas and pointed out places of interest. After that, she'd released us on the world to wreak havoc.

Every night, I'd spent a few hours running across town, mapping it in my head. The capital city of Pernula was huge so it was still far from a completed map but I was fairly confident about navigating it. However, I was nervous now as I stepped across the threshold and into the dimly lit pub.

Stale ale and sweat wafted through the air. I crinkled my nose as I surveyed the room. Wooden chairs and tables that had seen better days were crammed into the rectangular space and packed with people. I had debated at length how to play this but had finally come to the conclusion that the best course of action was to simply be me. Pretending to be someone I was not had never worked out well for me in the long run, but the Oncoming Storm was still alive. Granted, it had been a bit touch and go at times but I was far better at being me than I was at being someone else. I raised my voice to a shout.

"I heard this is the place to recruit people for an under-the-table mission."

Dead silence fell across the tavern as all its patrons turned to look at me. I met their stares with an even gaze.

"Who the hell are you?" a burly man to my right challenged. "And why're you talking the elven language?"

"I'm not from here." I swept hard eyes across the crowd. "I'm from Keutunan."

A murmur coursed through the room. "You're from the Lost Island?" someone asked towards the back.

The Lost Island, huh? So that was what they were calling our home. I actually quite liked that name.

"Yes," I replied. "My name is the Oncoming Storm."

Scattered laughter broke out. "The Oncoming Storm? What kind of name is that?"

Anger pulled at my soul. They were laughing at me. People who laughed at me usually got a knife through their windpipe but I figured one minute into the conversation was a bit too soon to start killing people. Shame.

"Yes, that's what I said." I gave them an irritated shake of my head. "Now, we can stand here and discuss differences in naming culture or we can get down to business. I have a mission for–"

I broke off when I felt fingers hovering over the bag of pearls tied to my waist. First they were laughing at me and now they were trying to steal from me. My hand shot out and snaked around the thief's wrist. Twisting his arm behind his back, I slid in behind him and pushed a stiletto blade against his throat.

"If you ever put that hand on me or any of my possessions ever again, you'll lose those fingers," I growled in his ear.

A few snorts could be heard across the room. "Yeah, good luck with that."

The name *the Oncoming Storm* should draw gasps of fear not bursts of laughter. These people had no respect for me. I would have to build my reputation from scratch. Rage clawed at my chest. Why did everything always have to be so godsdamn hard?

I shoved the thief away from me and shot another stiletto into my palm. "Come on then."

The man who had tried to steal my pearls leered at me while snickers rose from the crowd. Unrestrained anger surged through my body. I gave into it. Darkness filled my eyes as tendrils of black smoke whipped across my skin. Sharp intakes of breath echoed through the tavern. *That's more like it.*

"Ashaana," someone whispered.

There was that word again. The word that was incredibly important but the one I couldn't ask anyone about.

I leveled black eyes filled with rage on the man in front of me. He shrank back and raised his hands. Spreading my arms wide, I turned in a slow circle around the room.

"Anyone else?" I ground out between gritted teeth. The watching Pernulans stayed in their seats. "Good. Can we finally move on to business then?"

A few of the people around me nodded. I tried to pull the darkness back into my soul but it refused to leave. It was like trying to pull a boulder with a piece of string. Damn. I really needed to figure out how this thing worked. However, that was a problem for another day. Seeing as I could do nothing about it, I decided to just roll with it and continued explaining my job offer with black smoke swirling around me.

"Now, here's my offer. The day after tomorrow I need a flash mob to appear in a particular street at a particular time. You won't need to do any fighting, killing, stealing, or anything else that actually requires some sort of skill set. You only need to block the road." I lifted the leather pouch. "I will pay in pearls. Any takers?"

Uncertain glances bounced across the crowd until a man with tattoos along his heavily muscled arms shrugged and stood up. "Sounds like a good deal. I'm in."

After that, most of the tavern's occupants followed suit. People shifted from standing to sitting and back again as I gave instructions about the time and place and the target they were blocking. My purse was a lot lighter when I'd finally briefed everyone and handed out the pearls.

"I am very good with faces," I said and moved my still black eyes between everyone who had received payment. "If you don't show up, I will know and I will hunt down everyone who doesn't keep their end of the bargain." Lightning crackled over my skin. "And trust me, that is something you want to avoid."

Wood creaked as some occupants shifted uncomfortably in their chairs.

"Besides," I continued, "I'll have more jobs coming up and I pay well. So, keep your word and we can do lots of business together." Spinning around, I strode towards the door. "Be seeing you," I called over my shoulder before stepping into the warm night.

Only when I was halfway back to the school did the darkness finally retreat into the deep pits of my soul. It left me drained, but hopefully that stunt I'd pulled would spread across the Pernulan Underworld and spark a rumor about the Oncoming Storm on this continent as well. It would make my job so much easier if people actually took me seriously. Regardless, I was fairly confident that the people from the tavern would at least keep their word and block the road in two days' time. I grinned and broke into a jog. Marcellus would have no idea what hit him.

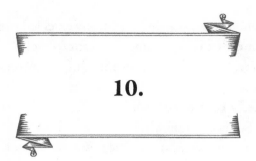

10.

"You really think this will work?"

I lifted my shoulders in a brief shrug. "I guess we'll find out."

Horse hooves on stone echoed from down the street. Elaran and I shrank back into the shadows as the sound drew closer. From our vantage point on a side street, we watched a grand dark brown carriage roll past. The white horse that drew the intricately carved coach flicked its tail as it passed our alley. Only a few people strolled along the street but they all quickly moved out of the way.

"Any second now," I whispered.

In a heartbeat, the peaceful scene shattered like a smashed mirror. Doors banged open in front of the equipage and a stream of men and women poured out. It was people I recognized instantly: my recruits from the tavern. Sparkling satisfaction coursed through my body. They had taken me seriously.

Further down the street, more people welled out. They only numbered about half of my recruits. I glanced towards Elaran.

"Damn," he swore.

"Those were the only ones you manage to recruit?"

"No!" He glared at the measly crowd he'd managed to gather as they mixed with mine. "I paid at least twice that amount to be here." My elven companion shook his head. He sounded embarrassed. "I don't understand why only half of mine showed up. I did pay them."

"I think I know." I gave him a teasing smile. "You're not scary enough."

"Says the girl who's a head and half shorter than me."

I released a soft chuckle. "Yeah, so that's saying something about how terrifying *you* are."

"Not scary enough, huh?" Elaran muttered under his breath with his eyes locked on the crowd before he turned back to me. "Are we doing this or what?"

"Ready when you are."

The grumpy elf gave me a short nod. We moved out. Slinking through the mass of bodies in a practiced fashion, we advanced on the coach. All around us, men and women paced to and fro like some kind of disoriented anthill. No one said anything. They just shifted places with each other only to move back again. I suppressed the urge to chuckle.

"What in Werz's name is going on?" an irritated voice I knew well bellowed from inside the carriage.

Despite my previous studies back in Keutunan and Norah's rigorous lessons every day since we arrived here, I still wasn't fluent in Pernish. But I extrapolated based on context and managed to understand enough to figure out the gist of what was being said.

Marcellus stuck his head out the coach's window. "Who the hell are all these people?"

"I'm sorry, General. I don't know," the driver called. "They just appeared out of nowhere."

"I don't care. Just get them to move! They're announcing the candidates today. We cannot be late!"

Elaran and I split up and set course for either side of the carriage. When I slunk past the window, I had to force myself to twist away so that Marcellus wouldn't recognize me, but all I wanted to do was stop and gloat. The horse whinnied and flicked its tail restlessly. I met Elaran's eyes on the other side of the animal and gave him a quick nod. He nodded back.

A stiletto blade shot into my hand and in one swift motion, I cut the strap securing the white horse to the coach. I assumed Elaran had been successful as well because after a brief glance in my direction, followed by a nod from me, he put two fingers to his lips and blew three shrill notes. The sea of people parted in an instant. I smacked the horse's backside and darted into the crowd.

The white horse shot forward. A startled yelp rang out from the driver as he was pulled from his seat by the bolting animal. Hidden in the mass of people still lining the street, I watched him land heavily on the ground before he dropped the reins. The horse sprinted down the empty corridor created by our flash mob and disappeared from view. A wide grin spread across my face as I slunk back towards the side street we had waited in earlier.

General Marcellus had jumped out of the coach and was busy shouting profanities at the driver and the horde of people around them when Elaran finally arrived at the alley as well. The crowd lingered for another few moments, staring blankly at the angry general, before they drifted off in different directions as if nothing had happened.

"So... that worked out rather well, didn't it?" I commented.

I had the pleasure of seeing Elaran's mouth quirk upwards in a smile. "Yeah, it did."

"We should probably get going." I grinned. "So that we don't miss his grand entrance."

The auburn-haired elf and I took off along the side street. We jogged at the fastest pace we could without wearing ourselves out in the heat that blanketed the city. Though, I had a feeling that Elaran was running slower than he otherwise would have so that I could keep up. But me being the proud and stubborn person I was, I pretended not to notice. The streets were uncharacteristically empty. At this time of day, they ought to be teeming with life. However, I suspected it was due to the very important event taking place outside Blackspire right now. The important event that General Marcellus would now be late to. Rounding the last corner, my elven companion and I ran headfirst into a wall of bodies.

The wide square in front of the obsidian palace was packed to the limit with people. A few onlookers even leaned out of windows on the nearby buildings. Excited chatter filled the air as they all studied the people on the podium. Where the box had been a week ago, a large stage now stood. Upon it were several men in various outfits. I started pushing my way through the crowd towards the unadorned wall we had watched from last week. Elaran followed.

"He's not here yet so I'm guessing it worked?" Haela called when she saw us making our way through the rows of people.

I heaved a deep sigh as I finally cleared the mass of bodies and arrived at the wall. Leaning back against the warm stones, I released another long exhale before turning to the excited twin and the rest of our group. "Yep, sure did."

Elaran detached himself from the crowd and took up position next to Haemir. "How are things going here?"

"They've already announced the candidates for High Priest and Master of Knowledge but since Marcellus isn't here yet, they're now just waiting for him so they can announce the ones for General as well." Zaina waved a hand at the podium. "The election supervisors have announced several times that they're just waiting for Marcellus to show up."

"So, he's not exactly making a fine first impression," I summarized.

"Nope," Haela confirmed.

"Perfect." I turned back towards the stage to look for the last member of our group. "How's Shade doing?"

"Good, I suppose." Liam pointed to the side of the podium. "He's on the left."

The wall we occupied was close enough that we could both see the stage well and hear what the candidates were saying, but it was at a strange enough angle that if you weren't specifically looking for us, you wouldn't notice us. Shade stood straight-backed at the edge of the dais with a calm mask on his face. I furrowed my brows.

"Is he wearing... new clothes?" I asked.

The Master Assassin wore a crisp black suit that fit his body perfectly and accentuated his lean muscles. It had to have been tailor-made for him.

"Yeah," Zaina said. "If he's gonna appeal to the good people of Pernula he can't very well walk around looking like an underworlder, now can he?" Her dark eyes sparkled. "He looks good, right?"

"I guess so." I tore my eyes from the well-dressed assassin and turned to the smuggler. "Is it actually called Underworld and Upperworld here too?"

The Pernish native gave me a carefree shrug. "No. It's not actually called anything here because people just pretend that the Underworld doesn't exist. But I liked those names so I think I'm gonna steal them."

"Oh, go right ahead. It would make things a lot easier for us too."

Just as Zaina opened her mouth to respond, a commotion on the other side of the square interrupted us. A very disheveled-looking man broke through the crowd and stalked towards the stage. Marcellus climbed onto the podium, his chest rising and falling in heavy breaths as if he had run there. Which he had. Because of us and our stunt with the horse and the flash mob. He straightened his rumpled clothing and ran both hands through his messy dark brown hair to smoothen it.

"Now that we are all here, *finally*," the plump election supervisor added with acidity, "we can at last present the candidates for the position of General of Pernula." He swept his arm towards Marcellus. "Our first candidate is someone you know well. It is our current General: Marcellus."

The tardy general stepped forward and raised his hand in greeting. Disappointment flashed over his face when the crowd's cheers were only lukewarm, but he recovered quickly and raised his voice so that it would carry across the square. Zaina translated for our group.

"Fine citizens of Pernula," he began. "I do sincerely apologize for being late. I was held up on my way here."

"You knew when this event started," the election supervisor with the double chin commented. "You should have planned accordingly."

General Marcellus shot him such a scorching glare that I was surprised the outspoken supervisor didn't get burn marks. However, he did snap his mouth shut while taking a step back. The furious general turned back to the gathered audience.

"As I said, unforeseen events happened that made me late but I am no less excited to be here. It has been an honor to represent you as your General these last years and I will gladly do so next term as well."

Clapping and a few cheers rose from the spectators as Marcellus once again raised his hand before stepping back. The leading election supervisor strode forward again.

"Next up, we have a new candidate who is participating for the first time," he called across the sea of people before motioning at the black-clad man on the left of the stage. "Please welcome Shade!"

If I could have captured the moment when Marcellus connected the dots, I would have watched it on replay forever. At the mention of that very distinctive name, his brows scrunched up and he drew back a little. Then, when he saw the familiar assassin striding towards the middle of the podium, his jaw all but dropped to the floor. Shock, utter disbelief, and then boundless rage flashed past on his face. Shade gave him a sly smile before turning to face the crowd.

"Honorable citizens of Pernula," he said in flawless Pernish.

Okay, so someone had studied a bit more Pernish back in Keutunan than he had shared with the group. Why was I not surprised? Him and his bloody secrets.

"It is a pleasure being here today," Shade continued. "I believe that it is time for a change in military leadership. General Marcellus has done an admirable job in the past but after his failed invasion of the Lost Island, perhaps it is time for him to step aside? I am here to offer an alternative. With a successful career leading fighters and advising other rulers, I believe I am the perfect candidate to lead Pernula into a new era. An era of greatness."

Silence fell across the square as the gathered Pernulans tried to decide what they thought about this new contender making bold claims. Zaina released a loud and very long whoop and clapped her hands. That broke the spell. Clapping ensued from the rest of the audience and a few more cheers rang out. Not nearly as many as when Marcellus had talked but enough that people would remember Shade's speech on a positive note when they thought back on the day's events. The Master of the Assassins' Guild bowed slightly and stepped back.

After that, the rest of the candidates were announced but it completely passed Marcellus by because his attention was solely on the Keutunian assassin. Eyes that burned with hatred stayed fixed on his competitor's face but Shade kept his cool mask and pretended not to notice.

"That concludes the candidate introductions," the election supervisor eventually called. "Our next event will be the debate in a few weeks' time. I look forward to seeing you there. Until then, participants, I wish you luck with your campaigns. May the best man win!"

The men on the stage bid the spectators farewell in whichever way they preferred. General Marcellus raised a gracious hand to wave, one of the High Priest candidates lifted some kind of staff, and Shade simply inclined his head before exiting at the back of the podium. All around us, the crowd started breaking up. Lively chatter about today's event floated from every corner, and more than one onlooker gestured wildly while debating something with their companions. I kept my eyes on the dark-clad man making his way across the square.

"Nice speech," I said as Shade stopped in front of our group.

"Yeah, you managed to both boost your own skills and deliver a heavy blow to Marcellus in the same sentence." Haela grinned and rubbed her hands. "I like it."

"Thank you," the assassin said. "And I noticed that our... distraction worked. Well done. Now we need to plan our next move."

"Or..." the female half of the twins began, "and I'm just throwing this out there, we could celebrate? Like normal people do when they accomplish something."

"Ha! I like this one." Zaina chuckled and nodded towards Haela.

"See!" the black-haired elf continued. "Let's go get something to eat and drink."

"I second that," Liam added. "I'm hungry too."

I nudged an elbow in his ribs. "Yeah, but you're always hungry."

My best friend gave me a mock scowl while his eyes glittered with mischief. "Yes, because unlike some, I can't survive on sarcasm and snarky remarks alone."

Haela let out a long *oh* while her brother leaned forward and put a hand on my arm. "Want some ice for that burn?"

While grimacing at the twins, I gave Liam a soft shove to the shoulder. "Moron."

The Master of the Assassins' Guild released a deep sigh and shook his head. "Fine. I guess we do have to eat."

An excited whoop escaped Haela's throat as she jumped and drove a fist in the air. "Alright, let's go celebrate!"

Our group of seven laughed at the energetic elf who never turned down a good time. It was so easy to just move on to the next problem all the time and forget to celebrate the victories. Unless you had someone like Haela, that is. I smiled as Zaina led us away from Blackspire. Good thing not everyone was as cynical and pessimistic as me.

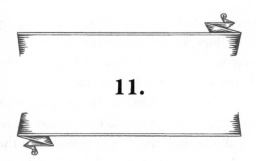

11.

Cheerful tunes drifted from the other side of the courtyard where a group of musicians played and the sound mingled with the murmur of chatting people. From our large table in the corner, I studied the space. It was some kind of outdoors tavern. Chairs and tables filled the stone courtyard and servers moved between the tables with sweet-smelling pastries. A café, Zaina had called it.

"I got us all a piece of pearl cake," the Pernish smuggler said as she dropped into her chair. "It's kind of like our national cake."

Liam's eyes sparkled. "I can't wait to try it!"

The wide tree branches above us cast leaf-shaped shadows on his excited face. I smiled. That boy loved everything sweet. We didn't have to wait long before a server approached with a large tray. He placed seven plates with slices of cake and seven mugs of some pale, yellow liquid on our table before withdrawing again.

Zaina lifted her mug. "To new friends, the promise of a ship..." Her mouth drew into a wide smile. "...and to kicking Marcellus' ass!"

Laughter rang out at our table, but eventually everyone pulled themselves together enough to reply, "To kicking Marcellus' ass!"

Sourness from the drink made my tongue curl but it was also very refreshing. Taking a bite of the cake, I realized that the drink complemented it well. The pearl cake was delicious, and very sweet, which was balanced nicely by the sour drink.

"Zaina, it's time," Elaran said. He didn't sound angry or bitter. Only tired. "You need to tell us about the other elves now."

The Pernish smuggler swallowed another piece of cake and took a sip from her mug. "Yeah, you're right." She blew out a long breath. "Gods, where do I even start?"

I put my spoon down and leaned forward on the table. We knew that Pernula was only one part of this continent and that there were other lands and people out there, but in the week since we arrived, we had been so busy setting our grand plan in motion that we hadn't had time to discuss it. Now, it seemed as though we were finally about to find out.

"Okay, so just as there are other nations of humans," Zaina began, "there are also other nations of elves. You're wood elves and there are wood elves here too so I'm guessing some of your people left and settled on the Lost Island centuries ago. But there are also other types of elves. Like mountain elves, dark elves, star elves-"

"How did you know we were wood elves?" Haemir interrupted.

"Your eyes." Zaina motioned at the twins and Elaran. "All wood elves have yellow eyes."

"Huh."

Our table fell silent as we all pondered this new piece of information. So there were lots of other nations and people out there. The world was much bigger than I'd ever dared dream.

But why weren't other elves as common in Pernula? As if he had heard my thoughts, Elaran spoke up.

"When we first arrived, you said it was a good thing we were wood elves because it would've been a problem if we were star elves. What does that mean?"

"Now we come to the complicated part." Zaina drummed her fingers on the table. "There's a war going on. It's been like that for many, many years now. And the star elves are the ones behind it."

"If it's been going on for so long, why hasn't it reached here yet?" Liam asked.

"Because it's elves! They have such ridiculously long lifespans. To rush isn't exactly in their vocabulary." She glanced at the three elves present. "No offense."

Haemir held up a hand. "None taken. But what's this war about? Why did the star elves start it?"

A warm breeze ruffled the leaves above our heads as Zaina considered how best to explain. I took another sip of the sour drink.

"We're not exactly sure," she finally admitted. "They don't really explain their motives, they just... conquer. Many nations, human and elven, have already fallen and they're not stopping. They keep advancing across the continent, slowly but surely. It probably won't be that many years until they declare war on us too."

Joyous music and mirthful chatter continued to drift across the courtyard but our table had grown silent. So that was why the Pernulans had tried to invade Keutunan. If it hadn't been our island they'd tried to take over, I would've understood the need behind it. But it *was* our island, and we needed that peace treaty.

"So, yeah," Zaina said, "that's why it's a good thing your ancestors were wood elves and not star elves."

A somber mood settled over our group. Haela smacked her lips.

"This was so not what I had in mind when I said *let's celebrate*." She stabbed a spoon in Elaran's direction. "No more talk about gloom and doom. Now we're gonna be happy about our victory. Maybe plot a bit more mischief." The determined twin pushed to her feet. "And I want another piece of cake."

The serious atmosphere dissipated and was replaced by surprised laughter. Leave it to Haela to raise everyone's spirits. Sometimes, I really was jealous of her social skills.

While conversion broke out again and a few of our group left to get more cake, I studied the black-haired assassin. He had remained silent during Zaina's story, and that unreadable mask he so often transformed his face into had been lodged in place the whole time. I wondered how much of this he had already known. With him, it was impossible to tell.

Shade's black eyes flicked to mine and he gave me a knowing smile when he caught me staring at him. I blew out a long breath through my nose and shook my head. He was a man of many secrets. I just wondered how many of them would come to light during this adventure. Taking another sip of my drink, I gave him a sly smile back. We would just have to wait and see, wouldn't we?

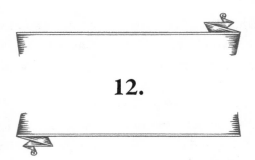

12.

Full of cake and lemonade, as Zaina had explained the drink was called, we left the cozy café behind. Hopefully, we would get to visit the Lemon Tree Café many more times before our mission in Pernula was over.

"Alright, I need to go take care of some things with my gang but you can find your way back to the school, right?" Zaina said.

She had previously explained that their Underworld wasn't organized in guilds, it was made up of gangs. I still found that word funny. Gang. As if they were a bunch of unruly street urchins. I suppressed the chuckle building in my chest and instead nodded in response to her question.

"Good. I'll see you tonight then." She fired off a quick salute before trotting off down the street.

"I've actually made friends with a nice couple who sell hats," Liam said. "I promised to join them for tea this afternoon."

I raised my eyebrows. "Oh?"

"Yeah." He lifted his shoulders in a light shrug. "Norah introduced me to them. They're actually pretty influential with people who sell clothes and stuff so if I can get them on our side, they'll be pretty good for our campaign."

Why had I bothered to raise my eyebrows? As if Liam making connections was in any way a surprise. That boy could make friends with an anti-social pine cone if he really wanted to. *Everyone* who met him liked him.

"We've actually also got somewhere to be," Haemir said and waved a hand at his sister. "There's this... debate club, kind of, that we've been working on getting invited to."

"Great, stay on that," Shade said. "I'm going to head to Blackspire and pay Marcellus a visit." He turned to me and arched an eyebrow. "Wanna come?"

At first, I drew back a little in surprise but a grin quickly descended on my face. "For sure."

Elaran huffed and crossed his arms. "I guess I'll just go back to the school then. And... strategize."

I had to twist away and pretend to look at a passing couple so that the grumpy elf wouldn't see the amusement on my face. Once I'd finally managed to wipe the self-satisfied smile off my lips, I turned back.

"Sounds like a plan," I said. "See you guys later then."

"Later!"

"Yep, see you!"

After we'd exchanged goodbyes with the rest of our group, Shade and I started towards the palace. A horse carriage thundered down the road, which made people leap out of the way. I nimbly stepped around it before rejoining the assassin on the other side.

"So, we're gonna break into Blackspire?" I said.

He snorted. "Yeah, right."

When I just furrowed my brows and kept staring at him, he seemed to finally realize that I was being serious. His pleasant-sounding laugh filled the air.

"You seriously believed we were going to break into the castle, *the castle*, blind and in broad daylight – and you still agreed to come?"

I lifted one shoulder in a shrug. "Well, yeah."

Shade tilted his head slightly to the right while studying me. "You really are quite something, aren't you?" He let out another brief chuckle. "No, we're going to do something even better."

He paused dramatically, waiting for me to ask what it was, but I just spun my hand in the air a couple of times, motioning for him to get on with it.

The Master Assassin shook his head. "We are going to walk straight in through the front doors."

Now it was my time to stare at him in surprise. "And how exactly are we gonna accomplish that?"

"Wait and see."

Damn assassin and his damn secrets. Again. However, I knew it was no use trying to pry the information from him. If he didn't want to share, he wasn't going to share. And besides, I didn't want him to see how much it irked me when he did stuff like this. So instead of asking more questions, I just gave him a lazy shrug.

We moved through the rest of the Inner Ring in comfortable silence. Zaina had explained that the city was divided into three rings, starting from Blackspire with the Inner Ring, then the Middle Ring, and lastly the Outer Ring. The inner one was the most expensive and then property value decreased the further out you got. Despite that, Pernula's Underworld gangs seemed to somehow be present in every ring, which I found rather fascinating.

"When we get to the gate, let me do the talking," Shade said, interrupting my musings.

"Fine."

In front of us, rays hit the palace's slick black surface, making it gleam like a dark jewel in the midday sun. Two guards in full armor protected the gate we approached. Before we reached them, I had time to wonder how insufferably hot it must be standing there in those clothes while heat bore down on them from above.

"Who are you?" the blond one on the left demanded.

"Oh, you might have seen me up on the stage earlier today," Shade said in a pleasant voice. "My name is Shade. I am one of the candidates for the position of General."

The blond guard's partner nodded in confirmation. "He is. I remember him."

"Great," the Master Assassin continued. "I am here to speak with General Marcellus. Candidate to candidate."

Both men shifted their eyes to me. "And who is this?" the dark-haired one on the right asked.

"This is my assistant."

It took all my self-control not to burst out laughing. Assistant? I had to have been the most well-armed assistant they'd ever seen. He'd have been better off telling them I was his bodyguard.

"You're going to have to leave all your weapons before you enter Blackspire," the blond one informed us.

"Of course," Shade said with another pleasant smile.

After a curt nod from the guards, they pulled open the gate and ushered us through. Inside we were met by more armed men and also a bunch of clerks who recorded our inventory and promised we would get them back when we left. While I removed my blades, another clerk explained different palace rules that I only half listened to, until at last a bespectacled man arrived to guide us into Blackspire.

"You have a few left, don't you?" Shade asked me, knowing I would understand that he meant knives.

"Mm-hmm. You do as well, right?"

The Master of the Assassins' Guild gave me a lopsided smile in reply. I shook my head at the memory of the guards back at the gate. Such amateurs. In front of us, our guide blabbered on about the gardens on either side of the stone path we followed. Flowers and bushes didn't excite me that much but I pretended to be fascinated by them while mapping the area in my head. Though, it was pretty. Even I had to admit that.

"Here we are," the clerk said as we stopped outside two very tall double doors. "Now remember, don't touch any of the paintings."

Frowning, I was just about to question why in Nemanan's name someone would want to touch the paintings, but a sharp look from Shade stopped me before the comment made it past my lips.

"Of course," the eloquent assassin said instead.

The bespectacled man gave us a satisfied nod and then pulled open the doors. A long hallway met us on the other side. Red carpets, paintings, and other details of the same color, complemented the polished black interior. Craning my neck, I looked up at the high ceiling. Okay, this was rather beautiful.

"Follow me, please," our guide said and started down the corridor.

While he led us deeper into the palace, I continued adding to my mental map. By the expression on Shade's face, he was doing the same. After a while, we arrived at a pair of closed doors. The clerk knocked twice.

"What is it?" a voice called in Pernish from the other side.

"You have two visitors, General," our guide replied.

"I'm in a meeting."

"I apologize, General. I will tell Candidate Shade and his assistant to come back later." He turned to us. "I am sorry, but as you can hear, General Marcellus is busy. If you want you can—"

One of the doors was thrown open. In the doorway stood the man who had tried to kill us and take over our city.

"Candidate Shade," General Marcellus said and flashed a brilliant smile. "And the Oncoming Storm. I think I can make some time for you." He pushed the door open wider. "Please, come in."

The clerk who had guided us here inclined his head towards his general and stepped back. Shade and I exchanged a look before striding across the threshold. The door clicked shut behind us.

"We were just talking about you," Marcellus said while two blond men stood up from their chairs.

Oh. Them. I felt the comforting weight of the knives in my sleeves.

"If it isn't William and Eric Fahr." Shade's eyes had taken on a predatory glint. "The brothers who murdered the Queen Mother and betrayed their country."

"Shade," the younger Lord Fahr spat before turning cold blue eyes to me. "And I see you brought the thief who butchered my son."

"I did, yes. But in my defense, I didn't know I would find you here, advising a ruler of Pernula."

Marcellus barreled past and took up position in the middle of the room full of murderers. "Why are you here? And more importantly, why are you running for General in *my* country?"

The Master Assassin turned hard eyes on the General. "You tried to mess with my country. Now, I'm going to mess with yours. Well, *you*, specifically. You are going to lose this election. To me or someone else. Unless... you give me what I want."

"And what would that be?"

"Before this election is over, you will have signed a peace treaty between Pernula and the nations of Keutunan and Tkeideru."

Uncontrolled laughter exploded from General Marcellus' chest. "I have a better idea. How about I kill you right now and bury you in a shallow grave?"

Shade tapped a finger to his jaw, pretending to think hard. "You could. But don't you think murdering your opponent would, I don't know, taint the election? If I were to mysteriously disappear only hours after I challenged you publicly, how do you think the fine citizens of Pernula would react?"

Marcellus opened his mouth but then closed it again. The Fahr brothers just continued watching the exchange with venomous stares.

"How unfortunate that your horse ran away today so that you made a bad first impression," the assassin pressed on. "It would be a shame if something like that happened again."

The General's eyes widened as realization dawned but before he could say anything, a vicious grin settled on Shade's lips.

"Come find me when you're ready to sign that peace treaty." And with that, the Master of the Assassins' Guild turned and strode towards the door.

After giving the Fahr brothers a smile as sharp as one of my knives, I followed Shade out the door. It banged as I pulled it closed behind us. I let out a soft chuckle as we started towards the exit. Damn. Shade sure was an arrogant bastard if I'd ever met one. And I kind of liked it. I would've handled the situation in that room in almost exactly the same way.

We'd had our ups and down over the years. And by that, of course, I mean we'd threatened, blackmailed, and outright tried to kill each other on more than one occasion. Not sure if that would qualify as *ups and downs* for other people, but for us, it was pretty normal. Anyway, I was glad we were on the same side this time. I glanced at the athletic assassin next to me as we finally reached the outer doors. The two of us working together. Not just trying to manipulate each other but *really* working together. I released another soft chuckle. Oh, imagine the damage we could do.

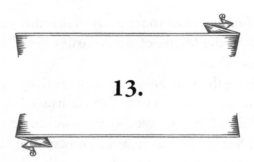

13.

"You'll be fine."

"No, I won't!" I crossed my arms and scowled at my five companions. "Why do I have to be the only one doing this?"

Despite there only being six people present, the school's living room felt very cramped. Liam, Shade, Elaran, and the twins stood in a half circle in front of the door I'd tried to escape through after Elaran had shared the latest plan he'd concocted while strategizing.

We'd spent the last week and a half running small scale interference with Marcellus' campaign. Some more stalling, a few acts of sabotage, and a hired mob or two shouting profanities during his speeches. All the while, Liam and the twins had worked their connections in the Upperworld. But now, Mr. Strategizing had come up with a new plan. And I hated it.

"You're not the only one doing it," Liam pointed out. "You're just the only one doing it in the Underworld."

"Exactly. Why can't Shade work that angle?" I flicked a hand at Elaran. "Or you. It was your bloody idea. I'm not the only one on Team Underworld."

Haemir gave me a look of understanding but went ahead and crushed my argument anyway. "Shade can't be seen making connections in the Underworld, you know that. The Pernulans hate that part of the population and pretend they don't exist, so if it became known that Shade mingles with those people, it would hurt his campaign."

"And I'm not scary enough for them to take me seriously." Elaran gave me a challenging stare. "As someone pointed out."

"I still think you should be covering the Underworld too." Shade studied the archer through narrowed eyes. "It is your job, after all."

The grumpy ranger threw an equally annoyed look back at the assassin. "My efforts will be much more effective elsewhere. And frankly, I don't care what you think. You're not in charge here."

"Oh, wanna bet?" A vicious smile flashed across Shade's lips.

"Guys!" Haemir cut in before swords were drawn. "Focus." He turned back to me. "The point is, it doesn't matter if *you* are seen making friends with shady people because even though they know you're part of Shade's team, your reputation doesn't affect his. And Elaran is right, you know how to behave in those circles. The rest of us don't. That's why it has to be you."

For a moment, the room fell silent. All eyes were on me. I knew that what he said made sense but I still didn't like it.

"Ugh!" I groaned and threw my arms in the air. The wooden floor creaked as I paced back and forth in front of my so-called allies. "I hate you all."

Liam patted me on the arm. "You'll be fine. Just talk to them and make friends."

"I don't know how to make friends!" I impatiently shoved a stack of papers out of the way and leaned back against the desk by the door.

Haela chuckled at the defeated look on my face but came and sat down next to me. "Of course you do. How did you make friends with all of us?"

"I don't know!" I blew out an exasperated breath and waved a hand at Liam. "He just showed up one day and refused to leave. And you three," I motioned at Elaran and the twins, "I infiltrated your city and tried to kill your queen. And you," I turned to the Master Assassin, "you and I spend as much time at each other's throats as we do... actually, I don't even know what we're doing when we're not threatening, blackmailing, or trying to kill each other."

The room burst out laughing. I studied them from under furrowed brows. Yeah, I really had no idea how in the world we had become friends. Though I was glad we were.

"Alright, alright," I muttered and pushed off the table. "I'll do it. I'll just go and make some friends." The wooden planks vibrated as I stalked to the door. "Right, no big deal. Just... make some friends."

More laughter followed me as I stomped through the corridor. A warm evening met me outside when I yanked the door open. As I moved through the streets painted gold by the setting sun, I tried to boost my confidence. I'd killed a king, for Nemanan's sake! How hard could making some new friends be?

MOONLIGHT SPILLED THROUGH the tightly packed buildings as I moved towards my fourth tavern of the night.

"Hmm... I only had to break one finger, threaten to kill three people, and throw two knives that time," I mused. "I think I'm getting the hang of this *making friends* thing."

A few sharp turns through narrow alleys took me to the pub I'd visited when I recruited that first flash mob. Sweat and other odors met me this time as well when I strode across the threshold. Candlelight flickered over quite a lot of faces I recognized. I'd recruited most of them for one job or another these last couple of weeks.

"The Oncoming Storm," a man said as I moved towards the bar. It was the tattooed one who'd been the first to accept my flash mob proposal. "Back again. Got another job for us?"

"Nope," I replied. "This time, I'm only here to drink."

After receiving payment, the bartender slid a robust mug filled to the brim with ale across the counter. I picked it up. *Now what?*

Everyone was already seated in groups so if I wanted to join them, I would have to walk straight up to a table and just sit down. Or ask them if I could join. Neither of those options sounded like something I wanted to do.

Come on, you have to talk to people to make friends. Just walk up to the guy with the tattoos and ask if you can join. My stomach twisted at the thought but my mind kept pushing. *Just do it! You killed a king. You can ask a stranger if you can join his table.* I took a half step forward. *Nope.* Transforming the motion, I instead swung the disobedient leg over my other one so it looked like I was only crossing my ankles. Why did I have to be so incredibly awkward? It was ridiculous.

"Hey," the muscular man with the tattoos called, breaking my lament over my nonexistent social skills. "Don't mean to be nosy or anything but I've been wanting to ask, you're with that Shade guy, aren't you?"

"Yeah," I replied. "How did you know?"

A deep laugh rumbled in his broad chest. "Not that many people from the Lost Island here so figured you kinda had to know each other."

Only my very impressive self-control prevented me from facepalming. *Obviously.*

I let out an embarrassed laugh. "Right. Good point."

"Why don't you come sit down so we don't have to shout across the whole room?" He pulled out an empty chair at his table and nodded towards it.

"Sure," I said with a light shrug as if it was no big deal and not the exact thing I'd been trying to do ever since I walked through the door.

The tattooed man and his two companions scooted over and made room by the table as I walked over. Fire flickered when they pushed the candle towards the center to make room for my mug. I dropped into the offered chair, making the scraggly wooden thing creak.

"Why's he here?" my host asked, picking up the thread from before.

"Shade?" I took a swig of bitter ale. "To win the election, I suppose. Beyond that, I'm not sure. I never really can tell what his endgame is." That much was true at least.

"Huh." He scratched at the bun that gathered up his dark brown hair. "What about you? Why're you here? You work for him?"

I snorted. "I don't work for anyone. I'm here to kill two people who fled here from our city."

The muscled man raised his eyebrows while his two friends studied me with curious looks on their faces.

"It's a long story," I added. "And yeah, I suppose I help Shade too."

"Ah, so you *do* work for him."

"I work *with* him." I raised a finger in the air. "Big difference."

Another rumbling laugh escaped his throat, making the large battle axe across his back shake. The other two people chuckled as well. Patrons from the other tables glanced in our direction and I had a feeling that some of them were eavesdropping on our conversation. Good.

"Oh by the way, I never caught your name," I said when the laughter at our table had quieted down.

"Yngvild." The tattooed man reached a calloused hand across the mess of mugs, candles, and spilled ale. I shook it. "And this is–"

"Vania," the blond woman opposite him filled in and nodded in my direction.

The third man lifted a hand. "I'm Kildor."

I nodded at Vania and Kildor in turn. "Good to meet you. My friends call me Storm."

A slow smile spread across Yngvild's face. "Storm."

"So how do you know each other?" I motioned at the three of them. "Are you from the same gang?"

"Yes."

"No."

Yngvild and Vania turned to look at each other, two pairs of pale blue eyes meeting across the table.

"What do you mean *yes*? We're not a gang, Yngvild," the tall woman said.

"Alright, maybe not a gang," the axe-wielder muttered. "But we look out for each other. Most of us in this pub do." He raised his voice. "Ain't that right, all you eavesdroppers?"

Mugs and utensils clattered as the rest of the tavern scrambled to make it look like they weren't paying attention.

Kildor chuckled. "True. Not that we haven't been offered to join a gang or anything."

"Oh?" I raised my eyebrows. "Whose? Why did you turn it down?"

Vania cast a sharp glance at her friend. "Best not mention any names."

"Yeah," Yngvild filled in. "Let's just say we don't like how he runs his gang."

Sensing that this was a delicate subject and not one to push too early, I just nodded in acknowledgement and took another drink of ale. Conversation moved from gang politics to tales of adventure. They shared stories from their lives, which is when I found out that Yngvild and Vania were from another country, one that was now controlled by the star elves. I even shared a few tales of my own. Despite my earlier reservations about making friends, I actually found myself enjoying it.

When we'd downed enough drinks to make the edges of my vision go all fuzzy, I decided to call it a night. Only one more thing left. The real reason I was in this tavern that night.

"Oh, by the way," I said loudly, as if I was too drunk to keep it down. I mean, I *was* drunk, but I wanted the whole room to overhear. "Remember I said I'm a bit involved in the election? You're not gonna believe what I overheard. Marcellus is gonna name the Fahr brothers his senior advisors."

My three table companions looked back at me with confusion in their eyes. *Right. That doesn't really mean anything to them.*

"They're the two lords from Keutunan I talked about before," I elaborated.

"The ones you're here to kill?" Kildor asked.

"Yeah, if I can pull that off." I swept a conspiratorial gaze across the room. "Let's hope I manage that before they become the senior advisors because trust me, we're gonna be so screwed if that happens. They hate underworlders—"

"Underworlders?"

"Well, us. That's what we call our kind back home."

"I like it." Vania gave me an approving nod.

"Yeah, me too," I said. "But if Marcellus gives the Fahr brothers power, they're gonna try and wipe out your Underworld too."

Vania crossed her lean muscular arms over her chest. "Let's hope you kill them first then."

"Yeah." I pushed off from the chair. "I've gotta head back. And plan that assassination," I added with a wink.

My drinking companions laughed in response. "Don't be a stranger," Yngvild called as I weaved through the tables.

"I won't. Promise." When I reached the door, I lifted a hand. "I'll see you around."

Cool night winds refreshed my mind when I stepped outside. Or *cool* might be a bit much but it was at least better than the baking heat Pernula suffered during the day. I shook my head to clear it. Everything was still blurry around the edges but at least I'd accomplished my mission. The rumor that Marcellus was going to give the position as senior advisor to the Fahr brothers instead of his own countrymen was now live in the Underworld. It hadn't gone as smoothly at the other taverns as it had here, but I'd at least managed to start the rumor there too.

A wicked grin spread across my face as I let go of the door handle and started back towards the school. This, in addition to the others' rumormongering in the Upperworld, was going to land Marcellus in so much trouble.

Air rushed out of my lungs. Doubling over, I tried desperately to refill them while also trying to figure out what had just happened. Something hard connected with my jaw. Stars flickered before my eyes as I hit the stone street. Between the alcohol and the surprise hits, I was having trouble gathering my wits.

Rough hands grabbed my arms and hauled me into the nearest alley before slamming me down on my knees hard enough to make my bones rattle. The edge of a sword appeared along my throat while the point of another pressed into the back of my neck. I blinked at the scene in front of me. A slim man with dark beady eyes stared down at me from across the alley.

"The Oncoming Storm," he said. "I knew someone was recruiting in my territory but I wasn't sure who until two foreigners so kindly informed me."

"Eric and William Fahr. How very helpful of them," I muttered. "And what do you mean by your territory?"

The man to my right pressed his sword harder into my throat. "Show respect when addressing the Rat King."

Bursting out laughing was a really bad idea, I knew that, but it was very difficult not to. The Rat King? What a ridiculous name. Thankfully, I managed to stave off an ill-timed chuckle.

"Yes, this is my territory." The Rat King straightened his gray suit. "Consider this your first and final warning. Stop recruiting in my territory."

The implied *or else* was loud and clear. I scowled at him but said nothing.

"I also have a message for you from the Fahr brothers. Since they so kindly informed me about you, and since it's such a fun message, I figured I would deliver it for them." Malice seeped into his eyes. "They said: back off or your friend will meet with some terrible accident. It's a big city. A lot can go wrong, after all."

Threats brewed in my throat but before I could spit them out, the Rat King pressed on.

"Don't let me catch you infringing on my territory again." He flicked a wrist at the two men holding swords to my neck. "Make sure she remembers."

Before the Rat King had even fully turned around, the first blow struck. More pain shot up my side as a kick connected with my ribcage. I reached for a knife but another fist knocked me to the ground. While punches and kicks rained down on me from above, all I could do was try to stay conscious. The battering eventually ended and footsteps disappeared down the alley. My ears rang. I coughed blood onto the street.

"Well," I gasped and wiped blood from my mouth. "That could've gone better."

Everything ached. I flopped over on my back and for a few minutes, I just lay there on the rough stones while heaving deep breaths. Tomorrow, I would be sporting some wicked bruises but I was pretty sure that nothing was broken.

So, the Fahr brothers had set some local gang leader on me. Clever. They were stepping up their game. But so were we. I closed my eyes and released a long exhale before pushing my body into a sitting position. Time to head back to the school and cook up some more trouble for the pretentious brothers and the arrogant General. Smiling hurt, but I couldn't stop a vicious grin from spreading across my face. It was *so* on.

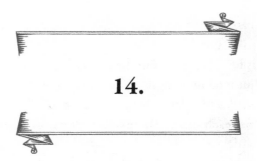

14.

My body protested loudly at every tiny movement but I ignored it and pushed down the handle of the kitchen door anyway. Inside, I was met by the heavenly scent of fried eggs and pork.

"What the hell happened to you?" Zaina exclaimed as she looked up from the frying pan.

The rest of my friends were seated at the sturdy table on the other side of the room. Shocked expressions settled on their features as well when they took in the state of my face. Liam shot up from his chair.

"Are you alright?" he asked, making a move to round the table.

I waved him back in his seat and strode towards one of the empty chairs. "I'm fine." After I had carefully lowered myself into it, I turned to Zaina. "I ran into the Rat King."

While I recounted the events of last night, the Pernish smuggler brought the last pan of eggs over. She put it down on the table and motioned for everyone to dig in before turning back to me. "Damn. Sorry about that. It seems like he's gotten more powerful in the months I've been gone. Smart move by Marcellus, though. We're gonna have to stop outside recruitment now. Any jobs we do are gonna have to be limited to what the seven of us can pull off because antagonizing the Rat King won't lead to anything good."

"Who is he?" I asked around a mouthful of fried eggs.

"Some jumped up gangster," Zaina said. "He's pretty savage, though. He rules his gang with an iron fist and he pits his own people against each other. There's no protection or loyalty, only obedience or death."

"Well, he sounds fun," Haela commented while scooping more food on her plate.

"Right. Well, apparently, the Fahr brothers sent him." I flicked my eyes to Liam. "They threatened you again. Said if I didn't back off, from ruining Marcellus' campaign I assume, you'd meet with a terrible accident."

Liam's dark blue eyes filled with sadness and exasperation but before he could reply, Shade cut in.

"It's an empty threat."

"How so?" Haemir asked.

"They can't kill him, or any of us, until after the election. If any of us die under mysterious circumstances then it would taint the election. And Marcellus can't have that." The Master Assassin looked to me. "That's why this Rat King only beat you up instead of killed you."

"I know." I squeezed my hand into a fist on the table. "But spreading rumors isn't enough. I want Marcellus humiliated."

A cackle rose from Haela's throat. "I actually had an idea about that. What if we drug him?" Mischief sparkled in her eyes as she swept her gaze around the table. "Before he goes on stage for the debate."

"We make him look like he's drunk in front of hundreds of people." Elaran ran a hand over his tight side-braid. "Yes, that could work really well for us."

"So how do we do it?" Liam asked.

A still warm frying pan hissed while our scheming group considered the question.

"If we do it too early, he will claim health issues and just cancel his appearance," Shade finally said. "We have to do it at the debate." His intelligent black eyes found mine. "*You* have to do it at the debate."

"You want me to..." I paused and massaged my forehead. "Let me get this straight. You want me to drug someone? On stage? While hundreds of people are watching?"

"Yep."

"How am I supposed to do that?"

"You're a thief," Elaran cut in and pushed a plate out of the way. "Figure it out."

"Yes, I'm a thief. I steal stuff, I don't manipulate elections!"

Haela gave me a bright smile "Just think of it as you're stealing his... sanity."

Even I couldn't help laughing at that. I shook my head. "Okay, fine. But I need to see the debate hall to make a plan."

"I can probably get you in," Zaina said. She scratched her sharp jawline. "Just give me like an hour. I need to set up a few things first."

I nodded at her.

"Alright, good," Shade said. "Storm and Zaina will start looking into that. And the rest of you know what to do."

"Yes, we know what to do, thank you," Elaran said, biting off each word.

Acid dripped from the stares the assassin and the ranger shot each other but they didn't continue the argument. While we cleared the table, I wondered how a full-blown fight between those two would end. I chuckled softly as I followed the others out the door. I would even pay to see that.

SUN BEAT DOWN ON ME as I sat cross-legged atop the stone wall surrounding the school. Heat from the stones beneath me seeped into my legs while I waited for Zaina. Across the fenced-in yard, Liam played with a group of students. I studied him.

His blue eyes glittered and a wide smile accentuated his beautiful features. When a boy caught him in a game of tag, he threw his head back and released a rippling laugh. It was a truly heartwarming sound. I couldn't remember the last time I'd seen Liam this happy. His whole soul practically glowed.

When my friend noticed me studying him, he patted the boy on the shoulder and jogged over to me. "Did you know that Norah doesn't charge tuition?" he asked, breathless after the wild game of tag and the jog.

"No, I didn't."

Liam leaned back against the wall I sat on. "All these kids are from poor families who wouldn't normally be able to afford school. Isn't that amazing?"

"It is." I smiled at him. "Norah is a kind person."

A wistful look swept across his face. "She's more than kind. She's... extraordinary." He shook his head in a quick jerky fashion. "I mean, the work she's doing is extraordinary."

I gave his shoulder a soft push from atop the wall. "So, how are things going with you and Norah?"

His cheeks took on a deep red color that had nothing to do with the heat or the run. "I don't know if there is a me and Norah yet."

"But you want it to be?"

"I..." Liam hesitated and kicked at a stray stone in front of his boot. "I mean... I..." He snapped his eyes to the side of the yard. "Oh, look! Zaina's back. You should head over so the two of you can go look at the debate hall."

I arched an eyebrow at him but he glanced away, that deep red color still on his cheeks. "Alright. But we're gonna finished this conversation later."

Liam coughed. "Right. Sure. You should..." He pointed towards Zaina. "I'll just..." He waved a hand towards the kids.

"Uh-huh." I chuckled. "See you later, moron."

My friend mumbled something and drifted back towards the students. I'd never seen him this embarrassed before. It was quite fun. And it confirmed my suspicion: the boy was in love. A wide smile spread across my own mouth as I jumped down from the wall and trotted to where Zaina waited. After everything he'd been through, it was nice to see him happy.

"Hey, is everything set?" I asked once I reached the Pernish smuggler.

"Yep." Her eyes lingered on the dark bruise across my cheekbone. "You ready?"

"Always. Lead the way."

She blew out an amused breath and jerked her head. "Alright then, follow me."

Morning business was in full swing. We had to dodge vendors, customers, and horse-drawn carriages on every road. The smell of baking bread along one street was replaced by exquisite perfume on another, only to be ruined by a large heap of animal droppings as we rounded the corner. I was starting to get used to the incredible amount of people who lived in this city, but at times it was still overwhelming.

"Whoa!" I stopped dead in the street and stared into the window of a shop. "Is that *magic*?"

Zaina drew up next to me and peered inside. A small upside-down pyramid floated in the air above a metal plate. The shop clerk held it up to a customer inside the store and pointed at different areas of the contraption. When the customer shook his head, the seller instead pointed to a pearly white orb the size of a palm with some kind of transparent air shield around it.

"Yeah, it is," Zaina said. "But it's just items with a simple spell on them. It's nothing compared to what it used to be. At least, that's what people say."

"What does that mean?"

The dark-haired smuggler motioned for us to continue walking. "Apparently, there used to be these great mages but they haven't existed for... centuries? I think. Of course, there are still people with different kind of powers." She threw a quick glance at me. "Like you. But there haven't been any great mages since the dragons disappeared."

I stared at her. "Dragons *are* real?"

"Yeah. Or they were, at least." She shrugged. "No one knows if the dragons disappeared because magic did or if magic disappeared because the dragons did."

"Wow." I weaved through a group of people blocking the road in front of a hatmaker's shop. "The world is so much bigger than I thought."

Zaina gave me a bright smile. "And there's so much more still to see."

It took great effort not to ask any more questions about magic. There was so much I wanted to know but it wasn't exactly a safe topic. I had sworn not to ask about Ashaana and I also had a feeling that it was best not to mention that Elaran and the other elves from Tkeideru could practice magic. So instead of voicing what was really on my mind, I continued pushing my way through the crowd in silence until another thought struck me.

"I've been meaning to ask," I began. "Norah is what, eighteen?"

"Nineteen."

"Liam told me the students don't pay to go to her school." I turned to the smuggler and furrowed my brows. "How did she manage to buy a whole school? And how can she keep it running?"

"The school runs on donations." Zaina let out a brief chuckle. "My sister is a very charming person and when she asks people for donations, they happily part with their money."

I released a soft laugh too. "Yeah, I can imagine. But how did she afford buying it in the first place?"

"She didn't." My walking companion fell silent. For a moment, only the chatter of people and rattle of carriages filled the space between us. "I traded my ship for it."

My mouth dropped open. "You... you what?"

Zaina lifted her toned shoulders in a shrug. "It was a small one, not like the warship we arrived on, but still... it was enough for my smuggling operation up and down the coast. And enough to buy a school." A sad smile blew across her striking face. "We've been on our own for a while. She's my sister. I need her to be happy, and being a teacher makes her happy."

Not only was the world more complicated than I'd imagined, there were also a lot more layers to Zaina than I'd originally thought. No wonder she and Haela got along so well. And the two of us too, for that matter. We all had a someone, family by blood or choice, who we would do anything for.

"We're here," Zaina said, breaking my wandering thoughts. She motioned at the large rectangular building in front of us before moving towards one of the short sides. "I've bribed the guard at the back."

As promised, the man guarding the small back door let us in after Zaina dropped one of our pearl pouches into his palm.

"How long do we have?" I asked.

"About ten minutes. So make them count."

A narrow corridor met us inside the door. After a quick nod to my criminal companion, we snuck forward. Labeled doors dotted the hallway but my excitement over being able to read the signs on them was tempered by the fact that they said unhelpful stuff like *storage* and other useless things.

"Whoa," I commented when the corridor dumped us on the floor of a great hall.

Stairs to our right led up to a gigantic stage while a vast sea of chairs spanned the area in front of it. Remembering that we only had a few minutes, I jogged up the wooden steps to the podium.

It was bare save for the row of lecterns pushed against the stage wall and a stack of empty glasses and water pitchers.

"Hmm..." I mused while studying the carved wood. "I could lace his lectern with a drug that can be absorbed through the skin." I shook my head. "No, that wouldn't work. I won't know which lectern is his until he gets on stage and by then it'll be too late. Damn."

Darting back and forth across the podium, I mapped the audience's viewpoints and the potential spots where I could move unseen. The results were disheartening. I threw my head back and let out a frustrated sigh. Beams. I snapped my gaze back to the chairs and then the stacks in the corner.

"Ohh this might work!" I thundered down the stairs and ran past a startled Zaina.

"We only have another minute or two," she called after me as I disappeared into the mass of chairs.

"I know," I called back before stopping at a random point in the audience and tilting my head back. Sprinting through the gathered furniture, I did the same at other spots throughout the room. A grin spread across my lips. "They won't see a thing."

When I finally reached the confounded smuggler again, I was thoroughly out of breath. "Alright, I have a plan."

"Good, because we're out of time."

"Can you get me a liquid drug?" I asked while we jogged back down the corridor. "Not a powder or a pill or something, but a liquid."

Zaina was quiet for a moment. "Yeah, I think I know something that'll work."

"Great!" That wicked grin was back on my face. "There are a few more things I'll need but yeah, I know how to drug Marcellus."

"I can't wait to see it," Zaina said with an equally excited smile as we slipped through the door.

Noise from people and carts enveloped us when we rejoined the city. How about that? It turned out that I would be able to steal Marcellus' sanity. On stage. In front of hundreds of people. I chuckled as we steered back towards the school. Thieves. We sure are a versatile lot.

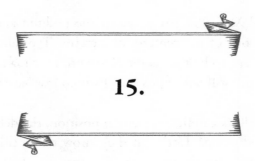

15.

Anticipation hung in the air. Excited murmuring drifted from the crowd seated in the chairs below and all the way up to my ears. I shifted my weight on the beam.

"Ladies and gentlemen," a voice boomed across the room. "Welcome to tonight's debate. Yesterday, you got to know the candidates for Master of Knowledge. Tonight, you will hear from the candidates for General."

He was speaking Pernish but I understood him anyway. In the weeks we'd been here, Zaina and Norah had taken every opportunity to talk to us in their language. Being forced to hear and speak it all the time, in combination with Norah's lessons and my own studies back in Keutunan, had finally led to some kind of proficiency. I still spoke with a heavy accent but I could now understand what others were saying fairly easily.

"Please welcome our six candidates," the debate leader called, making his double chin flap.

Enthusiastic clapping and cheering filled the room as the six men running for General entered the stage. Shade was once again wearing his crisp black suit that highlighted his athletic body and his face held a calm and confident expression. His entire being dripped with authority. As usual.

General Marcellus strode across the podium and took up position at one of the centermost lecterns. Typical. Of course he would want to be the center of attention. It made my job a bit trickier but still not impossible. I would just have to be extra careful.

When all six candidates were in position, the debate leader began introductions. Little did they know that a thief skulked only a short distance above their heads. The hall had been constructed so that all outside light pooled onto the stage, leaving the sea of chairs and the ceiling in darkness. I snuck across the beam until I was directly above Marcellus' lectern.

"We will start this debate with a question from the audience since we have received the same question from quite a few people," the heavyset moderator said. "General Marcellus, how do you respond to the rumors that you are going to make two foreigners your senior advisors?"

Marcellus drew back slightly. "I... what?"

"Yes, word has it that you are going to forgo your own countrymen in favor of William and Eric Fahr," the debate leader explained while I unpacked my gear. "You have been spending a lot of time with them, which some people find curious but not unsettling, per se. However, a lot of your fellow countrymen find this news that you will name them your senior advisors completely unacceptable. How do you respond to this?"

General Marcellus worked his mouth up and down a few times while I unrolled a spool of stiff but almost translucent thread. The flustered general cast a glance at Shade. I could almost see the flames burning in Marcellus' eyes but the assassin only looked back with a mask of mild surprise on his face. After one final scowl, General Marcellus tore his eyes from Shade.

Gathering himself, he coughed and took a sip of water from the glass perched on the edge of his lectern.

"Good people of Pernula," he began and held up both hands. "I can assure you that these rumors are only that: rumors. It is simply a smear campaign orchestrated by my enemies."

Slowly and carefully, I started lowering the thread.

"Why are you spending so much time with them then?" someone called from the audience.

Marcellus ran his fingers through his dark brown hair. "They are simply advising me on a matter–"

"So they are your advisors?" a shout rose from the crowd.

The thread was now dangling just above eye level. It was slightly in front and to the side, but still, if Marcellus looked up, he would see it. Now, I only needed to wait for a distraction.

"They are not my advisors!" Marcellus called across the increasingly dissatisfied crowd.

Shade cleared his throat. "General Marcellus, if I may, I think what the audience wants to know is, what position will these two foreigners have if you become General?"

Marcellus whipped his head towards the assassin. *Now.* I lowered the thread all the way down and tied the other end tight around the beam.

"You..." the furious general growled but before he could do something that would harm his reputation even more, he snapped his gaze back to the gathered Pernulans.

Shit. I yanked the thread from its destination. It swung above the lectern, just out of sight. Releasing a long breath, I held it steady.

"Yes, what place will they have in your administration?" an agitated voice called.

"Exactly! What are you hiding?"

"Why are you lying about this?"

Unrest spread through the crowd like wildfire. Our rumormongering had been quite effective, it would seem. All eyes were on Marcellus as he tried to sort through his anger and shock to deliver a satisfactory answer. I could almost see the smoke coming out of his ears.

"People," he called.

The audience continued mumbling and shifting restlessly. Marcellus blew out a frustrated breath and stalked towards the front of the stage. *And that's my cue.*

"People!" he bellowed across the room again.

I lowered the thread into position. After taking a deep breath to steady my hands, I snatched up the syringe and put the needle to the thread. The plunger edged inwards as I pushed it down.

"I assure you," Marcellus continued and raised his hands, "William and Eric Fahr have no place in my administration."

One drop, then two, then three drops of clear liquid ran down the thread. I squeezed out a fourth one and watched it race towards its destination.

"The position of senior advisors will go to esteemed members of the Pernulan elite. As it should."

It was impossible for me to follow the drops all the way down, of course. I would've needed an elf's eyesight for that. Therefore, I didn't know exactly when they had arrived but based on their speed down the thread, I made a rough estimate.

"Rest assured, William and Eric Fahr are helping me with a current matter but once that is settled, they will not occupy any positions of power in Pernula."

And... now! I yanked the thread and started pulling it back up. With the crowd finally placated, General Marcellus returned to his lectern and let out a long exhale. After smoothing his hair, he took two large gulps of water.

And now you're mine. The drug I'd just dripped into his water glass would start working within a minute or two. An evil grin flashed across my lips. We had managed to both drug him and make him publicly disavow the Fahr brothers. All in the span of a single day. Scheming foreigners from a backwater island, one. Military leader of a gigantic nation, zero.

"Now that these vicious rumors have been put to rest, can we continue the debate?" General Marcellus said.

"We can," the debate leader with the double chin replied. "The next question–"

"Actually," Marcellus interrupted. "Would you mind if I asked one of the other candidates a question? I promise you, it is of outmost importance for the good people of Pernula."

The moderator hesitated a moment but after General Marcellus flashed him a brilliant smile, he motioned for him to proceed.

Malice seeped into the smooth-talking General's eyes as he turned to Shade. "Candidate Shade. In your city, you are the Master of the Assassins' Guild."

Sharp intakes of breath sounded throughout the room. I closed my eyes. *Damn.*

"Tell me," the General continued, "why does an assassin, a *foreign assassin*, think he can become the leader of our great nation?"

Silence echoed throughout the room while everyone waited for the Master Assassin to explain himself.

To be honest, I was surprised it had taken Marcellus and the Fahr brothers this long to play that card but I'd been fervently hoping they wouldn't because it screwed us royally. Once everyone knew that Shade was an assassin, we would lose support from practically all of the upper class and most of the working class. Underworlders were not regarded favorably in this city.

"I am," Shade said. "In Keutunan, I am indeed the Master of the Assassins' Guild. The part I find funny about this question is that you, General Marcellus, are the one asking *me* why I would be a competent military leader for this city."

"You find that funny?" Marcellus raised his eyebrows at the assassin. "Why is that?"

"Because *you* lost to *me*." Shade gave a short shake of his head as if that had been obvious. "When you tried to invade my city, you lost. To me. You had three warships, a horde of soldiers, and an inside man in King Edward's inner circle but still you failed. And even in the face of those overwhelming odds, I beat you. You are asking me why I think I would be fit to lead this country instead of you. I think the answer is obvious."

Arrogant bastard. He hadn't exactly pulled that off all by himself. But to be fair, I knew why he said it, so I decided to let it slide.

"I didn't..." Marcellus coughed and wiped away sweat from his brow. "I didn't lose..." He put both hands to the lectern to steady himself.

That would be the drug finally working its magic. After clearing his throat, Marcellus emptied the glass of water in a few quick gulps. *Why yes, do drink even more of the spiked water. That will surely help.*

"I didn't lose t' you," the drugged General pressed out between lips that didn't seem to be quite working.

Shade arched an eyebrow at him. "No? Then why aren't you currently ruling Keutunan?"

"Cuz you cheat'd an..." Marcellus slurred before trailing off. He squinted at the room while his hands gripped the lectern so tightly his knuckles turned white.

"I'm sorry, I don't understand what he's saying," Shade said in an innocent voice, and turned to the debate leader. "Is he drunk?"

The leader of the debate shifted uncomfortably on his feet and cast a confused glance at Marcellus. Turning away from the rest of the audience, he lowered his voice. "General, are you drunk?"

"I'm nah drunk." General Marcellus slammed a fist into the wooden lectern so hard the glass jumped and tipped over the edge. It shattered as it hit the floor. "Don't know... goin' on."

Another candidate seemed to realize what a great opportunity this was to get ahead of the competition because he raised his voice. "Are you sure? He looks very drunk to me."

The other men on the stage caught on as well and nodded in agreement. Marcellus shook his head as if to clear it and took a step back. Big mistake. Without the support of his lectern, he stumbled and tripped into the one on his left. The crowd gasped.

"Ladies and gentlemen," the moderator called across the chaos spreading below. "I am afraid we will have to cancel tonight's debate. General Marcellus is not feeling well. Please file out in an orderly procession."

I didn't even try to hide the wide grin that covered half of my face. He'd sent some thug to beat me up. How was this for payback?

While the audience got to their feet, I snuck back towards my exit point so that I could blend in with the crowd.

My friends had all been in attendance tonight but they would most likely leave by the front door. They knew I would slink out the back so we had set up a rendezvous outside. Disgruntled and disappointed muttering hung over the crowd as we shuffled towards the door.

"Storm?"

I whipped my head around to find two tall people staring at me. "Yngvild? Vania?"

"Gods, what happened to your face?" Vania exclaimed while the mass of bodies continued pushing us towards the exit.

When we finally broke through the door, I pulled them towards a deserted part by the outside wall. "The Rat King paid me a visit."

"Shit."

"Yeah." I looked between the two blue-eyed warriors. "He was the one you talked about before, right? When you didn't want to mention any names."

Vania drew her pale eyebrows down and gave me a curt nod.

"Figured as much. He told me to stop recruiting in his territory." I lifted my shoulders in an apologetic shrug. "So I'm afraid I won't have any more jobs coming your way anytime soon."

"It's alright." Yngvild clapped a large hand on my shoulder. "You should still come by to drink, though."

"I will." I smiled at them both before jerking a thumb over my shoulder. "I've gotta go."

"Wait," the tattooed warrior said before I managed to turn around. "Is it true? That Shade is the Master of the Assassins' Guild in your city?"

"Yeah, he is."

Vania barked a laugh and turned to her muscular companion. "Told you sneaking in to watch was a good call. An assassin in the game and General Marcellus showing up drunk. This is the most entertaining election in years."

Laughter rumbled in Yngvild's chest before he turned to peer at me curiously. "The drunk thing, you didn't happen to have anything to do with that, did you?"

"Me?" I pressed a hand to my chest and put on my best innocent face. "I have no idea what you're talking about."

"Uh-huh." Both warriors chuckled.

"He's going to have so much explaining to do at his dinner next week," Vania said.

My ears pricked up. "What dinner?"

"You don't know?" The blond warrior looked genuinely surprised. "Marcellus is hosting a dinner for the elite next week. All the thieves are talking about it. Since so many lords and ladies will be at Marcellus' place, a lot of houses will be empty. Perfect time to break in."

A wide grin spread across my face. "It is indeed." With that satisfied smile still on my lips, I gave both Vania and Yngvild an appreciative nod. "Oh, you have been most helpful. Drinks are on me next time."

"I'll remember that!" Vania called as I trotted away.

Lifting my hand in goodbye, I continued towards our prearranged meeting place. This was perfect. Now, I only needed to get the others on board. But, knowing them, I was sure they would be.

"Hey, there she is!" Haela called when I came into view. A radiant smile full of mischief beamed on her face. "That was amazing! Did you see when he stumbled off stage? Ha! That was so funny."

"Yeah, it was rather great, wasn't it?" I came to a halt next to Liam and Haemir. "But he screwed us when he outed Shade as the Master of the Assassins' Guild."

Haela threw a mock scowl my way. "Party pooper."

I rolled my eyes. "Yeah, yeah. But seriously, none of the voters are gonna back Shade now. We can't win."

The Master Assassin looked unfazed. "We don't need to win, remember? We just need to make sure Marcellus becomes desperate enough to sign a peace treaty."

Elaran crossed his toned arms over his chest. "So, what's our next move?"

Shade shot him an annoyed look. "Weren't you supposed to be the strategist?"

"I know exactly what our next move will be," I said, ignoring the arguing grumps. "And it's gonna be so much fun."

Grins spread across the faces of my companions as I explain the scheme I had in mind.

We were constantly trading pieces on the board. First, we had sent flash mobs to interfere with Marcellus. Then, he had taken those away by sending the Rat King after me. We had humiliated him during the debate and he had responded by crushing our chance to win the election.

Now, it was our turn. We might no longer be able to win, but we were going to make damn sure that he wouldn't either. It was time to make our next move.

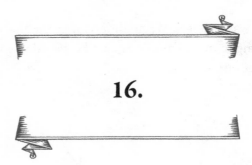

16.

Candles burned brightly in the windows as Shade, Elaran, Haela, and I snuck across the manicured lawn. Technically, Haela wasn't on Team Underworld but she had refused to be left out of the fun this time. And she was right. This was going to be fun.

"You know what to do," Shade said. "Meet at the storage closet when phase one is complete."

The three of us nodded and took off in different directions. In the days leading up to Marcellus' planned dinner for the elite, we had scouted his house and ironed out our plan of attack, so now all that was left was to carry it out. I arrived at my entry point and grabbed a hold of the windowsill.

After checking that the room inside was empty, I climbed onto the wooden plank. The next one was too high up to reach so I had to use the top of the window instead. It creaked beneath my weight. I sent a quick prayer to Nemanan before launching myself up. My fingers found the upstairs windowsill. The muscles in my arms tensed as I drew myself up and peeked into the room.

A shadow moved inside. I ducked down. *Shit.* I scrambled to find purchase with my feet because I wasn't sure how long my arms could bear my weight alone. My shoulders breathed a sigh of relief when I finally found a crack to stick my toe into. I risked another peek. A dark figure swept out the door just as my eyes took in the room. When the door clicked shut, it was empty.

Pulling myself up, I made it onto the ledge. The window was fastened by a simple latch on the inside so I slid a lockpick through the crack and lifted it up. After opening the side of the window that I didn't currently occupy, I climbed into the ornately decorated room.

There was no knowing when Marcellus or his servants would be back so I had to move quickly. A large vanity table next to the window showed me my first target. I snatched up the small container and darted back to the window.

Using one of my knives, I carefully pried open the stopper and flung the liquid out onto the lawn. Once it was empty, I removed a bottle from the inside of my vest and started dumping its contents into Marcellus' empty one. After pushing the cork back on, I returned it to the table.

Next target. I yanked open the drawers until I found what I was looking for. He even had three of them. How vain could you be? I shoved them all inside my vest.

A plank creaked outside the door. *Shit*. Light spilled into the opening. The window was too far away to reach in time. I dove into the nearest closet and drew the door shut just as two men strode across the threshold. My heart pattered against my ribcage.

"Be quick about it," Marcellus ordered as he dropped into the chair in front of the mirror. "My guests will be here soon."

Through the tiny crack in the closet door, I watched the cranky General's servant make a mocking face behind his back.

"Of course, General," he said.

The manservant picked up the bottle I'd tampered with and started applying the contents to Marcellus' hair. I saw General Marcellus crinkle his nose in the mirror.

"Give me that," he said and snatched the bottle from the servant's hand. "What is this?"

"It's your hair oil, General," the man said.

Marcellus brought the bottle to his nose and sniffed at it. "It smells... like a stable."

Inside the closet, I had to bite my cheek to keep from laughing. *That's because it's saddle oil, you pompous fool.*

The confounded General ran his fingers through his dark brown hair. "Ugh, it's all sticky. Something's wrong with this bottle. Comb it out."

"Yes, General."

Drawers banged and the contents inside rattled as Marcellus' servant searched with growing distress for a comb. I grinned as I felt the weight of the three I'd stolen.

The servant wrung his hands. "General, your combs are missing."

"What?" Marcellus tore through the drawers himself but when he came up empty too, he slammed them closed and shot to his feet. "My hair. Looks. Awful," he ground out between gritted teeth. "And it smells like a stable. I need to get dressed because the guests are arriving soon. Find something to fix it!" He stalked out the door.

I almost felt bad for his servant who shuffled out the door behind him. Almost. Seeing Marcellus this flustered brought me too much joy. I slipped out from the closet and sprinted to the window. Time to go. There was one more thing to do before phase one was complete.

The grass outside smelled of expensive hair oil. I chuckled to myself as I ran across it and made for the back door leading to the kitchen. Heat and the delicious smell of food met me when I cracked it open. Cooks bustled back and forth, stirring, frying, and spooning finished dishes onto serving platters. This was going to be tricky. I slipped inside.

From my vantage point behind a pillar, I studied the room. The food that was already finished and to be served cold, I presumed, was clustered together on platters by the door. Getting straight there would be easy but unfortunately, I needed to make a pit stop first. A shelf above the farthest counter held an army of small containers and they were all conveniently labeled. Most of them specified things I'd never heard of but there was one I knew very well and based on the finished dishes waiting on the table, it would work perfectly.

The plump cook closest to me pulled a pan from the fire and strode towards the counter. I darted forward. Fried meat left a scent trail in the air as she swung around, oblivious to the thief flashing past behind her back. I crouched behind the counter. The second cook was still blocking the shelf that was my target so I couldn't move until he did.

"Hey!" the plump female cook called. "Are you sure you marinated this? It doesn't look right."

The male cook groaned only a few paces away from me. "Yes, I'm sure." He turned around and waved a ladle at her. "When are you gonna start trusting me again? It was one mistake. One!"

While their attention was occupied elsewhere, I jumped up from behind the counter and grabbed the target container before ducking down again. Now I only needed to make it back to the door. My muscles tensed in anticipation of the sprint. *And... now!*

Muttered curses floated across the room as the plump cook rounded the counter again. My movements screeched to a halt and I swung myself back to the counter's short side. Damn. The female cook blocked my exit on that side while the male one did the same on the other. Panic welled into my chest. I was trapped. Drawing a long soft breath, I pushed the dread aside. I needed to think.

Pots and pans hissed and clanked all around me while fires crackled on either side. Burning down the kitchen would most certainly defeat the purpose of what we were trying to do, so that was out of the question. What else could I do?

Very carefully, I lifted a hand and felt around on top of the counter. Something long and made of wood brushed my fingers. *Ah. That might work.* I just needed to time it perfectly. Still clutching the stolen container, I grabbed the ladle on the counter and threw it across the room. It clattered as it landed on the other side.

"What are you doing?" the plump cook demanded. She had turned towards the noise and the second cook.

Keeping my head below the countertop, I sprinted towards the door. When I reached the pillar, I swung around it and made for the table by the inner door.

"Why are you always blaming me?" the other cook grumbled from the kitchen. "I didn't do anything."

My target dish sat in a blue bowl on the table. I had no idea what it was but it was white so I dumped half the contents of my stolen container in it. It disappeared into it without a trace.

"Of course it was you. Who else would it be? Evil spirits?"

Making it all the way back to replace what I stole would be impossible, so I simply pushed the container onto the counter while the two cooks were busy arguing. Hopefully, they wouldn't think anything of it. And if they did, it would most likely only give them one more thing to fight about. The muttered curses grew fainter as I left the kitchen behind and slunk into the hallway beyond.

Dark wood and lush carpets filled the corridor. With my ears constantly on the hunt for footsteps, I snuck along it soundlessly. The storage room we were meeting at was at the end of the hall. It was little more than a broom closet where the maids stored their spare supplies but it was enough for our purposes. Most importantly, it was perfectly situated next to the dining room and the staircase to the second floor.

The point of a sword met me when I opened the door and slid inside. I gave the man attached to it an exasperated stare before shoving it out of my face.

"How many times have you greeted me with the point of a sword now?" I hissed. "Don't pretend like you couldn't tell it was me walking through the door."

"Yeah, well, it's been a while now," Shade replied. "I was feeling nostalgic."

"Did you get it done?" Elaran demanded from behind the assassin.

"Of course I did. You?"

Both the assassin and the elf nodded.

"Why are there holes in every. Single. One. Of my suits?!" a voice bellowed from upstairs loudly enough to make the boards above our heads rattle. "Fix it. Right now. Or you're all fired!"

"As I was saying," Shade confirmed with a satisfied smirk on his face.

The door was yanked open and a dark-haired elf darted inside. "Phew, that was close." Haela squeezed herself in and pulled the door shut before twisting around. "I hear your suit-cutting was successful, Shade."

"It was indeed," the assassin replied. "And your mission?"

Haela's yellow eyes twinkled. "Wait and see."

Packed together in the storage closet, the four of us waited for Marcellus' esteemed guests to arrive. I didn't know if he'd managed to get his hair and wardrobe malfunction sorted, but before long the chattering of men and women could be heard outside the door to our hiding place. When the scraping of chairs had risen and died down, we cracked open the door a finger's breadth to hear better.

"Welcome, my dear lords and ladies, to my humble home," General Marcellus said. "It is an honor to have you here. I hope this evening will be one of great food and interesting discussions."

"Hear, hear," some of the lords replied.

"Let us raise our glasses together in friendship," the General continued.

Inside the closet, Haela rubbed her hands and I was certain she would have done a little dance if we hadn't been crammed so tightly together.

"To friendship," the lords and ladies of Pernula echoed.

For a moment, everything was quiet. Then it started. Violent coughing rang out from the dining room as the guests swallowed the drink.

"Oh dear," a woman's voice called out. "What is in this wine?"

A man coughed repeatedly. "It tastes like... dust."

I tilted my head up towards Haela. "What *is* in it?"

The grin on her face almost reached all the way to her ears. "Dust."

All four of us chuckled at that. We continued listening to Marcellus profusely apologize for the wine, saying that the seller must have given him a bad bottle. Plates and glasses clinked as the servants no doubt brought in fresh cups of wine and platters of food. Polite conversation resumed while they ate. That is, until the next calamity hit.

"Oh dear," the lady from before called once again. An attempt at a delicate cough followed, but eventually turned into quite unladylike sounds. "I am sorry. It is just that, this is very salty."

"I am sure you are just oversensitive, dear," a man's voice said. "I will have some of that, please." Silence. And then more coughing. "Wine," he croaked.

A few more guests must have tried the dish before more calls for drinks rose. Once again, we listened to the mighty General Marcellus apologize for another disaster at his dinner table.

Now it was the mischievous twin's turn to look at me. "How much salt did you put in?"

"Oh, about half the container."

More soft chuckles sounded inside the storage room. Even from Shade and Elaran. Who knew that screwing someone over could be this much fun? Actually, I already did know that.

The dinner progressed without further hitches until the auburn-haired archer inside the broom closet decided it was time for his part of the scheme. He lifted a lid-covered box from the floor and pushed his way towards the door. I had to squeeze into Shade to make room for him to pass. Scratching sounded from the box when Elaran moved it.

"Where did you...?" I began.

"Don't ask," he muttered and pushed at the door.

It swung open on soundless hinges. Elaran moved towards the edge of the door leading into the dining room while the rest of us snuck up the stairs. Once we'd made sure that upstairs was clear, we gave him the signal to unleash hell.

From atop the landing, we watched the grumpy ranger open the box and tip it towards the dining room. Three gray and fur-covered creatures fell out and scurried towards the happily oblivious guests. Ear-piercing shrieks bounced off the walls just as Elaran made it up the stairs.

"Rats! Rats!" a woman screeched.

"Phase two begins now," Shade said and motioned for us to scatter.

Terrified cries continued echoing downstairs while the four of us split up and disappeared into different rooms. Feet stamped and chairs scraped as the ladies no doubt tried to get away from the rodents while their husbands tried to show their bravery by chasing them out.

We had already messed up this dinner so much for Marcellus but we weren't done yet. An evil grin flashed across my face as I got into position. We weren't even close to done.

Once the screaming and stomping had finally quieted down, we began our next scheme. A pot crashed to the floor in the room next to mine. Another shriek rang out, followed by thumping footsteps up the stairs and then into the room.

When they had disappeared back down again, another ceramic pot shattered. The person ran back up the stairs and stalked into the new room. After a few minutes, they retreated again.

I picked up the brightly painted vase on the desk. It was quite pretty. Shame. Shards flew across the planks as I threw it on the floor. Hunting footsteps thundered again but before they made it into the room, I was gone.

The person inside stomped around, muttering curses about evil spirits while I hung from the windowsill and waited for them to leave. Once they had, I climbed back in again. One more minute of silence before the crash of something large and heavy echoed throughout the house. *Show time.*

Deafening noise filled the room when the bookcase I pushed over slammed into the floor. In the rooms next to mine, more booms followed. I let out a wail. It was a high-pitched howl that would've given me the creeps if I hadn't known that it came from my own throat. Otherworldly shrieks rose from the other upstairs rooms as well. After one last note, I jumped out the window and scrambled down the side of the building.

Cries of utter terror sounded from the front of the house while I made my way towards the fence.

"Evil spirits!" a woman screeched as she ran out on the street. "Your house is haunted!"

I could barely keep myself from cackling when I landed on the other side of the wall. Matching smirks decorated the faces of my three companions when I joined up with them a few streets down.

Oh we had really done a number on Marcellus tonight. Haela was practically skipping all the way back to the school and even Elaran and Shade looked uncharacteristically gleeful. After this, Marcellus had to be close to his breaking point. A malicious chuckle slipped my lips. Maybe just one more thing to push him over the edge.

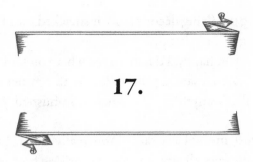

17.

Quiet. At last it was quiet. Late afternoon had brought an end to the school day and the constantly chattering and squealing children who occupied this building. I didn't know how Norah managed it. It would've driven me nuts to be surrounded by that many kids all the time. Liam seemed to like it, though. He and Norah had snuck off somewhere to prepare for the next school day. Or so they said.

"This is perfect!" Zaina barreled through the living room door and flopped down on the brown couch to my right. The assaulted furniture groaned in protest. "I just overheard another group of nobles discussing Marcellus' disaster dinner."

"I know, right?" Haela exclaimed and swung herself over the back of another sofa to land on its cushions. "Haemir and I heard the same thing at the debate club yesterday. It's only been a few days and his campaign has already taken a huge hit with the elite class!"

"Yeah," I mumbled and flipped the page in the Pernish textbook Norah had given me.

The excited twin seemed unsatisfied with my lukewarm reply because she picked up a frayed pillow and threw it at my face. "Why aren't you happy?"

Catching the flying décor before it smacked into my cheek, I blew out a sigh. "I am happy."

"If this is you happy, I'd hate to see what you look like when you're angry," Zaina said, a grin pulling at the corner of her lips. "Especially if it's anything like when I ambushed you in that alley."

"Oh, trust me," Haela said. "You really don't. She's pretty scary when she goes all attack mode. Surprising how much anger can fit inside such a small person."

I hurled the pillow back at her. "Funny."

"I know," she said, her eyes twinkling as she caught the projectile.

"I'm not jumping up and down with happiness because even though the nobles now have their reservations, Marcellus still has strong support with the workers and there are way more workers than nobles." I said. "So we need to make him think all voters are deserting him, not just the elite."

"Yeah, but Elaran and Shade are already checking out a lead on that." Haela gave me a carefree shrug. "They'll be back any minute now so we should have a plan for that soon."

"Exactly," Zaina said. "So, cheer up."

My muttered curses in reply drew laughter from the two optimists.

Draping her legs over the side, Haela stretched her graceful upper body across the couch and let out a groan. "I miss the War Dancer."

The Pernish smuggler sat up straight. "You've met a War Dancer?"

"What? No. It's a tavern back in Tkeideru."

"You named a tavern after the War Dancers?" Zaina chuckled. "I wonder how they would feel about that."

Raised voices sounded from somewhere outside but before I could get up to check, Haemir stuck his head through the open door to the living room.

"Hey, you hearing that?" he asked.

The three of us looked from one to the other before nodding in confirmation.

"You can hear who it is too, right?" Haemir asked his sister. When she nodded again, he went on. "We should go outside before this escalates."

Before what escalates? However, I didn't get a chance to ask that because the rest of the room scrambled out of their comfortable seats and followed Haemir out the door. After snapping the textbook shut and placing it on the low table, I did the same.

Afternoon sunlight filled the empty schoolyard with golden light. When I rounded the corner, I found two tall figures standing there on the smooth stones. *Ah. Them.*

"You arrogant bastard!" Elaran bellowed. "You're always trying to order us about."

"Right," Shade scoffed. "Because you never tell people what to do. Just because you're some kind of military leader in your city doesn't mean you are here."

"Same goes for you, *Master of the Assassins' Guild,*" the furious elf mocked. "*We* are not part of your guild."

Zaina and the twins had rounded the pissed-off warriors and taken up position by the wall next to them. Haela and Zaina seemed content to simply lean back against the stones and watch the exchange but Haemir took a step towards the fighters.

"Guys," he said, holding up both hands in the air. "Should–"

"No!" Elaran cut off. "I'm so sick of this pretentious human thinking he's better than everyone else. It's time to stop."

The Master Assassin raised his chin, a confident smirk on his face. "Or what?"

"Or you'll find yourself on your back with a sword to your throat. That should teach you a lesson in humility."

A haughty snicker dripped from Shade's lips. "Come try it."

The distinct ringing of swords being drawn echoed across the yard. I pulled myself up on the sun-warmed stone wall and crossed my legs. Leaning my elbows on my knees and resting my chin in my hands, I watched the two fighters stare each other down.

"Shouldn't we try and stop them?" Haemir asked, worry coloring his voice.

"Are you kidding?" I chuckled. "I've been waiting to see this since the day we left Keutunan. I only wish I'd brought snacks."

Out on the courtyard, the Assassins' Guild Master spun his blades once in his hands. Elaran replied with a derisive snort but crouched into an attack position. With a half-smile flashing across his lips, Shade twitched two fingers at him, telling him to get on with it. The elf flew across the stones.

Metallic ringing vibrated through the air as their swords connected. Elaran drove his right-hand blade towards Shade's ribs but the assassin blocked it while delivering a strike from above. The elf's other sword took care of that at the same time as he flicked the blade in his right hand. Shade slammed his weapon into it and kicked at the ranger's hip.

Elaran stumbled back but managed to twist out from the sword coming for his chest. The sharp edge produced a *whoosh* as it flew by. Shooting up from his evasive maneuver, Elaran leaped into the air and drove both swords towards Shade's head in a flying attack from above. The Master Assassin threw up his own twin blades. Metal clashed as the four weapons slammed into each other.

With a burst of force, they shoved their swords apart. Elaran drew his blade in a wide arc but Shade ducked and rolled under it. Coming up behind the elf, he drove his sword towards his opponent's exposed shoulder, but the skilled ranger swung his sword down across his back, absorbing the impact, while throwing an elbow into the assassin's jaw. Shade's head snapped to the side. Elaran twisted back around but before the elf had gotten into position, the Master Assassin landed a kick to the back of his knee.

A dull thud rang out as Elaran's kneecap connected with the ground. Tucking and rolling with the motion, he escaped the swords coming at him from above. While still crouching, he executed a swift swiping kick, clipping Shade's ankle and yanking his leg forward. The assassin lost his balance and slammed back first into the ground. Shade pulled his legs up towards his chest and rolled back on his shoulders. Kicking his legs upwards and pushing with his fists, he launched himself from the ground and landed in a crouch.

Across from the assassin, Elaran had gotten to his feet as well. Shade dashed towards him. Dodging the left-hand sword aimed at his head, the Master of the Assassins' Guild slammed his blade into the one Elaran had brought down to protect his ribcage. Steel ground against steel.

And like that, it continued. Thrust, parry, kick, slash, jump. All while one tried to gain advantage over the other. I unfurled my legs and let them dangle over the edge as the battle wore on. It was a rather extraordinary display. Both of them were excellent swordsmen and their reflexes were out of this world: twisting and swiping with the speed of lightning. Not to mention the force behind every hit. At one point, I was afraid the swords might shatter from the impact their strikes delivered.

Man, I probably shouldn't be antagonizing those two as much I was. If we ever got into a fight, a real fight, I would get my ass handed to me. Unless I could figure out how the darkness worked, that is. Still, I probably shouldn't test it. I tipped my head from side to side. But then again, it would be quite interesting to find out how a full-blown fight between us would turn out.

Metal clattered on stone as Elaran's left-hand blade flew from his grip, followed shortly by one of Shade's swords flying through the air and hitting the ground beside it. Looks of surprise flashed past on both their faces before they were at it again.

A flurry of silver filled the space between them as they continued their deadly dance. Shade ducked under Elaran's swipe, twisted around, and drove his blade towards the elf's neck. The sword-wielding archer had recovered from the evaded strike and changed the direction of his weapon mid-motion so that it sped towards the assassin's throat.

Silence. The clashing of metal and grounding of steel stopped as the warriors stared at each other. Astonishment filled their eyes. The edge of Shade's sword rested against the left side of Elaran's neck while the elf held the point of his own blade to the assassin's throat. Their chests heaved.

The Master of the Assassins' Guild looked down at the sword digging into his throat. "Impressive."

Elaran glanced at the blade pressed to his own neck. "Same." He gave the assassin an approving nod. "You're alright."

"Yeah, you too."

Both fighters lowered their swords. *Oh, come on!* And here I'd been looking forward to seeing at least one of them being taught a lesson in humility and it had ended in a tie? What a disappointment. From atop the wall, I watched Elaran hold out his arm. When Shade reached out as well, they clasped forearms and gave each other an appreciative smile. Hmmph. Did so not see that coming.

"Aww," I said because I couldn't help myself, and because I needed to vent my frustration by ruining the moment. "Is this the start of a bromance?"

"Shut up," Shade and Elaran called in unison. They turned back to each other and released a chuckle.

And now they were ganging up on me. Perfect. I shook my head. This was definitely the start of a bromance.

After retrieving their missing blades, both swordsmen swaggered over to where we'd watched their battle. I hopped down from the wall and saw Haela's eyes sparkle with the promise of a contest. Amusement shook my chest. I'd bet my fortune that once this was over, she'd challenge them both to another fight.

Zaina let out a low whistle. "Now I'm really glad I decided to ambush you that first night instead of trying to beat you in a fair fight."

"Right?" I added before realizing what I'd said. "I mean, not that I approve of you ambushing us, but I agree, stabbing people in the back is always the best option."

"Underworlders," Elaran muttered while shaking his head.

That drew laughter from the rest of our group.

"Speaking of backstabbing," Shade said. "We have some news. Apparently, there's a deal going down at a warehouse by the docks tonight."

"Yeah," the auburn-haired archer continued. "Marcellus has arranged for some kind of trade agreement between Pernula and some other cities down the coast that will lead to lots of business opportunities. It will make him very popular among the workers."

"They're closing the agreement tonight," Shade finished.

"Huh." I stroked my chin. "It would be a real shame if someone screwed that up."

The assassin cocked his head to the right. "Indeed."

A warm wind blew across the schoolyard, ruffling our hair. Haela threw her ponytail back behind her shoulder, her face beaming with mischief.

"Oh, I'm not missing this," she declared.

"Yes, you are," her brother said. "We're invited to that dinner tonight, remember?"

Excitement washed from Haela's features like a bucket of water to the face. "Aw, seriously?"

"Haemir is right," Elaran said. "You need to keep working that angle."

The previously excited twin drew her eyebrows down but didn't argue. After all, she was on Team Upperworld and we needed her to do her part there.

"You need any help from me?" Zaina asked.

Shade studied her. "Are you free?"

"I can be. I've got some things to take care of for my gang but if you need my help, I can move stuff around."

The black-eyed assassin shook his head. "It's alright. The three of us can handle it." He turned to me and Elaran. "Isn't that right?"

"Oh, for sure," I said, a grin spreading across my face, while Elaran backed me up with a nod.

"Alright." Shade nodded back. "Go get ready then. We're leaving in fifteen."

"There you are giving orders again," the grumpy elf said and lifted an eyebrow at the assassin.

Shade chuckled. "Sorry. Force of habit. Do you want to...?" He gave a short wave of his hand.

"Sure." Elaran turned to me. "Go grab your stuff. We're leaving in fifteen minutes."

Laughter bounced off the stones in the courtyard as the rest of our group voiced their amusement at the simultaneously astounded and offended look on my face. I stared at the power-loving dictators through narrowed eyes.

"Now both of you are giving me orders." I shot a stiletto blade into my hand and waved it in their faces. "That has to stop."

The fighters glanced at each other and, in one terrifyingly synchronized motion, drew their swords and spun them in their hands.

A smirk settled on Shade's face. "Or what?"

"Or I'm gonna reconfirm my policy that stabbing people in the back is a stellar move." After one last dirty look, I stalked across the yard.

"Where are you going?" Elaran called at my retreating back.

"To grab my shit. Now get ready and meet me outside in ten minutes."

Hearty chuckling echoed between the walls and followed me all the way to the door. Damn elves and damn assassins. First, they hadn't even given me a satisfactory end to their sword fight, and now they were ganging up on me. Once our mission was over, I vowed to find out everything I could about what I was and what Ashaana meant. Then, I'd knock some respect into both of them. But for now, I'd settle for revenge on Marcellus. Yanking the door open, I strode towards my room and the army of knives waiting in there. He was about to learn, once and for all, not to mess with the Oncoming Storm.

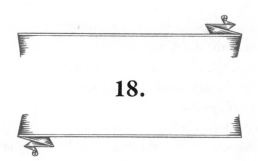

18.

Wood creaked as I rested my shoulder against the crate. From across the warehouse, Shade put a finger to his lips. As if I didn't already know that an ambush required silence and the element of surprise. Idiot. I rolled my eyes but gave him a nod.

According to the rumors, Marcellus and his trade partner were meeting here at sunset. There were no windows on the bottom floor of the building so I didn't know for certain, but I was sure the sun must've dipped below the horizon by now. Even though I knew it was pointless, I cast a glance through the large hole in the ceiling that was used to haul goods to the second floor. Only the edge of a wooden crane and another dark ceiling stared back. Where were they?

A heavy thud resounded outside the robust warehouse door. I whipped my head towards it. While my mind tried to connect the sound with a source, Elaran and Shade shot up from their hiding places as well.

"Something's wrong," Elaran said. He stalked towards the door and placed both hands on it. A groan escaped his lips as he put his full weight behind a shove. "It won't open."

Fear fluttered its poisonous wings in my chest. "What do you mean it won't open?"

"My guess, that sound we just heard was someone slamming a bar in front of the door," he said.

"It's a trap." Shade jerked his head towards the side of the room. "Get to the staircase."

We took off at a run.

"How could–"

An explosion roared through the building and broken boards shot towards us from the direction of the stairwell. I threw my arms up to protect my head. Jagged edges tore gashes in my arms as they flew past while a splinter made it through my defenses and left a cut in my cheek, just below my eye. I drew in a sharp breath between clenched teeth. Wood banged on stone as debris sailed through the air and clattered to the floor.

"You alright?" Shade called from somewhere to my left.

"Yeah," I shouted over the ringing in my ears. "Elaran?"

"I'm here!" he replied.

Heat met me as I lowered my arms and turned in the direction of our intended escape route. An explosion had torn out the staircase so that only a burning hole of scattered wood was left. Flames licked the walls on the whole right side of the building. This was bad. I wiped off the blood running down my cheek and darted to where I'd heard my companions call out.

A few red slashes marred Shade's left arm but Elaran looked relatively unharmed. Since he'd been the furthest from the stairs after checking the door, it seemed as though most of the projectiles had missed him. Good.

"Stairs are gone," I said as I came to a halt next to them. "We can't even climb through. Everything's on fire over there."

"A detonation this big, how did that happen?" Elaran pitched a piece of wood in the direction of the staircase, frustration evident on his face. "How did we miss that?"

"They could've snuck in from somewhere upstairs and planted it after our sweep. I don't know. We didn't have time to sweep the whole damn warehouse, remember?" Shade shook his head. "It doesn't matter. We need to get that door open. Grab pipes, logs, or whatever you can find."

We split up. My heart thumped in my chest as I rummaged through the room in search of something that could smash through the door. The flames crept closer along the wall. Crackling and popping of wood echoed as the whole building seemed to groan in response to the fire eating its hull.

A broken plank was the best I could find so I snatched it up and rushed to the door. Shade and Elaran were already there, trying to jam another flat piece of wood into the small gap under the door. Once it was in, they heaved. Cracks spidered throughout the makeshift lever. And then it snapped.

"Gods damn it!" Shade bellowed and hurled the useless piece across the room.

"Give me that." Elaran grabbed the plank I'd brought.

Dull thuds rang out as he banged it into the entrance again and again. The sturdy door vibrated with each strike but for all Elaran's strength, it barely produced a mark. He moved to the wall and started another assault. Chips flew through the air but it was with growing dread that I realized the progress he made was too slow. We would be dead before he got through. It wasn't that bad yet, but eventually the fire would swallow all the oxygen in the vast warehouse.

"What the hell is this building even made of?" he shouted as his improvised battering ram broke in two.

"Alright, both of you, get over here," Shade said. "If we push the door at the same time maybe we can make whatever's blocking the door snap too." The three of us put our hands to the door. "Now!"

My boots slipped on the sand-covered stones as I put every smidgen of strength I had into forcing the door outwards. Muscled arms tensed on either side of me as Shade and Elaran did the same. The door let out a groan but remained firmly in place.

Terror seeped through my body like a flood of ice water. We were going to die here. Rumbling, followed by another series of loud bangs, echoed across the room as burning wood fell from the flame-covered right side of the building and crashed to the floor.

Shade whipped towards me, panic swirling in his black eyes. "Can't you use the darkness or something?"

"To do what?" I threw my arms out in desperation. "Create more black smoke? It doesn't give me superhuman strength or anything that'll actually help get us out!"

The assassin turned frantic eyes on the elf. "Elaran?"

Guilt flashed over Elaran's face and he averted his eyes. "I can't."

I knew what he was asking, what *we* were asking, but we were quickly running out of options and if we were going to survive, we needed to get out. Now.

"Look, I know that using magic costs you part of your future but please, if you don't, we will all die." Shame burrowed into my chest at even asking something like that but impending death made desperate people of us all.

"It's not that. I *literally* can't." He punched a fist into the unmoving door. "Ever since we got here I just... I can usually feel the magic inside me but ever since we left the island, I can't even feel it anymore." He raked both hands through his hair. "The forest gave us our magic so... I don't know. I think we can only use it when we're close to it."

The hopelessness that washed over me at hearing our last hope crushed threatened to drown me so I shoved it out. Feeling would have to wait. Tapping my fingers to my forehead, I paced back and forth. *Think.*

"What about that?" I pointed to the hole used for hauling goods to the second floor.

"Don't you think I've considered that already?" Shade snapped. "It's too fucking high! I can't jump that high. Can you?" He whipped from me to Elaran. "Can you?"

Fire roared from the right side of the building. It had spread from the wall and the nonexistent stairwell to the crates on the floor and was now making its way towards us. Smoke burned in my throat.

"Okay, not jump then." I dropped my arm as an idea struck. "Throw. You're strong. Especially you," I said, looking at the elf. "If I jump while you throw me into the air, I could make it up there."

"Then what?" Elaran asked. "How do we get up there?"

"The crane." I pointed at the edge of the wooden structure peeking out of the hole. "I'll lower the rope from the crane."

"If you miss..." Shade began.

"I'll break my legs on the way down, I know. But we're out of options. So just don't... throw me off course or, you know, not high enough."

Burning wooden beams crashed to the floor as the fire spread further up the side of the building. Soon, the whole right side would come falling down on our heads.

"Get ready," I said and backed up as far as I could.

Under the square-shaped hole in the ceiling, Elaran and Shade got down on one knee and knitted their fingers together. I released a long exhale. *Here goes nothing.*

In a burst of speed, I sprinted towards them. Managing to time it right, I succeeded in placing my foot firmly in their waiting hands. Their combined strength launched me into the air.

For a moment, it was as if everything was suspended in time. No pain, no fear, no looming death as I sailed through the air. The edge of the hole came closer. I stretched my arms high above me. A strange sort of calm filled me as I realized that there was nothing more I could do. Either I would reach the edge or my upwards momentum would stop and I would plunge back towards the stones before salvation was within my grasp. And I could do nothing to affect the outcome.

Rough wood appeared under my fingers. *Yes!* But the sudden jerk as gravity once more pulled my body downwards yanked my right hand from the edge. My left hand tightened on the boards as I scrambled to regain my hold. Swinging my arm back up, I managed to get a firm grip on the planks. The muscles in my arms shook as I heaved myself upwards. Splinters and pebbles dug into my palms as I clawed my way up and onto the floor. Rolling over on my back, I let my chest heave for a second before climbing to my feet. I could breathe when I was dead.

A ridiculously ironic thing to say when I was trapped in a building where I couldn't breathe because it might kill me. Speaking of... why was the air better up here? I whirled around to find a small opening in the wall. When part of it had collapsed and the boards had fallen down to the ground floor, it had created a hole big enough to climb through. I swore I could spot the roof of the one-story building next to ours if I gazed through it. That was our way out.

I rushed over to the crane. We would have to hurry, though. Flames licked the ceiling and it wouldn't be long before it too came crashing down. I studied the wooden device. Operating it seemed easy enough, it looked like it would only be a matter of pulling the right lever, but moving it into position was the issue. It was facing the wrong way.

While sending a prayer to any god who would listen, I put my bloodstained hands on the side of it and pushed with all my might. The construction groaned but didn't move.

"Come on!" I screamed and retreated a few steps.

After backing up, I ran back to the crane and threw my full weight into it, shoulder first. Something at the base snapped lose. My shoulder throbbed but I put my hands back on the side of it and shoved. It moved. Hope fluttered in my chest.

Once it was in position, I pushed on the lever and watched the hook at the end of the rope plunge downwards. I ran back to the hole and stuck my head down. Fire roared in the ceiling above me.

"Are you on?" I shouted.

Shade and Elaran were scrambling to get a grip on the line. "Now!" they finally yelled.

I sprinted back to the operating panel and pulled the large lever in the other direction. The thick rope creaked as it was hauled back up again. When the heads of my two friends finally appeared in the hole, I couldn't stop the tears of relief rolling down my cheeks. Reaching my hand out, I helped them climb onto the floor.

"There's our exit." I pointed to the opening in the wall. "We gotta hurry!"

Shade coughed but managed a nod. I shoved them both forward and when they took off in a sprint, I followed. Crackling flames and popping wood drowned out my heavy breathing. We were almost out. Fresh air and cool stones waited only a short distance away. I couldn't believe we'd actually managed to make it out.

My stomach lurched. The board beneath me cracked and my leg disappeared through the floor. My other knee hit the planks with a thud but at least that part held. Heat seared my boot. The ceiling on the other side of the floor was on fire. I yanked my leg through the hole and shot to my feet. Over the noise of the fire and the crumbling building, my companions hadn't heard my mishap but now that they had arrived by the opening, they whipped around. Alarm flashed over their faces when they realized how far away I still was.

"Storm!" Shade called. "Hurry!"

Something huge snapped above me. I threw myself backwards as the ceiling above my head crashed down.

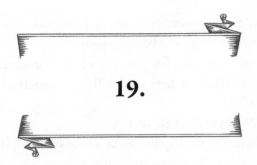

19.

Heavy beams, pipes, and wooden boards thundered to the floor in a cloud of smoke. Lying on my stomach, I coughed and lifted my head. My ears rang. When the dust had settled, I found a mountain of debris blocking my way.

"Storm! Storm!" frantic voices shouted from the other side.

"I'm here," I croaked but I knew they couldn't hear me. Coughing again, I pushed to my feet and made my way towards the wreckage. My heart sank. There was no way I was getting through this. "I'm here!" I yelled at the top of my lungs.

"Can you get through?" Elaran's voice called.

"No."

Silence for a few moments. "Hold on, we'll get you out."

I closed my eyes. They would never manage to clear enough of it in time. Something rumbled on their side of the barricade. My eyes snapped open.

"Listen to me!" I bellowed. "You are leaving through that opening. Right now!"

A loud bang sounded, as if someone had driven a fist into the debris.

"Damn it, Storm!" Shade shouted. "We're not leaving you!"

"I'll find another way out. Now go! Or I swear to Nemanan, I'll kill you myself!"

Another few moments of silence. Then, the assassin's voice could be heard through the barrier again.

"Then the same goes for you. If you don't find another way out, I'll come back in here and kill you myself! I swear to Ghabhalnaz."

"Deal! Now get the hell out!"

Since there was no way for me to make sure they'd left, I just had to trust them. Without sparing another glance at the wall of debris, I whirled around and ran in the opposite direction. Fire roared in the hole below when I sped past the crane. This was a three-story building, or at least it had looked like it from the outside, so there had to be another staircase somewhere. If I could just find it, I might be able to make it through another window or out onto the roof, and from there, jump to an adjacent building.

The cave-in must've given the fire more oxygen because it was spreading quickly now. Crackling flames followed me in the ceiling above. Leaving the room with the crane behind, I darted through a doorway into a long and rather narrow storage room. I skidded to a halt. Two people were blocking the way.

At the sound of my footsteps, they whirled around. A woman with copper hair supported a gangly man who dragged one of his legs behind him. They stared at me. Then the man drew the curved sword at his hip.

"You set the explosion!" he accused and pointed the blade in my direction.

"I didn't set any explosions," I called back. "I'm trying to get out, just like you. Now move! We need to get out of here."

The rafters above our heads creaked and shifted as the fire ate at their support. Smoke drifted in from the crane room. We didn't have time for this.

I drew my hunting knives. "I don't want to kill you but I will if you don't step aside."

His female companion whispered something in his ear but he cut her off by holding up a hand. "If you don't want to fight, go back becau–"

A piercing scream drowned out his words as the ceiling support gave out. I threw myself back into the doorway right before two massive beams slammed into the floor in front of me. Roof tiles rained down after them. Bright flames danced high up in the ceiling around the huge hole it had created. At least the oxygen now rushing into the room would prevent death by asphyxiation. For now. I scrambled to my feet and sprang forward, dodging the fallen logs while sticking my knives back in their holsters.

"Help," a woman's voice moaned.

Slowing my mad dash, I twisted my head towards the sound. One of the gigantic pieces of timber had landed straight on top of the sword-wielding man. His right arm and leg stuck out at an unnatural angle but the rest of his body was crushed underneath it. My stomach turned. Next to the dead man, the woman with the red hair lay. Her leg was pinned beneath the beam but because her companion's body provided a slight gap, it didn't look severed.

When I reached her, she was desperately pulling at her leg. I coughed from the smoke slowly filling the room. If I was going to help her, I had to do it quickly or we'd both die.

"I'll try to lift it while you pull your leg out," I said and put both hands under the gigantic piece of wood.

More splinters dug into my already bloody hands and my shoulder throbbed as I heaved with everything I had. Adjusting my grip, I crouched down again and pushed upwards with my legs while lifting with my arms. The monstrosity of a beam didn't budge. I flicked up my eyes. Fire painted the ceiling yellow and red. Slowly letting go of the fallen rafter, I shook my head and backed away.

"I'm sorry," I said.

The woman leaned her head back on the floor and released a soft laugh before waving her hand in front of her face as if to say that it didn't matter. "It's okay. I would've left me too." She blew out a deep sigh. "Shitty way to die, though."

Flames spread rapidly across the outer wall, making something further into the storage room rumble.

"I'm sorry," I said again before turning and taking off at a sprint.

I wish I could've saved her but even if I'd stayed and tried for another hour, I wouldn't have been able to lift the beam on my own. There was no point in two people dying over something that couldn't be changed.

Part of the wall gave out. I jumped to the side as more debris crashed into the floor. Two metal bars clanged as they bounced off each other. I stopped dead in my tracks. Two metal bars. I looked back down the room. No. It was too risky. And most certainly not a survivor's move. Tearing my eyes from the fallen rafters, I took a step towards my potential exit. Liam's face, full of horror, disgust, and disappointment when he'd learned that

I'd killed the Masters of the Builders' Guild and Scribes' Guild, flashed before my eyes.

"Gods damn it!" I swore and snatched up the metal bars.

Footsteps smattered on the floor as I raced back towards the trapped woman. Utter astonishment shone in her green eyes when she saw me shove one of the bars underneath the beam. I wedged the other one beneath the first and climbed onto the rafter not pinning her to the ground.

"Get ready," I said. "I'm gonna jump on this now and that should create enough force to move the beam so you can yank your leg out. But you're gonna have to be really quick. Can you do that?"

She nodded.

"Alright, go!" I leaped off the wooden platform and pushed my feet down as hard as I could when I landed on the iron bar.

The young woman had time to release a sharp breath and a short scream before the heavy piece crashed down again. I barely dared look.

"It worked," she breathed. She was staring at her now free leg that was resting on the floor.

"Great, let's go!" I snapped and hauled her to her feet.

When she tried to put weight on her injured leg, she released another sharp cry. I blew out a frustrated breath and draped her arm over my shoulder before practically dragging her forward.

Wood and metal smattered to the floor behind us. I picked up the pace. Every step drew a small moan from the redheaded woman and her eyes seemed to go in and out of focus. Excruciating heat seared my whole left side as I pulled us past the burning wall that had fallen and produced the metal bars I needed.

"After all the selfish shit I've done in my life to survive," I muttered between heavy breaths. "If I die because of this, I'm gonna be so pissed."

A staircase untouched by fire appeared in the distance. Relief tried to sparkle in my chest but I shoved it down. We weren't out yet. The woman's head lolled to the side and her eyes fluttered closed. *Oh, I don't think so.*

The sound of a hard slap rang out. Her eyes shot open.

"Ow," she groaned.

"Hey, no nodding off," I said. "I can't carry you. You have to at least partly walk on your own."

The green-eyed woman rubbed her stinging cheek. "You're a rather violent one, aren't you?"

I let out a strained chuckle. "You have no idea."

She was probably in a lot of pain. From her leg and whatever else had happened to her before I'd shown up. If she passed out, I wouldn't be strong enough to carry her out by myself. I had to keep her talking.

"So, why were you here?" I asked.

She squinted as if trying to remember. "We heard a rumor that a deal was going down with some rich traders. We wanted a piece of their goods. The explosion in the stairwell took us by surprise. Knocked us out for a while."

Huh. So they had just been unlucky enough to get caught in a trap meant for us. Apparently, Marcellus' lie to lure us here had been so well-crafted that others had gotten wind of it and believed it too. At least that made me feel a bit less pathetic for having fallen for it. But only a bit.

Her eyes were drooping again so I fired off another question. "That guy back there, was he your partner?"

For a moment, she didn't reply. I wanted to kick myself. Had I really just asked her about the friend she'd watched getting crushed to death only a few minutes ago? Idiot. Those nonexistent social skills really weren't going to fix themselves, were they?

"He was my gang leader," she finally said. "I was his second."

Her body was slipping down my arm so I stopped to hoist her back up. Loud crashes echoed between the walls as another part of the ceiling no doubt caved in. I started out again with renewed speed. The stairwell was so close now.

"So I guess that means you're the gang leader now," I said.

A coughing fit shook her frame. "Yeah. Not that I want to." She drew in a strained breath. "Being responsible for other people sucks."

"I know, right?" I said, surprise and recognition filling my voice, just as we finally made it to the stairs. Easing her arm off me, I leaned her towards the wall. "Wait here. I'm gonna get that door open."

I ran up the stairs, two steps at a time, and put my hands on the trapdoor at the top. My tired and bleeding body protested but I ignored it and shoved open the hatch. Only, it didn't move. I stared at it for a moment, refusing to accept what had happened. Or rather, not happened. Taking another step upwards, I put my shoulder and back to the wood and pushed. Nothing happened.

Pain shot up my arm as I pounded on the trapdoor. This couldn't be it. After everything it had taken to get here, we were going to die because of a jammed hatch. I slumped down on the topmost step and buried my face in my hands. Tears threatened to well up in my eyes. Bitter resentment seeped into my chest as I couldn't help regretting that I'd gone back and saved the trapped woman. If I'd just kept running, I would've noticed the jammed trapdoor sooner and I would've had more time to find another exit. Damn. I'd just wanted to get Liam's look of revulsion out of my head and now my first selfless act in years was going to get me killed.

No. More pain flashed up my wrist as I slammed my fist into the stairs. I refused to give up. Thundering down the stairs again, I tried to come up with another plan. The copper-haired woman swayed on her feet as I ran past. Flames were slowly eating their way through the room we'd come from but there had to be another way out. There had to.

A tattered drape hung on the wall opposite the staircase. *What an odd place for a curtain.* I grabbed the splotchy dark blue fabric and yanked it aside. It only revealed more of the impenetrable wall. A feral howl tore from my throat as I ripped the whole drape from its fastenings. I blinked. There, towards the middle of the previously hidden section, was a door. And it led straight into the outer wall. I sprinted forward.

The handle rattled as I shook it. It was locked. Finally. Finally something I could actually fix. Kneeling before the door, I pulled out my lockpicks and got to work. The lock clicked open within a matter of seconds. Pushing down the handle, I shoved open the door and was greeted by salty sea air. I took a deep breath and stepped across the threshold.

On the other side, a platform sticking out from the side of the building met me. It was bare save for the metal contraption I assumed was used to haul goods up from a boat underneath. No rope was in it, though. Stepping carefully, I snuck towards the edge and looked down. Blue-green water moved in waves beneath. Well, at least it wasn't a stone courtyard.

When I retreated inside, I found the redheaded woman slumped on the floor, her eyes drooping. Damn. I picked her up and dragged her through the door and onto the ledge. After going as far out as I could, I took a firm hold of her waist.

"This is gonna suck," I muttered and jumped off the edge.

Air whooshed in my ears as we fell. The impact when we hit the water was enough to knock the breath out of me and make me lose my grip on the woman. Kicking hard, I raced towards the surface. Salt-tasting winds filled my lungs again. I whipped my head around. Red hair floated in the water an arm's length away but it was disappearing fast into the ocean. I swam forward.

Drawing her to the surface again, I twisted onto my back and put her limp body on top of mine. After I'd looped my arms around her shoulders, I kicked towards the shore. I'd run out of strength to do shit like this before we'd even jumped off the ledge but kept at it anyway.

Stones slammed into my head and scraped along my back. Why were there stones in the middle of the water? It took my exhausted mind an extra second to understand that we had made it to the shore. Flipping onto my knees, I crawled up from the water while dragging the woman behind me. Shouts rose from somewhere near me but I was too tired to hear what they said.

Once I'd gotten our torsos onto land, I spared a glance at the woman's face. Her eyes were closed. Damn. Was she breathing? I thought I could detect a small rise and fall of her chest but I figured I needed to wake her up so she could get some of that water out of her lungs. Since I was no doctor, I had no idea what to do. So I did the only thing I could think of: I gave her face a hard slap.

Her eyes snapped open and she coughed water onto the stony shore. I let out a long exhale and slumped back against the wet stones. Water lapped around my legs.

The green-eyed woman lay down beside me and released a strained laugh. "You *are* a violent one."

I was too devoid of strength to chuckle so I just blew out an amused breath through my nose. Somewhere behind me, stones smacked against each other as boots trampled towards us. The voices were back too but I didn't care. I just closed my eyes and felt the gentle waves rise and fall over my thighs. Man, selflessly saving some random stranger was ridiculously dangerous and exhausting. I was definitely never doing that again.

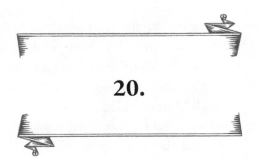

20.

"Oh no, don't even think about it," Liam said.

Dropping into the blue and green armchair, I flashed him a smile that said: *thank you for your concern but I don't care what you think.* I swept my gaze over the five people gathered in the school's living room. "I have a plan."

"Someone tried to blow you up," Liam protested again. "Yesterday!"

"Someone tried to blow them up too." I threw an arm in the direction of Shade and Elaran. "But I don't hear you telling them to sit this one out."

"Because they *got out.* When there was an opening, they climbed through, while you stayed behind in the burning building."

"I saved..." I began before realizing that I never asked the woman with the copper hair what her name was. "I stayed behind because the damn roof caved in and Shade and Elaran would've died trying to get me out. And then I saved... what's-her-face who was stuck in there too." I glanced away and picked at a loose thread sticking out of the armrest. "I thought you'd be proud."

"I am proud of you," my friend said in a soft voice. "But I'm also worried."

I rubbed my hands over the scars and half-healed bruises covering my forearms. "I'm fine. I'm a hard person to kill."

From across the room, Shade's piercing gazed locked on me while the corner of his mouth twitched upwards. "I've noticed."

"Like a cockroach," Elaran added.

Crossing my arms, I sent a scorching scowl his way. "You know, you really need to make up your mind about which unflattering animal I remind you of."

Laughter rose from our companions but before the rude elf could retort, Haemir pushed the conversation back on track. "You said you had a plan?"

"Yeah," I confirmed. "Marcellus tried to kill us—"

"Why did he even do that?" Haela interrupted and turned to Shade. "You said he wouldn't try to kill us until after the election."

The assassin gave her a lopsided smile. "Because we're too good at our job. We've messed with his campaign so much that he's getting desperate enough to take drastic measures. Now that he failed, though, people are going to start talking."

"Which brings us back to the plan I was trying to explain," I said and looked pointedly at Haela.

She grinned sheepishly.

I shook my head. "As I was saying, Marcellus tried to kill us. *We* know it. Now we just need to make sure that everyone else knows it too."

"And how are we supposed to do that?" Elaran muttered and crossed his arms. "He will have covered his tracks well. It's not like we're going to find barrels of gunpowder and spare torches just lying around in his house."

A satisfied grin crept across my face. "Unless, you know, we put it there." I lifted my shoulders in a light shrug. "Then, all we'd have to do is whisper it in a few people's ears and *whoosh*, a wildfire rumor and evidence to support it."

The room fell silent as everyone watched me. Somewhere above us, children stampeded through a hallway towards their next class.

"You want to frame the guy for something he actually did?" Haela barked a laugh. "Ha! I like it."

Elaran studied me from under furrowed brows but then nodded. "It's actually a pretty good plan."

"You don't have to sound so surprised," I grumbled.

Paper rustled as Shade pushed off the desk he'd been leaning on. "And if we embellish it further and tell people that lots of honest workers died in the explosion too, then we might finally push Marcellus over the edge."

"Remember that couple who sells hats I talked about?" Liam tapped a finger to his chin. "They're very influential among the merchants. If I tell them about workers dying, they'll be furious and they'll definitely tell others about it. We've gotten close lately so I should be able to just drop in on them today."

"Yeah," Haela said, "and if we tell the people in the debate club about it, they'll spread the word too. Like, come on, they're in a debate club. They *love* talking."

The plan was coming together. After glancing at each other, we all gave a collective nod. I jumped up from the armchair and strode towards the door. My sore muscles protested at the sudden movement but I pretended not to feel it so that Liam wouldn't worry.

"Alright, I'm gonna go get us some incriminating evidence."
I looked to Shade and Elaran. "I could use some help planting it,
though."

Shade's black eyes glittered as he tilted his head to the right.
"The master thief needs help breaking into a house?"

Stopping with one hand on the doorframe, I turned back
to the smug assassin. "No, the master thief needs two grunts to
carry the barrels of gunpowder for her." I flashed him a smirk and
rounded the corner into the hallway beyond. "I'll have it ready in
like two hours. Make sure you're here when I get back."

Grumbled curses mixed with scattered laugher followed me
to the door. Shade was right. Marcellus had become desperate
enough to try to kill us. If we got him busted for trying to
assassinate a fellow candidate, he might finally be ready to
surrender and sign that peace treaty. Blinding sunlight met me
when I stepped through the door. Just one final push, then we'd
be home free.

"ARE YOU SURE THIS WILL work?" Elaran cast a suspicious
glance between me and the door to the garden shed in which
we'd stashed the gunpowder.

Grabbing his sleeve, I yanked him back into the house across
the street as a crowd trampled past.

"I can't believe General Marcellus tried to kill his
opponent!" a woman exclaimed.

"That's what you're hung up on?" a man's voice asked. "I can't
believe he killed ten workers trying to do it."

"Ten?" another man said. "I heard it was fifty."

I glanced up at Elaran. "I'd say it's working just fine."

The building opposite Marcellus' house had been deserted, so after we'd planted the evidence in our target's shed, I had used my lock picking skills to get us inside. Now Shade, Elaran, and I stood pressed together just inside the front door. Darkness covered the world outside as we all spied through the crack in the door.

"Liam and the twins did their job well," Shade said. "The rumor has spread like a disease since just this morning."

"Yeah, the twins and Liam have done what they're supposed to but what about our part?" Elaran flicked an impatient hand in the direction of Marcellus' lawn. "The people still need to find the gunpowder. How can we be sure they're going to demand to search his house? And he's one of the *rulers* of this nation. Why would he even let them in?"

"Oh, you just leave that to me." I pulled up the hood of my cloak and slipped out the door.

A mob had gathered outside Marcellus' house but so far, the mighty General was nowhere to be seen. I moved through the gathered bodies like a wraith.

"Why isn't he out here?" I said as I slunk past a group of apron-wearing women. Putting a light hand on the back of a man discussing with his friend, I moved between them. "We need answers," I whispered as I pushed past them gently. Three married couples stood in a row further in. I grazed past them. "He needs to explain himself."

Before long, my comments were being repeated in different parts of the group. I withdrew to the back of the crowd. Disgruntled muttering came to a head when a robust man finally raised his voice to a shout.

"General Marcellus! People have died in an explosion you set. We demand an explanation."

Other voices rose in agreement. More and more people called out for an explanation until finally, the front door swung open and a furious-looking Marcellus stepped out.

"People of Pernula," he began, voice shaking with anger. "This is my home. Why have you come here and disturbed my privacy? This is the height of rudeness!"

"Rude?" I commented in a low voice to the people in front of me. "Isn't killing fifty honest workers the height of rudeness?"

The crowd stirred. "You don't get to talk about rudeness when you killed fifty people while trying to rid yourself of your competition!" someone called close to me.

I tugged my hood further down and moved to another part of the throng.

"This is absurd!" General Marcellus said. "I haven't killed anyone."

"He's lying," I whispered as I slipped past a group of men who smelled like seaweed and salt water. Three women who looked to be sisters parted as I slunk past while muttering under my breath. "He probably still has leftover gunpowder and torches from it on his property." I gently weaved through a cluster of soot-covered men. "We should demand to search his property for evidence."

Increasingly heated discussions rose from the mob as my passing suggestions spread from one group to the next. In the flickering candlelight I thought I could detect a hint of apprehension in Marcellus' eyes.

"We don't believe you!" a woman called.

"Prove it then!" another voice shouted. "Let a representative from us search your property then."

Red flushed the General's face and he stared daggers into the sea of people. "This is outrageous! You have no right to trample into my home. And at this hour. You should be ashamed of yourselves! If you have any concerns you will bring them to me in the morning. At Blackspire. Following the proper protocol."

Embarrassed murmuring rippled through the crowd. Some people glanced away while others kicked at stones on the ground like a bunch of students who had just been admonished by their teacher. Oh, he was good. A smirk settled on my hood-covered face. But I was better.

"He's stalling," I muttered as I made my way through the mob. A blacksmith stepped back to let me pass. "He probably wants us to wait until morning so he has time to get rid of the evidence." I spied a group of young men who looked more angry than abashed and wove towards them. Placing a light hand on one of their upper arms, I slunk through the agitated men while commenting loudly enough for them to overhear. "If he truly has nothing to hide, why wouldn't he let a representative in?"

"You just want to get rid of the evidence!" one of the pissed-off young men called. "Only someone who's guilty would refuse to prove his innocence!"

"Yeah! You have nothing to fear if you have nothing to hide."

"What are you hiding, General?"

Desperation flashed past on General Marcellus' face as the roar of the mob increased. He really had no other choice now. If he refused their request for a representative to make sure he was telling the truth, then all the people gathered here tonight would believe he was guilty. Then, they would tell the rest of their friends, and then they would do the same, until the whole city buzzed with the news.

"Fine!" Marcellus called at last and held up his hands. "I have nothing to hide. Choose a representative and then I will escort that person around my property until they are satisfied that I had nothing to do with the explosion by the docks."

A malicious chuckle slipped past my lips as I detached myself from the throng and made my way back to where my two companions waited. Marcellus could kiss his election goodbye.

When I finally slunk through the door of the building across the street, I was met by curious looks from both Elaran and Shade.

Throwing my hood back, I glanced between them. "What?"

"How did you do that?" Elaran asked.

"Let's just say this ain't the first time I've started a riot."

Both of them were silent for a few seconds before sudden realization slammed onto Shade's face with all the force of a basher's bat.

"*The King's Day Riot?* That was you?" Disbelief dripped from the assassin's voice. "King Adrian wanted my *head* for not catching the person behind it."

"I don't see how that's my problem." I flashed him a wicked grin before lifting my shoulders in a nonchalant shrug. "I was robbing three mansions. I needed a distraction."

"Wait..." Shade stared at me while comprehension and incredulity slowly filled his intelligent eyes. "No way. You're responsible for *both* the King's Day Riot *and* the Triple Robbery?"

A smirk decorated my lips as I gave him another light shrug. "I'm very good at what I do."

The Master of the Assassins' Guild released an impressed chuckle. "Clearly."

Elaran muttered something under his breath but it was drowned out by the rising cries outside the door. We all peered through the crack again. A growing crowd had gathered outside General Marcellus' garden shed.

"They've found the gunpowder," Elaran said.

I ran a hand over my chin. "I wonder how he's gonna try and explain his way out of this."

"Me too," Shade said. "But we probably shouldn't stick around to find out. If we're caught here, it was all for nothing."

"True." I let out a disappointed sigh but followed the assassin and the elf out the door.

Once I had relocked it behind us, we took off down the nearest side street. If this didn't make Marcellus desperate enough to sign the peace treaty then I didn't know what would. It had to be a done deal by now. There was, of course, one other possibility. We might have pushed him so far over the edge that all bets were off now. After this, he might send his entire army after us with a kill-on-sight order. I shrugged as we veered into another alley. Oh well, just another day in the life of a smart-mouthed thief.

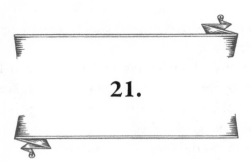

21.

Three hooded figures blocked the way. I yanked my hunting knives from their holsters while, on either side of me, Shade and Elaran drew their blades as well. The cloaked men took a step forward.

It had been four days since we'd outed Marcellus' hand in the explosion. Civil unrest had spread through the city and the General had been losing support by the day. We'd been bracing ourselves for some kind of retaliation, but so far nothing had happened. I had a feeling that was about to change.

The man in the middle removed his hood and the sudden light revealed the scowling face of General Marcellus. He seemed completely unfazed by the weapons pointed at him from across the alley as he strode forward between the gangly buildings encapsulating the side street. Behind him, his two companions dropped their disguises as well.

"You have been busy," General Marcellus said when he came to a halt a few strides in front of us. The Fahr brothers took up position next to him. "Framing me for the warehouse fire. Clever."

"It's not really framing when you're actually responsible for it," I pointed out.

"And that stunt during my dinner," Marcellus pressed on as if I hadn't said anything. "I wonder, how did you manage all that?"

Shade returned his swords to the sheaths strapped across his back. "Why have you come, General?"

"It is time to stop this nonsense."

"So, you're surrendering?" I said, a smirk on my lips.

"I am not surrendering," Marcellus growled at me before turning back to Shade. "But this foolishness has to end." He motioned at the two brothers beside him. "William and Eric Fahr will accompany you back to your accursed island and deliver the peace treaty I have drafted for your king and the queen of the elves to sign. And then, you will leave my country and my election alone."

"I will need to see the documents beforehand," the assassin said.

General Marcellus flicked an impatient hand. "Fine. They'll show it to you at the harbor before you board the ship."

"They will show it to me, but I'm not boarding your ship." Shade tilted his head slightly to the right. "We're taking our own ship."

"Suit yourself." Marcellus returned the assassin's gaze with a hard stare of his own. "If you do anything else to mess with my campaign, I will tear up the peace treaty and have you executed."

Before anyone had time to answer, General Marcellus whirled around and strode back down the street. After one last venomous look, the Fahr brothers turned around as well and followed the General's billowing cloak out the alley.

I glanced at my companions. "So we won?"

"It would appear so," Shade said.

Elaran shoved his swords back in their sheaths and crossed his arms. "We haven't won until that document is back home and signed by Faye and your king."

"Such an optimist, aren't you?" I rolled my eyes at the grumpy elf.

"You're one to talk."

The Master of the Assassins' Guild interrupted our arguing by clearing his throat. "We need to head back and let the others know."

"Yeah," I said. "Zaina needs to get the ship and crew ready."

When Elaran nodded as well, we all turned around without another word and started jogging back to the school. I could barely believe it. All our scheming had actually paid off. We had managed to make Marcellus desperate enough to secure a lasting peace between our nations. That is, if we could get the documents to the Lost Island. Elaran was right. We hadn't won until King Edward and Queen Faye had signed the treaty as well. And a lot could happen before that.

WAVES CRASHED ONTO the beach behind our backs. Shade, Zaina, and I faced the other five members of our group on the soft sand. A small rowboat waited a short distance away.

"Are you sure we shouldn't come too?" Haemir asked.

"I'm sure," Shade said. "In case this is just a trick to get us out of town for a while, you need to stay here and keep the campaign running."

"You think he will betray you?" Norah asked.

"I always plan as if people will betray me," the Master Assassin said.

Norah's face took on a sympathetic look. "Sad way to live."

"Good way to survive."

She nodded at the assassin before turning to her sister. "This time, you will come back."

"Yes," Zaina promised and put a hand on Norah's shoulder. "This time when I leave, I will come back."

Wind whipped through our clothes and carried the scent of the sea to our nostrils. I turned to study the boy next to the Pernish teacher. Liam's dark blue eyes were filled with worry.

"Be safe," he said, locking eyes with me.

"I'm just going back to Keutunan. You're the one still stuck in enemy territory." I blew out a soft laugh. "I should be telling you to be safe."

Next to me, Shade and Elaran clasped forearms.

"Keep them safe," the assassin said.

"Always."

I tore my eyes from the anxious faces arranged before us and strode towards the rowboat. Sand shifted beneath my boots. I didn't like saying goodbye and I was even less a fan of leaving our friends here, but Shade was right. If this was some sort of trick, we had to at least keep Shade's campaign running in his absence so that we could come back and continue our assault on Marcellus if need be. I took a deep breath of salty sea air as I reached the boat. Hopefully, we wouldn't have to.

SAILS SNAPPED IN THE strong northern winds. I leaned against the railing and studied the approaching island. The Lost Island. My home. Another gust of wind ripped through my clothes, sending a shiver coursing through my body. Thanks to the warm climate of Pernula, I had almost forgotten that we were far into fall.

"Have you missed it?" Zaina strolled over and placed her arms on the cool and damp wood next to me.

"The cold?" I snorted. "Not really."

She gave me an exasperated stare. "No. Keutunan."

For a moment, I considered her question in silence. "I don't know," I said finally. It was the truth. I wasn't sure if I'd missed Keutunan or not, which was strange, but I didn't want to talk about that so I decided to switch topic. "So this is what you want?" I turned my head to study the pirate next to me. "To be on a boat your whole life?"

Zaina stroked the railing in an affectionate gesture. "It's not just a boat. With this ship, there are no limits. No boundaries. I could sail to the end of the world if I wanted to."

"So it's about freedom?"

"Yeah." A wistful look drifted across her face. "I guess it is."

Turning our heads all the way to the side, we both watched in silence as Keutunan's harbor drew closer. We had caught up with the Fahr brothers' ship on our way here so now, both our vessels approached our destination together. After another few minutes of quiet, the Pernish smuggler spoke again.

"What do you want?"

Startled by her question, I frowned at her. "What do you mean?"

"I want to be a pirate. To sail my ship into the horizon. What do you want?"

"I want Liam to be happy."

Zaina released a soft chuckle. "Yeah, obviously. And I want my sister to be happy. But I didn't ask what you wanted for someone else. I asked what *you* wanted. For you."

What I want for me? Propping my elbows on the railing, I rested my chin in my hands. What did I want? Apart from keeping Liam safe, I had wanted an adventure and when I'd gone to Pernula, I had gotten that. But that wasn't really an answer to Zaina's question. In a perfect world, what would the rest of my life look like? I had no idea.

"I don't know." I blew out a sigh and shook my head. "I don't know what I want for me."

The pirate nudged an elbow in my upper arm. "Then maybe it's time to figure that out."

Before I could think of anything suitable to say, she straightened and strode back across the deck while snapping orders to the crew. My mind kept churning. Why were there suddenly so many questions that I didn't have an answer to? Had I missed Keutunan? I didn't know. What did I want? I didn't know. Tilting my head up towards the gray sky above, I let out a long exhale. Damn pirate. Why did she have to ask such difficult questions?

Fingers snapped in front of my face. "Pay attention."

I shook my head to pull myself back to reality and found a black-clad assassin staring at me. "What?"

"The rowboat's ready." He jerked his chin towards the other side of the ship. "Let's go."

With the turmoil in my head, I hadn't even noticed that we'd dropped anchor. Getting distracted was dangerous. If the Fahr brothers were up to something, I needed to stay sharp. I shoved the list of unanswered questions out of my mind and followed Shade across the deck. Worrying about the future would have to wait until I was finished worrying about today.

Wood creaked as I climbed onto the pier. I drew a deep breath. Crisp and cold and pine needles. The air really smelled different here compared to Pernula's warm spices scent.

"The Fahr brothers and the Pernish delegation are right behind us," Shade said. "We need to hurry. I have to fill in Edward before they arrive at the Silver Keep."

"Yeah."

We took off across the pier. To be honest, I wasn't entirely sure why I was there. I couldn't show my face in the Silver Keep because I was a thief and I didn't really have a specific role to fill. When we crossed into the Merchants' Quarter, I decided to voice that to Shade.

"You told everyone else to stay behind in Pernula," I stated. "Why did you ask me to come?"

The Master Assassin turned his head to gaze at me while darting around a group of women doing their afternoon shopping. They gasped as we flashed past.

"I needed someone. In case shit hits the fan."

"And you trust me to watch your back?" I arched an eyebrow at him.

"Not particularly, no." He cracked a teasing grin. "If things get ugly, I just need someone to throw to the wolves so I can get out unscathed."

"Funny," I said drily.

"I know."

A very tall and muscular man with a shaved head stepped out of a side street. I skidded to a halt in front of him and blinked twice. He seemed as surprised to see me as I was to see him. All around us, people bustled past on their afternoon errands, pulling hoods and cloaks around themselves to stave off the biting wind.

"Bones!" I exclaimed.

"Storm." His mouth transformed into a wide smile. "It's so good to see you. I didn't know you were back."

A few strides ahead, Shade paced restlessly. "I need to..." He pointed towards the keep.

"Yeah." I nodded. "I'll catch up."

"Stay in the ceiling," he said before sprinting up the street.

I turned back to the Thieves' Guild gatekeeper. "It's good to see you too. I literally just got off the ship." I jerked a thumb over my shoulder, towards the harbor. "How is everything?"

A hearty laugh rumbled in Bones' chest. "Quiet, now that you're gone."

"I'm that bad, huh?" I chuckled and gave his shoulder a soft push. "But everyone's okay?"

"Everyone's okay. Told you, I always take care of the guild." He looked behind me as if searching for something. "Where's Liam?"

Despite the cold weather, the street was busy so I put a hand on Bones' arm and led him towards the wall of a watchmaker's shop. It offered some protection against the winds and even more against potential eavesdroppers.

"He's still in Pernula," I said. "I can't go into detail but the mission we're on isn't done yet. It will be soon, or so we hope. But he and the elves stayed behind just in case."

Bones' gray eyes peered down at me. "That doesn't sound like Liam. He doesn't usually agree to let you go alone."

Now it was my turn to release a warm laugh. "Perceptive as always. Liam... met someone."

The gatekeeper raised his eyebrows.

"That's why I think he didn't mind staying behind," I said. "You should see his face. I've never seen him this happy."

Another wide smile spread across Bones' face, making his eyes twinkle. "I'm glad to hear that."

Down the street, a clock announced that the hour was full. Bones jerked his head up.

"I have to go," he said. "My shift's about to start."

"It's alright. I've gotta go too." I nodded towards the Silver Keep. "I'll swing by the guild later and we'll catch up, yeah?"

"Sounds good." The muscled gatekeeper surprised me by drawing me into a tight hug. "I've missed you, trouble."

"I've missed you too," I said into his broad chest.

Releasing me from the embrace, he gave my shoulders a squeeze before disappearing into the crowd again. Okay, maybe I had missed Keutunan after all. Or perhaps not the city as much as my friends in it. Speaking of, there was an assassin in need of my help at the Silver Keep. Or in need of someone to throw to the wolves in case shit hit the fan, as he had so eloquently put it. I pulled my cloak tighter around my shoulders. I guess we were about to find out which of the two it was.

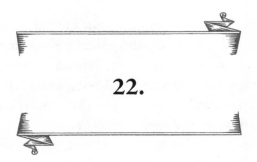

22.

The young black-haired king sat straight-backed on the obsidian throne. I shifted my weight. As usual, I was perched on the beams in my favorite eavesdropping spot high up in the ceiling. It was as if the person who'd designed the room had added a place for spying on purpose. If you stood down on the floor, you wouldn't be able to hear the people on the dais if you were standing further away and they spoke quietly. But up here, the acoustics were phenomenal. I could hear almost everything.

From my vantage point, I could also see both the raised marble dais that King Edward and Shade occupied, as well as the floor in front of it where the rest of the crowd had gathered. Crowd was definitely the right word.

In addition to the Fahr brothers and the small group of Pernulans who accompanied them, the throne room was filled with lords and ladies from Keutunan. At first I had struggled to understand why, but then I'd realized that it had to be in order to make the peace treaty as public as possible. Smart. It would be much harder for General Marcellus to back out of it now.

King Edward rose from his throne and strode to the edge of the platform. Shade followed and kept guard behind his shoulder.

"Esteemed council members, lords, and ladies," the smartly dressed king said. "We have gathered here today to make history. The great nations of Keutunan and Pernula are going to sign a treaty to ensure the safety and well-being of our citizens. And then, Queen Faye will do the same in Tkeideru. This is the start of a new era of peace and plenty for all of us."

He looked admirably calm considering the fact that the two brothers in front of him were responsible for killing his mother and betraying his country. I craned my neck and watched Lord Fahr the elder motion for something to be brought forth. One of the Pernulans placed a small wooden box in William Fahr's hands.

"King Edward," the blond lord said and stepped towards the dais. "Please accept this gift from General Marcellus as a sign of friendship."

Shade made to intercept him but Edward waved him back. Lord Fahr held up the intricately decorated box towards the king and bowed his head.

"I thank General Marcellus for this gift," King Edward said as he plucked the case from the blond lord's hands. After inspecting it closely, no doubt for hidden traps, he opened the lid.

Something white and shiny became visible against the dark wood and red cushions inside. I squinted at it. It was too far away to see exactly what it was but I had the strangest feeling that I'd seen it somewhere before. King Edward picked up the pearl-colored sphere and placed it in his palm to show the rest of the audience.

"Ow!" he hissed.

Shade ripped the white orb from his king's hand. A red smear marred one side of it but the stain seemed to disappear into the ball, giving it a slight pink hue for a few seconds. Lightning flashed in the assassin's eyes when he saw the blood dripping from Edward's palm.

"Ha!" William Fahr called. "I knew it!"

The confused crowd let out a startled yelp at the load cry. What in Nemanan's name was going on? And where had I seen that white ball before?

"What is the meaning of this?" King Edward demanded. "Explain yourselves."

"The meaning of this is to expose the truth. My friends," Lord Fahr said and turned towards the gathered nobility. "You have been lied to for many years now. My brother and I began to suspect the truth and that was why we were forced to flee."

King Edward fixed the blond brothers with a hard stare. "You were forced to flee because you shot the Queen Mother and betrayed our city to the Pernulans."

William Fahr placed a hand on his chest in offense. "We were trying to liberate our noble city from a corrupt ruler."

"Corrupt? The only corrupt people in this room are you."

The blond lord turned to Shade. "Place that ball on the dais and I will prove it to you."

The Master Assassin glanced to his king. We all knew that they couldn't refuse because that would only work in favor of the Fahr brothers. King Edward gave Shade a brief nod. With lightning still flashing in his eyes, the assassin strode forward and placed the white orb on the edge of the platform. An air shield shimmered to life around it.

"Who do you trust most?" William Fahr asked the nobles around him. "Whose honor is beyond question?"

"Lord Raymond," several people said.

The senior member of the Council of Lords stepped forward. "Lord Fahr, this kind of behavior is unacceptable."

"When you find out the lies the king has poured into your ear, you will change your mind. Now, please pick up the orb."

Lord Raymond stroked his mustache but then heaved a deep sigh and approached the ball. After studying it for a few seconds, he reached for it. A *zing* sounded as soon as he touched the air shield around it. Lord Raymond jerked his hand back. He looked at his fingers with a puzzled expression on his face and then bent down again to give it another try. Another *zing*. He snatched his hand back.

"I cannot get through the... glowing air around it," Lord Raymond announced.

"Of course you can't," William Fahr said, a victorious grin on his lips. "No one in this room can. Except..." he trailed off and swept his arm in a dramatic arc. "Ladies and gentlemen, may I present Ciaran Silverthorn."

The silence was deafening as we all stared at him in shock. *No way. It couldn't be?* I watched the scene below with wide eyes. *Could it?*

"This is absurd," King Edward said, aghast. "My brother died when he was a child. His body was returned burned–"

"Burned beyond recognition," Lord Fahr filled in. "Yes, that is what we have all been told. And *beyond recognition* really is the key phrase in that sentence. A child was returned but it was not the crown prince." He stabbed a finger at Shade. "This is Crown Prince Ciaran."

A buzz went through the crowd as they shifted, pointing and whispering. Shade's face was an unreadable mask while the king bore a deep frown. I stared at the events unfolding beneath me. This was insane.

"What an outlandish claim," King Edward said as if he'd heard my thoughts. "Even for you, Lord Fahr."

"Is it?" The blond lord motioned between the two men on the dais and the gathered nobles. "Their facial features may not be that similar, but that is true for a lot of siblings. But everything else. Can you not see it? They have the same hair color, the same eye color, and the same pale complexion."

"Yes, we and thousands of other people in the city," the Master Assassin said and tilted his head slightly to the right.

"And that!" Lord Fahr exclaimed, pointing to Shade. "That... mannerism. Usually when someone cocks their head, they do it in either direction but King Edward only ever tips it to the right. And so does this assassin."

Surprised murmurs drifted through the audience. The pale light filtering in from the tall windows illuminated the well-dressed lords and ladies. Looks of recognition slammed onto face after face.

"King Adrian did that as well," a man in a dark blue waistcoat called.

"Yes, I remember that."

"It's true, the late King Adrian did it too."

King Edward shook his head and blew out a weary sigh. "This is absurd. You are telling me that my dead brother is alive and all you have to back it up are similar hair and eye colors and a vague mannerism."

Lord Fahr lifted a finger in the air before lowering it to the white orb lying forgotten on the dais. "And that. That is a neat object that the Pernulans use to guard small valuables. It is protected by blood magic. It draws blood from the person who picks it up, you all saw it do that to King Edward, and now, only those who share the same blood can get through the shield around it."

A gasp rippled through the crowd just as a memory snapped into place in my mind. I knew where I'd seen that ball before. In the window of the shop selling magic artifacts that Zaina and I had passed. Could it really be true?

"Come, try to touch it," William Fahr said and beckoned to the crowd.

After an initial second of hesitation, a flood of lords poured forth to try. All of them snatched their hands back when they reached the air shield. The unreadable mask was still firmly in place on Shade's face but Edward's confidence was wavering. He looked between the ball and the assassin.

"You could touch it," he said.

On the floor, realization dawned on the nobles as well.

"That's King Adrian's lost heir."

"That's the son who presumably died."

King Edward tore his eyes from the white orb that no one else could touch and trained them on Shade. He tipped his head to the right as he studied the assassin. I wasn't sure what he had seen in his face, I could read nothing in it, but the king jerked back a step as if someone had slapped him, and stared at Shade with wide eyes.

"You knew?" the young king said and let his mouth drop open.

Shade swallowed. "Your Majesty, this is not the time or the place."

"I don't care!" Edward yelled. "I thought I'd lost my whole family. I thought I was alone. And all this time *you've known*!"

"Your Majesty..." the black-eyed assassin began again before he was interrupted by a raised voice from the nobles.

"But that means *he* is the rightful heir. He is the rightful *king*."

Matching smirks decorated the faces of Lord Fahr and his brother. Clothes rustled as the audience shifted in the silence that had fallen.

"So you see," William Fahr said. "You have been lied to this whole time. But that is not the end of it. These two brothers have—"

"Enough!" King Edward bellowed in a voice dripping with authority. "Ladies and gentlemen, we will resume this meeting one hour after sunrise tomorrow. Everything will be answered then. Now, please see yourselves out."

No one moved. The nobles in their brightly colored clothes remained rooted in their spots. Lightning flashed in Edward's black eyes.

"Get out!" he screamed.

Ladies gasped and clutched their skirts as they hurried towards the exit in a flurry of colorful fabric. Their husbands followed, whispering among themselves.

The black-haired king snapped his fingers and pointed at the Fahr brothers and the Pernish delegation. "They will remain in the guest wing under guard until tomorrow." He turned hard eyes on the treacherous brothers. "Have that peace treaty ready.

As soon as this nonsense is sorted, we are signing it and then you are leaving my city."

Metal clanked as the Silver Cloaks escorted the last group out of the throne room. I should probably have left as well but I was too shocked by this revelation to care about the indecency in eavesdropping on private conversations. Could Shade really be the lost heir? I shifted my weight on the beam and peered down at the only two people left in the room.

"You're my brother?" Incredulity was written all over Edward's features.

The impassive mask had dropped from Shade's face and he now looked worried and... ashamed. I don't think I had even seen him look like that before. The assassin opened his mouth but then closed it again and glanced around the room.

"I..." he began but then trailed off.

Edward kept staring at him until the disbelief faded and shocked certainty took its place on his young face. "How long have you known?"

Shade just looked back at him with a pained expression.

"Answer me!" the king yelled.

"My whole life."

"You...?" King Edward shook his head and exhaled forcefully. Raking his fingers through his glossy black hair, he paced back and forth in front of the assassin. Shade remained silent. Suddenly, the king jerked to a halt and whipped his head towards him.

"My mother," Edward said. "My mother realized it. That day when we were attacked by the Pernulans and Lord Fahr." He drew in a sharp breath. "She took a bullet for you!"

Shade glanced away. The agony on his face was so strong it almost cut the air when he moved.

The young king took two strides towards the assassin and shoved him backwards. "She pushed you out of the way and took the bullet meant for you. My mother died because of you!"

Edward drove his fists into Shade's chest while continuing to push him away. The assassin just stood there and let his little brother beat him. His little brother. My head spun. But it all made sense. Everything Lord Fahr had said, and everything King Edward had said after the rest of the crowd had left. Not to mention that I already knew the white orb actually contained magic because I'd seen in it Pernula. I pressed a hand to my forehead. Shade was Ciaran Silverthorn. The lost crown prince of Keutunan. And he had always known it.

Down on the platform, Edward had stopped his assault. He looked drained. Like an empty shell that the tide had washed clean. The young king stared with unseeing eyes at the assassin that was his brother.

"I need time to think," he said.

Before Shade could answer, he turned around and made for the door in movements far jerkier than usual. The Master of the Assassins' Guild stared after him. When the King of Keutunan had disappeared from view, he pressed both hands to his head. For a moment, he just stood there, unmoving like a statue. Then, the spell broke and he let his arms drop.

He shot across the dais and reached for the magic orb. The air shield around it retracted as he snatched it up and hurled it against the wall with all his might. A deafening scream tore from his throat and echoed throughout the room. Glass shattered and shards clinked to the floor as the ball hit the marble wall behind the throne. Then, for a moment, everything was still. Shade cast one last look at where Edward had disappeared before he too strode across the floor and vanished through another exit.

Up on the wooden beams, I was still trying to put my scrambled mind together. How long had the Fahr brothers really known about this? Based on William's victorious call when Shade took the orb, it seemed as though they hadn't been certain until this very moment. How had *they* seen it and I hadn't? In hindsight, it all made sense but I would never have guessed it before today.

I shook my head. We'd expected that the lords Fahr would try something during the reception but never in my wildest nightmares had I imagined that it would be this. The only question was, what would they gain from it? Except the general confusion that followed, of course. As I made my way down from the ceiling, I racked my brain for answers to any of the numerous questions swirling around in there, but when my boots hit the floor soundlessly, I still didn't have any. What was I supposed to do now? I had no idea.

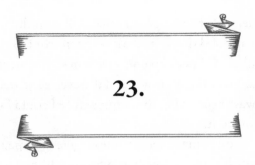

23.

Loud crashes echoed through the hallway. I wasn't even sure what I was doing there. Why I had followed him. I usually stayed out of other people's messes but there had been something in his eyes that I just couldn't get out of my head. Stopping in front of a thick wooden door, I stared at it for a moment. After drawing a soft breath, I pushed down the handle and slipped inside.

A knife flew at my face. I jerked to the side. The blade produced a sharp thud as it burrowed into the doorframe. Turning my head, I looked from the weapon to the man who'd thrown it.

"You know," I said, "if that had been... well, anyone but me, they would've died."

"If you just knocked like everyone else, I wouldn't need to throw knives at you," Shade retorted.

"Ah, but see, I thought we had already established that I'm not a knocking-on-the-front-door kind of girl." I flicked my eyes between the overturned desk, chairs, and bookcases littering the room. "Besides, I figured even if I had knocked, you wouldn't have been able to hear it over all that crashing furniture."

"Funny."

"I know, right?"

Shade leaned back against the still standing wardrobe behind him and slid down its dark wooden front. Sitting on the floor, he pulled his knees up and threw me a disinterested stare. He looked... vulnerable, in a way I'd never seen before. For a moment, I wasn't sure what to say but before I could figure it out, Shade beat me to it.

"So, have you come to lecture me or give me a pep talk?"

"I'm probably the last person who should be lecturing you on keeping secrets. And motivational speeches ain't really my thing." I lifted the bottle in my right hand. "I brought this, though."

He snorted. "Where did you get that?"

"I swiped it from an unattended room nearby." After taking a few quick strides across the room, I plopped down on the floor next to the assassin and passed him the bottle of alcohol I'd stolen.

Shade uncorked it and took a long drink before handing it back to me. I tipped some of the clear liquor into my mouth as well and felt it burn as it made its way down my throat. Crossing my legs, I glanced at the assassin.

"So, you're the king, huh?"

Shade leaned back and rested his head against the wardrobe. "Yeah."

For a long while we just sat there in silence, passing the bottle of booze back and forth. I had no intention of pushing him because sharing personal details wasn't exactly high up on my list of enjoyable things either. If he wanted to talk, he would. Otherwise, we'd just drink.

"I wasn't supposed to care," Shade said at last.

I glanced at him from the corner of my eye but said nothing.

"I've been trained not to have emotions," he continued. "Since I was a child, I've been molded into the perfect weapon. Ruthless. Cold. For Ghabhalnaz's sake, I killed my own father and I didn't even bat an eye! But now..." He gulped back some more alcohol from the bottle and barked a humorless laugh. "Oh, if my old Master could see me now, he would beat me within an inch of my life."

"Your old Master?"

The weary-looking assassin was silent for a while, as if trying to decide how much to share, but eventually tipped his head back and released a long sigh.

"Yeah. The man who took me, he was the Master of the Assassins' Guild before me. Apparently, King Adrian had betrayed him, or something, he never said. But he wanted revenge."

"So he kidnapped his heir," I summarized.

"Yeah. And not just that." Shade shook his head. "He raised that child to hate his family, to crave power, and to wipe the whole Silverthorn line from existence."

Clothes rustled against wood and stone as I turned to stare at him. What a childhood that must've been. His mouth had taken on a hard set and something I couldn't quite identify burned behind his eyes.

"It was the perfect revenge," the Master Assassin went on. "His own son, his eldest son and heir, was destined to kill them all and take the throne for himself in the name of the Assassins' Guild."

"So what changed?"

Shade blew out a tired chuckle. "Edward. After I'd killed Adrian and become a trusted advisor to Edward, he was going to meet with some terrible accident and I would take the throne for myself."

I noticed that he referred to the previous king as *Adrian* instead of *my father* but I decided not to comment on it.

"I was almost there," Shade continued. "It was all within my grasp, everything my old Master had worked towards for almost twenty years, but then... I couldn't do it." A crazed laugh slipped from his lips. "All because the fucking Master of the Assassins' Guild realized he had feelings."

Arching an eyebrow at him, I passed him the half empty bottle of liquor. "You decided not to kill your little brother and steal his throne, I'd say that's a pretty understandable decision."

The dark-eyed assassin grabbed it and took another long drink. "Yeah, but don't get me wrong, I still want it. My whole life I've been raised to crave it, and I still do. The throne. Power. Supremacy. You have no idea *how much* I want it."

"But you care about Edward more?"

"Yeah, and trust me, no one is more surprised by that than me. I hated him. Hated them all. My Master taught me that all the horrific things I'd had to endure during my childhood, during my training, was because of them. If it weren't for their actions, I would've had a happy and safe life. That's what he said. And I believed him. Hate and anger and a lust for power were all that sustained me all those years."

Knowing how all-consuming anger and hate could be, I just gave him a nod in understanding.

"I wasn't supposed to care. Why do I have to care?" Shade picked up a book and threw it across the room. It sailed through the air in a flapping of paper and hit the floor by the overturned desk with a thud. "It's so fucking inconvenient!"

"I know, right? Caring about people is so damn complicated and annoying. Like, why do we even have to have feelings at all?"

The assassin pointed the bottle at me with a look of surprised recognition on his face. "Exactly!"

Grabbing the dark brown bottle from his hand, I hoisted it in the air. "Well, here's to the cold black heart that we apparently don't have. May we one day find it."

Shade chuckled and raised a pretend bottle in the air next to mine. "To a cold black heart."

A sound came from the door. I squinted across the sea of furniture, books, and decorations cluttering the floor. Had I imagined that? Then I heard it again. A knock.

The Assassins' Guild Master stabbed a finger in my direction and threw me a pointed look. "See! Everyone else knocks."

I snorted. "Whatever."

Shade ignored my sarcastic comment and instead raised his voice to a shout. "Come in!"

The thick wooden door cracked open and Edward stuck his head through. He drew back a little when he noticed the state of the room and the two drunk underworlders still sitting on the floor.

Shade scrambled to his feet. "Edward."

"I'm sorry," the king said as he squeezed into the room. "I didn't mean any of that. You're not the reason my mother... *our* mother is dead. I was just angry and confused. But I'm not anymore." The sadness washed from his face and a genuine smile spread across his lips. "I have a brother! And not just any brother. *You.*"

Bracing myself on the wardrobe, I climbed to my feet as well. I might not have much respect for other people's property or private conversations but even I felt that this particular conversation was one I shouldn't be here for. The room swayed a little as I straightened.

I pointed an unsteady hand at the door. "I'll leave you to it."

King Edward gave me a grateful nod. "The reception will start in only a few hours and I would very much like it if you're there for that. In case Lord Fahr and his brother try something else. That room you've stayed in before, you can sleep there if you want."

Considering how much I'd had to drink, I didn't feel like heading back to the Thieves' Guild. If I did, I would have to talk to people and I was way too tired and intoxicated for that. Not to mention everything Shade and I had shared this night which had gotten both my head and my heart all tangled up.

"Thank you," I said. "I'll do that."

Right as I was about to disappear through the door, Shade's voice halted me.

"Hey, Storm!"

I stopped and peered back at him.

He locked steady eyes on me and held my gaze. "Thanks."

The corner of my lips quirked upwards in a smile and I gave him a slow nod before slipping out the door.

Well, this day had certainly taken an interesting turn. In the span of a few hours, the lost heir to the throne of Keutunan had been revealed, two brothers had been reunited, and I had gotten drunk with the Master of the Assassins' Guild.

Soft carpets muffled my steps as I steered towards my temporary bedroom.

Shade had shared much more with me than I ever thought he would and I felt like I understood him a bit better now. A bit. I mean, he was still an arrogant bastard.

A grin crept across my face as I neared my room. Good thing I was too.

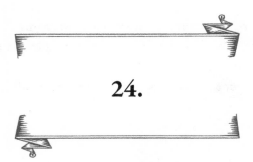

24.

Morning brought clear blue skies and a pale fall sun casting its rays through the tall windows of the throne room. The huge silver chandelier in the ceiling below me hung empty but the rows of candelabras on the floor had all been lit. Fire flickered on the sunlit walls. I snuck across the beams to my favorite eavesdropping spot.

Shuffling feet sounded from the marble arch. Twisting my head, I found a procession of finely dressed lords and ladies making their way through the rows of burning candles. When the Keutunian nobles had all taken up position throughout the room, the last group was brought in. A squad of Silver Cloaks escorted the Pernish delegation and the two treasonous brothers.

"Lords and ladies, welcome," King Edward said once he had risen from the throne. His face bore an incredibly disarming smile. "Yesterday was a very eventful day, would you not agree?"

Scattered laughter erupted from the audience as they nodded their agreement.

"I think I speak for us all when I say that the news that my brother, Ciaran Silverthorn," Edward motioned at the black-clad assassin behind him on the dais, "was alive came as a complete surprise. Though, a very welcome one. We talked long into the night and I can share with you that our reunion was a happy one."

In a matter of a few sentences, the mood of the nobles had shifted. When they had arrived, they'd looked anxious and suspicious but now, that was all gone. Instead, looks of understanding and sympathy filled their faces. King Edward sure knew how to move a crowd.

Shade stepped forward and held up a hand to the audience. "Esteemed nobles, I apologize for the deception. Though I have known the truth about my heritage for a while now, I was reluctant to share because I didn't want to create trouble for my brother and his reign." He squared his shoulders and raised his chin. "Let it be known that I make no claim on King Edward's throne."

The gathered nobles raised their eyebrows in surprise.

"Edward is the rightful king of Keutunan," the assassin pressed on, his voice powerful and certain, "and I will never try to take his crown, for as long as he lives. Long live the king!"

"Long live the king!" the rest of the room cheered back.

Given everything I'd learned last night, I knew that it must've been very hard for him to say something like that. His face, however, revealed nothing except strength. I blew out a breath through my nose and cracked a wry smile. The things we do for the people we love.

On the platform below, Edward nodded at Shade before stepping forward. The Master Assassin once again took up position behind his shoulder.

"Now, let us get back to making history," King Edward said with another infectious smile on his face.

The satisfied lords and ladies chuckled.

"Lord Fahr," the king went on. "You have brought a peace treaty from General Marcellus of Pernula. Bring it forward and in front of these respected witnesses, we shall sign it and begin a new era of friendship and prosperity."

Lord Fahr the elder motioned for his younger brother to pass him the intended scroll. I studied them. Eric had trouble hiding a smirk but his older brother looked calm and composed. Were they up to something?

William Fahr held up the scroll adorned with a large seal in red wax. "In my hand, I have the treaty between General Marcellus of Pernula and King Edward of Keutunan." He strode forward between the rows of flickering candelabras, hand still in the air.

All eyes were on him as he stopped a short distance from the marble dais. Lord William Fahr lowered his hand slightly and then snapped his whole arm to the side.

A collective gasp rang out. Everyone watched in stunned silence as smoke and flame devoured the promise of peace.

"You are going to regret that," King Edward said in a voice as hard as his obsidian throne.

Lord Fahr dropped the burning document. Flaky ashes swirled on the white marble floor as it landed.

"I doubt that," William said. He turned to the gathered nobles while Silver Cloaks closed in on him from every direction. "You see, my friends, the king will now arrest me in order to prevent you from hearing the truth."

"What truth?" someone called.

"Yes, what is the meaning of this, Lord Fahr?"

"I am afraid I will not have time to explain," the blond lord said. "King Edward and his guards will silence me before letting the truth come out."

The black-eyed king held up his hand and the Silver Cloaks stopped advancing. "Speak your mind then, traitor. Explain to these fine people why you just burned their only chance at peace."

Lord Fahr the elder gave the king a smug smile before turning back to the nobles. "The just and fair rulers of Pernula will not make peace with a corrupt king. As I tried to explain yesterday before King Edward so rudely sent us all away, these two brothers are guilty of more than simply keeping their true identities secret."

A nervous ripple spread through the crowd. Shade looked neutral as always but Edward's slight shift told me that he was worried as William opened his mouth again.

"They are both guilty of patricide!"

Startled cries rose from the audience, followed by disbelieving murmurs. *Oh. Shit.* Technically, that was true. Edward had been part of the plot to kill King Adrian, and Shade had actually drawn the knife across his throat. How in Nemanan's name had Lord Fahr found that out? As if he had heard me, the treasonous lord continued.

"Last year we were told that King Adrian had died in an animal attack while in the woods." William Fahr swept his gaze across the sea of people. "That was a lie. He was assassinated by that man." He stabbed a finger at Shade. "On the orders of your current king."

Edward looked as if someone had punched him in the gut but he recovered quickly and roared across the room. "How dare you! Once again you are standing in my halls, making outrageous claims with nothing to back it up." The young king turned to his nobles. "Do you really believe that I am capable of *murdering my own father*?"

The crowd stared back. After another few seconds of contemplation, most of them shook their heads.

"Arrest these traitors," King Edward said.

"I have proof!" Lord Fahr called as the Silver Cloaks started moving again. "A soldier who survived the slaughter, who saw Ciaran Silverthorn, also known as the Master of the Assassins' Guild, murder his own father."

Icy dread seeped through my chest. Could someone really have survived the massacre? But why would they have stayed silent until now? Memories of darkness, earsplitting screams, and a forest drenched in blood flashed before my eyes. Fair enough. If someone had seen what I'd done to their friends that day, they would probably not have been in a hurry to draw my attention by telling everyone what had happened.

The mood of the crowd shifted again. Shade's assassin ties were working against him and people whispered restlessly that there might be truth to Lord Fahr's words. Panic welled into my chest. How were they going to explain their way out of this one?

A brown-haired man separated himself from the group of Pernulans and made his way towards the brothers Fahr. Candlelight flickered across his face.

"Soldier," William Fahr said and motioned at the approaching man. "Tell us what you saw."

The whole room held its breath as the surviving soldier opened his mouth. A *whoosh* sounded. Then a thud. Everyone stared in shock at the witness as he only produced strained gurgles. The polished hilt of a knife gleamed in the firelight where it protruded from his throat. His knees buckled. Before he'd even hit the floor, the brown-haired man was dead.

"Everyone get back or I'll kill him!" Shade bellowed across the throne room.

Every head on the floor snapped back to the raised marble dais. On it stood the Master of the Assassins' Guild with a knife pressed tightly to King Edward's throat. Cries of terror and outrage rose from the crowd. I stared at them, my mind reeling. What the hell was he doing?

"I don't know how you found out that I was the one who assassinated King Adrian," Shade shouted at Lord Fahr. "But you were wrong about one thing. I don't care about my little brother's life and I have most certainly not been plotting *with* him. After the devastating loss of his father I inserted myself into his life in order to gain his trust and eventually take the throne for myself." The assassin sneered at the audience. "But now you've screwed that up. So back up, or I will kill your precious king."

Ah. Now I understood. Clever. But awful. And insanely selfless. There might have been a way to rectify the situation later that would exonerate both brothers but Shade wasn't willing to risk it, it seemed. In that split second, he had decided that his little brother's safety and happiness were more important, so instead of gambling on a potential later solution, he had sacrificed his own future here. Oh, the things we do for the people we love, indeed.

"Do as he says," Edward called.

While the gathered nobles, Pernulans, and Silver Cloaks backed away, Shade used his free hand to flash a quick sequence. We didn't have many universal Underworld hand signals but after the assassination of King Adrian, we had agreed on a few. Like the one for *lying*, *trap*, or the one Shade was currently showing me: *cover*.

Cover? With what? I sprang into action and dug around my various pouches. Some small glass vials clinked. *Of course*. While fishing out the first one, I moved into position. Then, I dropped the tiny bottle. Glass shattered as it hit the floor and it sounded like something huge caught fire. A thick black cloud spread in front of the platform, concealing Shade and Edward from view.

As soon as the smoke cover was in place, the assassin whipped the blade from Edward's throat. "We don't have much time."

Shade was whispering but because of the extraordinary acoustics in the ceiling I mentioned earlier, I was still able to hear him if I strained my ears.

"I don't know how many smoke bombs Storm has so we have to be quick," he continued.

"Why did you do that?" King Edward demanded.

"I have to take the fall for this. If they find out that you were involved, it will be the end of everything. That's why we have to make them believe that I'm your enemy and you were just duped by me."

The black smoke was thinning so I dropped another vial. Shards flew across the marble floor and more smoke bloomed from the ground.

Shade put his hands on Edward's shoulders and locked eyes with him. "You have to banish me."

The king jerked back. "What? No!"

"You have to." The assassin threw his arms in the air in a display of utter frustration. "It's the only way to save your rule."

"I'm not banishing you!"

Sadness crept into Shade's voice. "It's that or kill me. Those are the only two options to keep you safe and your reign untainted."

Turning the last vial of blackout powder in my hands, I let out a low whistle. Shade's head jerked up. I dropped the bottle into the dispersing cloud and watched it shatter.

"That was Storm," the assassin hissed. "That's the last smoke cover. You have to do this. Please." Desperation filled his voice. "I need you to be safe. We can figure something out later but for now you have to banish me. Get Frank and Albert to arrest me. We have to make it look real."

Edward shook his head, tears streaming down his cheeks, but he raised his voice and called for his two most trusted guards. Frank and Albert barreled out of the small door behind the throne. I watched the pained expression on the young king's face as he explained the plan to the two Silver Cloaks. Shade sheathed his knife and held out his arms, palms up. Albert grabbed his offered arms and twisted them behind his back while Frank drew his sword and pressed it to the assassin's throat. King Edward wiped the tears from his cheeks just as the black smoke dissipated.

"Ladies and gentlemen," the king called. "This is a sad day for all of us."

A row of Silver Cloaks had kept any of the guests from leaving and now when King Edward snapped his fingers, they advanced on the Fahr brothers once again.

"First the traitorous Lord Fahr and his brother, who betrayed our country to a foreign power and shot my mother, once again stabbed us in the back by burning the peace treaty."

He watched with hard eyes as the guards arrested the two blond lords. "And now we learn that my father was also murdered. By none other than my own brother!"

The Keutunian lords and ladies stood unmoving on the floor. Shock, fear, and anger were present on every face.

"Ciaran Silverthorn," King Edward called. "You have committed a crime so heinous that you should be executed. However... I cannot watch another member of my family die. If I do, my heart will shatter."

Sympathy for their king softened the agitated expressions of the nobles.

"Therefore, I hereby declare that you are banished from the city of Keutunan." Edward's face betrayed nothing as he stared into the sea of people. "Under pain of death."

My heart bled for the two young brothers who had both found and lost each other within a single day. Life. Such a cruel thing.

Lighting flashed in the king's black eyes as he trained them on William and Eric Fahr. "You will share the same fate. The only reason that I am not executing you right now is because you are here under the flag of diplomacy and I will not dishonor that sacred bond. Even though you have. You are also banished. If you ever show your faces in my city again, you will be killed on sight."

The crowd murmured in support and stared daggers at the banished men.

"If any of you are still here after the tide has left tomorrow morning, you will be executed. Use this day of grace to get your ships ready to leave. Once you are on them, I do not care what happens to you." With that, the king flicked his wrist and the guards started pulling the prisoners away.

His face might be a mask of determination but I could tell from Edward's eyes that his heart was being ripped apart from the inside. As the rest of the room left, he simply remained standing there, staring into nothingness. How cruel could fate be? He had just yesterday found out that he wasn't alone and now he was forced to send his only remaining family away. As I made my way down from the ceiling, I prayed to Nemanan that this wouldn't break him completely. Then, it would all have been for nothing.

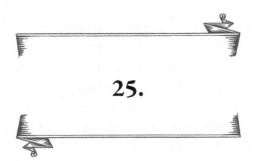

25.

Hatred burned in his eyes like wildfire. Even from a distance, I was afraid I'd suffer severe burns just by looking at him. I snuck along the wall. Shade hadn't spotted me yet but that was no surprise. He was standing at the mouth of a side street, staring at the Silver Cloaks who dumped Eric and William Fahr outside the gate to the Silver Keep. For the assassin to get out here this quickly, Frank and Albert must've let him go as soon as they were out of sight.

"If you're not gone with the next morning tide, you will die," the guards said to the Fahr brothers before retreating into the keep.

Shade's hands twitched at his sides. Crap. He was about to do something stupid. I darted through a group of merchants and skidded to a halt in front of the assassin before he exited the alley.

"Get out of my way," he growled.

"No. I know what you're thinking and it's a bad idea."

"I don't care what you think." Shade thrust out his arm and shoved me aside.

Damn assassin and his damn stubbornness. I yanked a hunting knife from its holster and slammed it in place at his throat before he took another step. The wildfire in his eyes mixed with a lightning storm, creating a truly terrifying visage, as he turned to stare at me. I didn't back down.

"Get that knife out of my face," the Master Assassin said in a voice as quiet and deadly as poison.

"I will. When you get that dumb idea out of your head."

He moved like a viper. Twisting into the space between us, he drove the side of his left hand into my wrist and the heel of his right into my chest. The knife clattered to the ground as I lost my grip and staggered backwards. A boot behind my kneecap pulled my leg forwards again and an elbow to my back sent me crashing into the street. While I pushed myself onto my knees, Shade flashed back in front of me. He grabbed a fistful of my shirt and yanked me to my feet. With a knife to my throat, the assassin backed me into the wall.

Anger danced in his eyes. I coughed as Shade shoved me into the rough stones and leaned down over the blade. Yep. Provoking the insanely furious Master Assassin had been a bad move.

"Did that make you feel better?" I asked before he could start threatening me again.

The question seemed to catch him off guard because he drew back a little.

"I know what you were gonna do," I pressed on. "You were gonna go out there and kill the Fahr brothers right there in the street. That's a stupid move. What would happen to Edward then? As long as they're in the city, anything you do will just hurt him. Is that what you want?"

Shade gripped the handle of the knife tighter but didn't push it further into my throat. That was good at least. But it was *my* hunting knife and that annoyed me more than anything else.

"William Fahr murdered my mother and forced my brother to banish me," the black-eyed assassin ground out between gritted teeth.

"And Eric Fahr kidnapped my best friend, turned my own guild against me, and almost killed me multiple times," I countered. "I hate them too. But we can't kill them until they're aboard their ship. Otherwise, *your brother* will be in trouble."

A mad grin spread across Shade's face. "Once they're aboard. Yes. We'll do it tonight, when they're back on their ships."

I glanced pointedly at the blade to my throat. "We?"

"We." He removed the knife, twisted it in his palm, and offered it to me hilt first. "William's mine. Eric's yours."

My mouth drew into a wicked grin as I took the offered weapon. "Deal."

Shade straightened and smoothed his black clothes. "I have a lot to take care of before this day is over. I'm leaving, maybe forever, I need to get my guild ready to leave as well."

"You're taking your guild with you?"

"I'll leave a few loyal ones so they can start a new Assassins' Guild for Edward but yeah, I'm taking my guild with me."

I lifted my eyebrows. "They won't be mad that you're forcing them to move to another country?"

Shade let out a short chuckle. "No. The only upset people will be the ones I order to stay behind. Loyalty is everything in our guild." He turned around and made for the mouth of the street.

"Hey!" I called. "Aren't you gonna apologize for almost slitting my throat?"

The Assassins' Guild Master twisted around. "You put a knife to my throat as well. Are you going to apologize for that?"

I crossed my arms over my chest. "No. You were being an idiot."

Shade's rippling laugh drifted through the air as he strode away. "See you tonight, Storm."

While muttering curses at his retreating form I returned the hunting knife to the small of my back. Pulling up my hood, I trotted away in the other direction. It was still only morning so I had a full day to fill before we were leaving again.

Whatever else the future might bring, I was going to return to Pernula with Shade because I needed to go back for Liam. What I'd do after that was a problem for another day. Today, I had plans. I wanted to visit Apothecary Haber and buy some more blackout powder, talk to my Guild Masters, grab a drink with Bones at the Mad Archer, and stock up on some more gear. Oh, and plan an assassination. Fun times ahead.

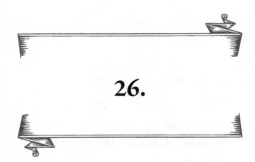

26.

Darkness had drawn its shroud over the harbor and filled the Pernulan ship with shadows. I snuck across the wooden planks. Eric Fahr's desk was locked but that didn't stop a sneak thief extraordinaire. My lockpicks solved the problem in no time.

I had spent the day getting ready to leave. Haber had been happy to see one of his most well-paying customers and I'd shown my appreciation by almost emptying his stock. Better to have too many exploding orbs and vials of blackout powder than not enough. My Guild Masters had been called away on the emergency Underworld Conclave Shade had summoned to no doubt explain this very odd situation, but I'd managed a brief meeting with them beforehand. The best part of my day, however, had definitely been the afternoon I'd spent with Bones at the Mad Archer. I really had missed him.

The door was yanked open. I slammed the desk drawer closed just as Eric Fahr strode across the threshold. His eyes widened. The ship rolled underneath my feet but I drew my hunting knives and crouched into an attack position.

"What have we here?" the blond lord said. "If it isn't the Oncoming Storm herself."

I spun the knives in my hands. "I'm glad you're happy to meet your death."

"My death?" He snorted and flicked an impatient glance at my blades. "Oh, put those silly things away before you hurt yourself."

Rounding the desk, I flashed him a malicious grin. "The only one getting hurt is you."

Lord Fahr snatched up a pistol from the bookcase next to him and trained it on my head. I froze. His mouth drew into a nasty smile.

"You were saying?" He snapped his fingers and pointed at the set of drawers to my right. "Blades over there. The ones on your legs and all the ones behind your shoulders too."

With deliberately slow movements, I removed my knives and placed them in a neat pile on the flat surface.

"And the one in your boot."

I knelt on the floor and put a hand inside my boot to release the blade strapped inside. After rising again, I dropped it with the others. Eric jerked his pistol and motioned at the rickety chair in front of the desk. What an amateur. I still had three knives left.

"Sit," he ordered. "And hands where I can see them."

Staring daggers at him, I complied and lowered myself into the chair while keeping my hands raised.

"You thought you could come in here and do what?" Lord Fahr said. "Steal from me? Kill me? I have said it before and I'll say it again. You are out of your league, girl."

I answered with a disinterested stare.

Eric moved to the set of dark wooden drawers I'd left my weapons on but he didn't go for them. Instead, he picked up one of the numerous glass bottles and poured liquor of a dark amber color into the lone glass waiting next to them. He picked up the glass and leaned his hip against the dark wood.

"By the way," he said, "I know you have more knives in there somewhere but if you as much as twitch your fingers, I'll shoot you."

"What do you want?" I growled.

He cocked his head and gave me a patronizing smile. "Remember what I said in that courtyard all those months ago? Tell me it hurts. All I want is for you to hurt the way I hurt after you murdered my son." The arrogant lord took a long drink from his glass. "We have finally arrived at that point in time."

"That right?"

"Oh, yes. I'm going to take my time with you." He swirled the liquor in his glass. "But don't worry. I won't let you die before I make you watch as I slowly torture your friend to death."

I blew out a snort. "You shouldn't make promises you can't keep."

"This is a promise I will—" A violent coughing fit interrupted Eric's speech. The pistol shook in his grip in rhythm with his chest. "A promise I—" His chest convulsed again and metal clattered against wood as he threw his pistol hand out for support against the furniture.

"You know," I said and swung my feet up on the desk while lowering my hands, "you really should know by now. I'm a very good thief. I don't get caught." A malicious grin decorated my features. "Unless I want to, of course."

Eric dropped the half empty glass as if he'd been burned.

I smacked my lips. "There's poison in that, in case you were wondering."

Lord Fahr raised the pistol. Rage covered his face as he fired. Nothing happened.

"Yeah, I also stole the bullet and black powder you'd preloaded that gun with." I shrugged. "Thief, you know."

The pistol hit the floor next as Lord Fahr could no longer make his fingers work properly. He staggered towards the door while working his mouth up and down. Panic flooded his blue eyes as no sound came out.

"That would be the poison cutting off your vocal cords," I informed him.

He finally made it to the door and put a hand on the smooth wood. A sharp thud rang out. Lord Fahr opened his mouth as if to scream but nothing made it past his lips. I flicked a lazy gaze at the throwing knife pinning his palm to the door.

"How did I know that you would drink from that particular bottle, I hear you ask?" I crossed my ankles on the desk. "Well, I didn't. That's why I put the poison in the glass."

Eric pried uselessly at the blade piercing his hand while his feet were slipping beneath him.

"Of course, I couldn't be sure that you would drink anything at all." I nodded at the dropped firearm. "That's why I also coated the handle of that pistol with poison. It's two different kinds, you see. One you drink and one you absorb through the skin." I squinted at the desperate man trapped by the knife. "Both seem to be working, though."

After swinging my feet off the desk, I strode towards the door. Lord Fahr's legs were about ready to buckle. I looked him up and down before yanking the blade from his flesh. He dropped to his knees. I twirled the knife in my hand before putting it under his chin and tilting his face towards me.

"You should've just cut your losses," I said. "You tried to kill me several times. That, I could've taken, though. But the minute you went after Liam, you signed your own death sentence."

Only strained gasps and gurgling answered me. I cracked a smile.

"Oh, who am I kidding? You turned my guild against me. Your fate was sealed the moment you launched your first attack." I studied the kneeling man before me. "How does it feel to know that you were beaten by a girl half your age?"

Angered simmered in Lord Fahr's eyes, pushing the panic out. But he could do nothing about it so I just pressed on mercilessly.

"After all your plotting and scheming, it was all for nothing. You will die here. Alone. The last of your line." I bent down over the knife and threw his own words back in his face. "Does it hurt? Tell me it hurts. All I want is for you to hurt."

Eric Fahr, of course, couldn't answer me. After removing the knife from under his chin, I put a boot to his chest and shoved him backwards. He slumped to the floor with his back propped up against the wall. I watched the light dim from his eyes.

"So ends the line of Fahr. House of spies and traitors."

After strapping on all my knives again, I climbed out of the window I'd arrived through and into the cold night.

STARS GLITTERED IN the dark water. I watched the moonlit ships float in the harbor in front of me while a figure approached from behind.

"You took your time," I said.

Shade came to a halt next to me on the edge of the roof. "Yes."

For a moment, we just listened to the silver-speckled waves crash against the shore. Our cloaks fluttered in the cold northern wind.

"Are we bad people?" I asked.

"We are who we are."

"That's not an answer."

The assassin turned his head to look at me. "If we hadn't killed them, what would've happened?"

I was silent for a moment. "They would've kept sending people to kill Liam until one of them got lucky."

"Yeah," Shade said. "Same with Edward."

Another few minutes passed without either of us speaking. Winds whipped through my clothes. I drew my cloak tighter around me.

"That's not the only reason I did it, though," I said, steel seeping into my voice. "He hanged me. I was one second away from dying at the end of a rope in front of a cheering crowd. And even worse than that, he made my guild, the only home I've ever known, he made them brand me a traitor. I wanted revenge."

The Master of the Assassins' Guild glanced at me from the corner of his eye. "I did too."

"So..." I began but left the rest of my conclusion unspoken.

"So," Shade picked up. "We are who we are."

Somewhere up the street, a clock struck midnight. Without another word, we climbed down from the roof of the pavilion and made our way towards the hidden dock at the edge of the harbor. A rowboat bobbed up and down in the dark water. I watched it move until three hood-covered figures approached from across the pier. Two of them stopped further away, while the smaller one continued towards us.

King Edward threw his hood back. "I don't want you to leave."

Shade put a hand on his brother's shoulder. "I don't want to leave either but I have to. Just for a little while, until this storm quiets down. Both Fahr brothers are dead but we still have to deal with Marcellus."

"This isn't fair," Edward said. "We've only just started to become brothers and now... now I don't even know when I'll see you again."

The Assassins' Guild Master drew his brother into a tight hug. "We will see each other again. And we will always be brothers. No matter how far apart we are, that is never going to change."

The King of Keutunan buried his face in Shade's shoulder. "Family. Always."

They drew back and Shade wiped a tear from Edward's cheek. It might have just been light from the stars but I could've sworn the assassin's eyes were glistening as well. He put a hand to his little brother's chin and lifted it up.

"Never forget who you are."

And with that, he released Edward and turned around. We both watched the Master Assassin stride towards the rowboat and jump inside. I turned to the king.

"You will see him again," I said.

I didn't know why, but it felt like the right thing to say. And I truly believed it. Somehow. King Edward nodded, pulled up his hood, and retreated to where his guards waited. I climbed into the small vessel with Shade.

No one said anything as we made our way across the dark water. The heavens covered our surroundings in a blanket of stars but the beauty of it was lost to the torrent of pain I could see in Shade's black eyes. Leaving had almost broken both brothers.

My mind churned as Zaina's ship grew larger in front of us. In addition to the Silverthorn brothers' agony, we had another problem. Marcellus' peace treaty had been a sham. That meant we still needed to figure out how to stop a war between our nations. If I decided to stay, that is. I didn't know yet what I would do after I'd gone back for Liam. Fortunately, I had a long journey across the sea to figure it out. Well, in the brief windows when I wasn't hurling across the railing, at least. My stomach turned as we reached the side of the ship. I was so not looking forward to that.

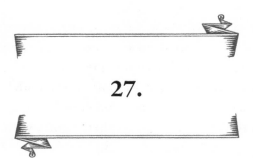

27.

"Wait, let me get this straight..." Liam began, his eyebrows raised high. "*You* are the lost crown prince? The real heir to the throne?"

Shade gave him a wry smile. "Yeah."

All eight of us were gathered in the school's living room. A thunderstorm had rolled in on our way back from Hidden Oaks Cove, as the smugglers' port down the coast was called, so we had taken shelter inside as soon as we'd arrived. Shade had just finished explaining what had happened on our trip to Keutunan and it was safe to say that Liam wasn't the only one wearing a look of shock on his face.

"Wow." Liam sat back on the frayed brown couch. "How about that?"

The Master Assassin hadn't gone into detail as to why he kept it a secret, and no one had dared ask. As far as I could tell, I was the only one who knew the full story. Or at least, the part he had chosen to tell me that night we got drunk on the floor. Mystery still swirled around him like smoke and I was pretty sure he kept more secrets than the rest of us combined. I wondered what else he was hiding.

"Yeah, nah, I'm not gonna start addressing you as Your Majesty or stuff like that," Haela announced with a mischievous grin on her face. She swung her arm over the back of the sofa and twisted to face the newly revealed royal son. "But does that mean we should start calling you Ciaran now?"

Man, I hadn't even thought to ask him that. I had just continued calling him Shade. How was that for social skills?

"No." The assassin shook his head. "I've been Shade far longer than I ever was Ciaran. It doesn't even feel like my name anymore."

Haela sent him another bright smile. "Shade it is, then."

A soft creak escaped the couch as Elaran shifted his weight. "You said Edward banished those two lords as well but when their ship arrived yesterday, they weren't on it." He flicked calculating eyes between me and Shade. "What happened to the Fahr brothers?"

The Master Assassin and I glanced at each other.

"I ran a sword through William's heart." Shade tipped his head to the right and blew out a short chuckle. "Eventually, anyway."

I lifted one shoulder in a lopsided shrug. "I poisoned Eric."

Liam closed his eyes. Pain was written all over his face. I squinted at him, trying to understand why in Nemanan's name that kind of reaction would be the result of learning that the person who had kidnapped him was dead. Norah seemed to notice it too.

"What's wrong?" she asked and gave his hand a gentle squeeze.

"More people dead because of me." He slumped back against the brown cushions.

Shade turned to look at him. "Not everything is about you."

"Eric's death is." Liam sat back up again and threw out his arm in a desperate gesture. "He only became our enemy because Storm killed his son."

I flinched at his words but they were true so I didn't know what to say. Liam pressed on.

"And she did that because of what Rogue did to me." He raked his hands through his curly brown hair. "And then Eric wanted revenge for a murdered son and now he's dead too. Father and son, both killed because of me."

Uncomfortable feelings carved into my chest like a rusty knife. I shoved them out. "But that's what our life is like!" I blew out a frustrated breath. "It's not some fairy tale. It's complicated and violent and messy."

"That's my point." Liam turned to me, his eyes full of agony. "Does it really have to be? It's not like that in Tkeideru. Or here among the merchants in Pernula. Maybe it's because of who y... who we are, that life is like that."

I stared at him in silence. The start of that unfinished word before he'd changed his mind twisted like a blade in my gut. Was I the reason his life had been so filled with blood and violence? Maybe I really was a bad person.

Zaina cleared her throat. "Either way, they're dead and the peace treaty is screwed. Now what?"

For a moment, no one said anything. Rain smattered against the windows while the wind howled between the buildings outside. Shade flashed us a confident smile.

"Now, we win the election."

Haela whirled around to stare at the assassin. "I'm sorry, the election in a foreign country that ends in *six days*. The one we have absolutely no chance of winning. Ever. That election?"

Shade nodded. "That would be the one."

Laughter bounced off the ceiling as Haela threw her head back and let out a string of merriment that lasted a good minute. We all watched her with amused expressions on our faces. Once the torrent had ended, she wiped a joyous tear from her eye and straightened.

"I knew coming on this mission was a good idea. Impossible stakes in a challenge we were never meant to win." The mirthful twin grinned. "Who could say no to that?

Haemir shook his head at his sister but cracked a smile. "I'm in too."

The auburn-haired elf on the other end of the sofa crossed his arms and drew his eyebrows down. "This is insane, Shade. I've said it before and I'll say it again: we can't win an election in a foreign country!" When his companions only looked back at him with knowing smiles, Elaran blew out a breath and threw his hands up. "But someone has to make sure you don't all get yourselves killed. And Faye would have my head if I let anything happen to you two idiots," he added and nodded at the twins. "So I guess I don't have much of a choice."

The rest of the room chuckled at the grumpy archer. My head and my heart were still in too much turmoil from our previous topic, so I'd been studying the raindrops racing down the window during most of the conversation, instead of participating. Now, I felt Shade's eyes on me.

"What about you?" he asked.

Turning my head, I found his intelligent eyes watching me. Strange emotions hid in the depths of his black irises but the look was so unexpected that I couldn't identify what it meant.

"Are you staying?" the assassin asked again.

Was I staying? I wasn't sure. The Fahr brothers were dead so the threat to me and the people I loved was gone. That meant I couldn't claim that I was doing it out of self-interest. Sure, if Marcellus won, he might attack Keutunan but now there was another way of stopping that. King Edward's mission to secure a peace treaty was already in shambles so we no longer needed to play nice. If I wanted to stop Marcellus from declaring war, really stop him, I could just assassinate him. My friends wouldn't like it, of course, because it would leave Pernula divided and weak in the face of a potential invasion from the star elves. But what did I care about that?

No, helping Shade win the election wasn't about survival. It was about him. I studied the assassin. If I stayed, it would be because I wanted to help him win. Because I cared about him. I heaved a deep sigh. By Nemanan, I really needed to find that cold black heart again.

"I mean, you'd have absolutely no chance of winning this without me," I said and flashed the Master Assassin a smirk. "So, I guess I'll stay."

Relief blew across his face for just a fraction of a second but when he noticed that I had caught his expression, he gave me a teasing grin instead.

"Good." His black eyes glittered. "That saves me from threatening and blackmailing you into it. My guild is here now, remember?"

"Oh, I thought you didn't need your guild for that." I gave him a quick rise and fall of my eyebrows while a wicked smile spread across my lips. "Are you finally admitting that you can't take me on your own?"

Shade's mouth dropped open and a surprised chuckle slipped out, but before he could decide on a comeback, Liam interrupted us.

"I'm staying too," he said and squeezed Norah's hand. "It's the right thing to do."

Norah smiled at Liam while Zaina looked from face to face, her dark eyebrows raised.

"You people really are insane," she announced, though the smile on her face was more impressed than anything else. "Alright. You're basically screwed with the elite, both because you're an assassin and because you're an outsider, so that leaves the workers. We might be able to swing some of them, though I'm not sure which factions. Any bright ideas?"

For a few moments, only the sound of the smattering rain filled the room. Which parts of the city would be most likely to support an assassin as General?

I tapped my chin. "Alright so they're not technically part of the working class but what about the Underworld?"

"They don't vote," Norah said.

"You mean they're not allowed to vote or they choose not to vote?"

"They can, they just don't." The dark-haired teacher looked pointedly at her sister.

Zaina blew out a sigh. "Oh I'm sorry for not being overly interested in politics." She shook her head at her little sister. "None of the laws benefit me so I don't care who makes them."

"Alright, so we just get the underworlders to vote then," Haela said, her eyes sparkling.

The Pernish smuggler swung her feet onto the table but after a sharp glance from Norah, she withdrew them again. She draped her arm across the back of the sofa instead.

"Sure, we could probably get some to do it but the problem is that our Underworld isn't organized enough to launch a successful campaign," she said. "There are some gangs, like the Rat King's crew, but it's mostly just people who look out for each other without wanting to challenge the other gangs for power."

"Like Yngvild and Vania," I concluded.

Liam turned to me. "Who?"

"The guys who..." I waved a hand in front of my face. "Never mind. But can't we get them organized then?"

"Even if you could," Norah said, "there's just not enough of them to make a difference in the vote. Our city hates underworlders, remember? So there aren't that many to find."

"What about the soldiers?" Elaran ran a hand over his tight side-braid and turned to Shade. "You don't have a lot of noble qualities but you're a good fighter."

Shade frowned at him. "Was that supposed to be a compliment?" When the archer only gave him a confused look in reply, he shook his head. "You kind of suck at giving people compliments."

"I agree," I interjected.

"The soldiers," Zaina cut in before another argument could start. "That's actually a pretty good idea. They respect strength, combat skills, and smart tactics more than anything. We could definitely get them to vote for you."

"But how?" Haemir said.

Shade pushed to his feet and strode to the window. For a while, he stood there and stared out as if the thunderstorm outside held all the answers. Our mission of simply messing with Marcellus' campaign had suddenly turned into a race to the finish line. Now, we needed to see this election through to the end and we didn't have much time to do it.

"Sorry, Zaina," I said and gave her a shrug. "Looks like we dragged you into something more complicated than we thought."

The dark-eyed Pernulan grinned. "Oh, don't you worry about me. After the crates of pistols you brought me from Keutunan, I'm a happy camper."

Haela sat up straight. "Can we use that? Pistols are illegal here so can we somehow convince people that Marcellus is making them so that he loses support with honest people?"

"No!" Norah said with force.

Furniture creaked as we all twisted to stare at the suddenly terrified-looking teacher. Only Shade remained gazing out the window with his hands clasped behind his back.

"Pistols are banned across the whole continent," Norah explained. "If the star elves find out that a city is producing guns, they will come and wipe it out. We can't risk it. Even for a rumor. If the star elves hear it, they will come here and kill us all."

"That's it!" Shade whipped around. His eyes were filled with plots and schemes when he faced us.

"Didn't you hear what she just said?" Elaran scowled at him. "We can't use that."

The Master of the Assassins' Guild flicked an impatient hand. "Not that. We con Marcellus into thinking that the star elves are attacking so that he looks incompetent and jumpy. It would completely discredit him."

Zaina let out a low whistle. "That could work."

"What if we also circulate a rumor that Marcellus is going to send out the bulk of the common soldiers as cannon fodder so that the higher-ranking officers can survive the battle?" I said.

Shade released a dark laugh. "I like the way you think."

Norah stood up and rounded the couch on her way to the door. "I don't like it. It will terrify people and make them panic. But... I will help you as long as you promise that the ruse will be revealed quickly." She stopped with a hand on the doorframe. Once she had seen Shade nod, she continued. "I need to get dinner started but those of you who will convince the merchants and nobles, you can come with me to the kitchen and we'll start planning our approach."

With that, she was out the door. She was a determined young woman, that Norah. I could see why she made a good teacher.

"Alright, you heard her," Zaina said and waved a hand at the empty doorway. "Team Upperworld, follow the bossy girl in the white skirt. Team Underworld, you're with me."

Scattered laughter echoed through the book-filled room as Liam and the twins rose from their comfortable seats and made their way towards the kitchen. After one last look to make sure that her sister had left, Zaina swung her feet onto the table and leaned back against the cushions.

"Ready to make some trouble?" she asked us.

I grinned at her as Shade, Elaran, and I settled in to scheme about Marcellus' fall from grace. "Always."

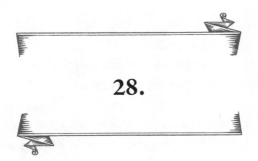

28.

The scent of rain on warm stones hung over the city and mixed with its usual aroma of spices. It had been early morning when the thunderstorm finally stopped. Now, people moved about on their usual morning activities while the sun did its best to soak up the puddles.

"Him," Zaina said and nodded towards a frazzled-looking man with a body shape that would make the average reed envious.

"You sure?" I asked.

"Yes. Now hurry before he makes it into Blackspire."

After a quick nod to the Pernish smuggler, I grabbed a fistful of Elaran's shirt and pulled him with me as I started out. "Let's go."

The grumpy elf yanked his sleeve from my grip but followed. We weaved through the crowd and towards our target as fast as we could without drawing attention.

"What am I even supposed to say?" Elaran muttered.

"I don't know," I answered. "Just make something up."

"Just make something up?" He drew his eyebrows down and cast me an irritated look. "Not everyone has *lying* as their second language."

"Now you're just being dramatic. You just need to stall for a minute or two. How hard can it be?"

"It's—" Elaran began but I interrupted whatever protest he had planned by giving his arm a hard shove.

"You'll be fine. Now get going before we lose him."

The elf muttered profanities under his breath but picked up the pace and circled around the group of women with stained aprons that separated us from the reed-thin man we were following. I continued moving with the stream of people. The merry chatter around me would soon be replaced by panic. Norah had made a great point. I did feel a bit bad for all the ordinary people who would get caught up in this scheme. Oh, well. Eggs. Omelets. You know.

"Excuse me," Elaran said a few paces ahead of me.

The frazzled-looking man drew up short as a tall elf stepped into his path. "Yes?"

"I'm meeting a friend at the Lemon Tree Café," Elaran said as I closed in behind them. "But I seem to have gotten turned around. Would you be able to point me in the right direction?"

"Oh, uhm, the Lemon Tree?" He pushed his glasses further up his nose and swung around. "Let's see..."

Not a sound escaped as I flicked open the top of the brown ledger in his hand while he was busy turning around.

"I'm not sure exactly," he continued and lifted his hand to point. "But it should be in that direction. If you go that way and then maybe you can ask someone else?"

The documents were in and the brown leather flap was closed before his other hand had finished showing the way. I slid into the crowd again.

"Thank you," Elaran said and started in the indicated direction.

I trailed him at a distance until I'd seen the thin man disappear behind the walls of Blackspire. With a few quick strides, I caught up to the elf.

"See, it wasn't that hard, was it?" I grinned up at the grumpy archer. "We'll make an underworlder out of you yet."

"Hmmph."

We both steered back towards the corner where Zaina waited. Amusement shone in her dark eyes when we approached.

"Done much reverse pickpocketing, have you?" she asked.

"Not really." I shrugged. "I prefer normal pickpocketing."

"Of course you do." Elaran shook his head before turning to Zaina. "Are you sure this will work?"

"Why is everyone suddenly questioning if I'm sure? Yes, I am. That's the guy who gets all the notes from all the different runners and brings the latest news to Blackspire every morning."

"Yeah but Marcellus isn't gonna believe that the star elves are attacking just because some documents said so," I pointed out.

"Correct." Zaina jerked her head and strode forward. "Let's go see Shade."

And she called her sister bossy. I shook my head but followed the pirate and the elf into the crowd. It was time to visit the new Assassins' Guild.

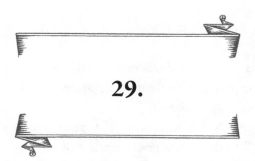

29.

A gigantic mansion made of white bricks rose before us. I craned my neck and stared up at the three-story manor complete with smooth round pillars and a carved wooden door. This was the new Assassins' Guild headquarters? By Nemanan, he must be incredibly certain that he would win because there was no hiding in this spectacle. This house was not a place for underworlders.

Releasing an impressed chuckle, I snapped my head back down and strode towards the door. Zaina and Elaran did the same.

"Shouldn't we knock?" Zaina asked in a hurried whisper as I placed my hand on the handle.

"I don't knock." I yanked the door open.

A sword slammed into my throat, stopping just short of drawing blood. I gave it a disinterested stare while pushing the edge of my own blade further into the neck of the man on my right.

"Hello, Slim," I said.

The blond assassin eyed the knife below his jaw. "The Oncoming Storm."

Behind me, Elaran heaved an exasperated sigh while I swore I could hear Zaina chuckling softly. I flashed Slim a satisfied smile before I made the stiletto blade disappear into my sleeve again. He kept the sword at my throat.

"Shade's expecting us," I said and lifted my shoulders in a nonchalant shrug.

Just as the words had left my lips, a man in tight-fitting black clothes swaggered down the stairs. He tipped his head to the right as his mouth drew into a lopsided smile.

"If you just learned to knock, you wouldn't be met by so many blades every time you walk through a door," Shade said and flicked a lazy hand at the blond assassin holding a sword to my throat. "Let them through."

Steel whizzed through the air as Slim removed his weapon. Shade had stopped on the bottom step and, with one hand still on the railing, he watched us. Around him, some kind of organized chaos took place. Assassins hurried back and forth with chests, crates, and furniture while dust swirled in the stale air. Getting the death guild back in business apparently took some work.

Elaran watched the room of killers mill about for another second before taking a step towards the staircase. Slim made as if to intercept him while glancing between Shade and Elaran's twin swords, but when the Master of the Assassins' Guild shook his head, he stood down. Zaina followed the elf. So, he apparently trusted us enough to come into the Assassins' Guild armed now. How about that?

Shade jerked his chin at me. "Let's go."

I rolled my eyes at his arrogant command but joined him anyway. The wooden steps were silent beneath our feet as we made our way upstairs.

"So, you didn't force me to strip off my knives this time," I commented. "Going soft, are we?"

Shade snorted. "Right. No, I've simply assessed your skills and come to the conclusion that you'd never be able to win a fight against me. So why bother?"

"Uh-huh. Keep telling yourself that. Besides, I could always just stab you in the back."

The Master Assassin glanced at me, his black eyes glittering. "Come try it."

Zaina cast us a curious look as we made it onto the landing. "Do the two of you ever do anything other than threaten to kill each other?"

"Sometimes we also blackmail each other," Shade supplied.

"Yeah, or actually try to kill each other." Grinning, I turned to Zaina. "A variety of activities, wouldn't you say?"

The Pernish smuggler snorted and shook her head while the assassin nodded to a door on our left. "In here."

No furniture occupied the room inside the white door. It seemed as though the team of redecorating assassins hadn't gotten to this part of the mansion yet, but at least it was private. Shade pushed the door shut and leaned back against it.

"Did you plant the documents?" he asked.

I nodded. "Yeah."

"Marcellus should be getting them any minute now," Zaina filled in.

"But now we need to make sure that he truly believes it," Elaran said. "How do we do that?"

"Liam and the twins are already spreading the word in the Upperworld," Shade said. "And I can have my assassins do the same in the Underworld. But what we need to really sell it is some kind of physical evidence."

Zaina strolled over to the window and gazed at the manicured garden outside while the restless elf took to pacing the room. Draped against the door, Shade crossed his arms.

"I was thinking," he began. "Can we get some fake soldiers to make it look like a real army?"

"I've considered that too," Elaran said. "But it won't work. If it was a human army, it wouldn't be a problem, but from what I've been told, wood elves and star elves look too different for us to just recruit some random elves."

By the window, with her back still towards us, Zaina nodded. "Yeah."

"But," the auburn-haired archer continued, "do they need to *see* the soldiers?"

I frowned at him. "What do you mean?"

Over by the door, Shade's eyes lit up. "He means, we can just make it look like an army is on the march without having them see any individual soldiers." The assassin gave Elaran an impressed nod. "Smart."

I looked between the two of them as the calculating elf nodded back. It had definitely been a lot more entertaining when they were at each other's throats all the time but to be honest, this joint scheming was kind of... attractive. I shook my head to clear it of stupid thoughts and get it back on topic.

"So, basically just smoke and mirrors then?" I said.

"Exactly." Shade grinned. "It looked like there was some kind of desert area to the west. Is that true?"

Zaina tore her gaze from the window and turned around. She tapped her sharp jaw. "Yeah, it is. We could kick up some dust there, for sure."

"What about fire?" I asked. "Can't we, like, set fire to some trees or something to really make it look like an invading force is coming?"

Elaran's pacing screeched to a halt. "We are not burning down a forest!" He threw me a scorching scowl. "You city people have no respect for nature."

I held up my hands. "Alright, calm down there, tree hugger."

"What did you call me?" he challenged.

"You heard me."

Elaran opened his mouth again but before he could launch into a full-blown lecture on the divinity of trees, Zaina interrupted.

"What about the Salt Woods?" she said.

All three of us turned to look at her, confusion evident on every face. The pirate leaned back against the windowsill.

"Setting stuff on fire is actually not a bad idea." She looked from me to Elaran. "But you're a wood elf so of course you don't want to burn down a forest." A knowing grin spread across her face. "I have a perfect middle way. There's a place called the Salt Woods out there in the desert. Apparently, it was the site of a battle long ago and the winners wanted to wipe the people who lived there from the face of the world so they salted the ground. Now, it's just a dry wasteland full of dead tree trunks."

Elaran's mouth twisted in disgust. "Humans. Destroying nature just because they can't get along with each other. Despicable."

"Yeah, it sounds like a real waste," Shade said. "Also sounds like it will burn well."

We all studied the heartbroken elf. His yellow eyes had taken on a look of pain and sadness that, to be honest, I didn't quite understand. Wasn't it just a bunch of trees?

A deep sigh escaped Elaran's chest and he gave us a determined nod. "Yes, it's better that way. Then maybe something will grow from the ashes instead."

"Alright, no time to waste." Zaina pushed off from the windowsill and strode towards the door. "We should do it this afternoon, while the forged documents are still fresh in his mind. I'll see to transportation."

Boots thudded against wood as we followed the smuggler back down the stairs. When we left our pocket of calm in the empty room, we were once again faced with the crowd of assassins getting settled in their new home. I lingered on the steps for a few seconds in order to let two black-clad men bustle past with a heavy-looking chest that clanked suspiciously like a pile of swords. By the door, Slim watched us all with the eyes of a hawk.

Zaina paused with her hand on the handle and looked back at the commotion. "If you could bring some of your assassins with you, it would be much easier to make it look like a big army."

"I can do that," Shade said.

"How many can you spare?"

"How many do you need?"

Zaina considered for a moment. "Twenty?"

The Assassins' Guild Master flicked his gaze to Slim. "Get it done."

"Yes, Master." Slim dipped his chin and disappeared into the next room.

"Great," Zaina said. "I'll have transportation ready for us by the main gate in about two hours so if you need to prepare stuff, you have some time." She pushed open the door and stepped onto the porch before casting a grin back over her shoulder. "Oh, and bring torches."

I blew out a soft chuckle. Here we were again, on the brink of another great scheme. This time, we only had to create a fake army out of nothing and completely ruin the credibility of the most respected military man in the whole city. What could possibly go wrong?

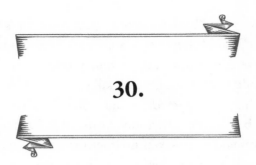

30.

Footsteps echoed in the alley behind me. A cold spike of realization shot up my spine. I was being followed. There was a side street up ahead and if I could just make it there with enough distance still between us, I could lose my pursuer. Picking up the pace slightly, but not enough to attract attention, I set a course towards it.

A man stepped into the alley. I drew up short. He had appeared from the cross street I had planned on using as my escape route which meant that they must've been tailing me from a distance for a while now to orchestrate this. The footsteps behind me drew closer. I swung around so that I could see in both directions of the alley while the building behind me protected my back. My two ambushers closed in on either side.

"The Rat King told you to stop running game in his city," the dark-haired man on my left said.

I scoffed. "Okay, first, this ain't *his* city. And second, he told me to stop recruiting people, which I have, and not to stop working completely."

"You really should be more respectful when speaking about the Rat King," the muscled man on my right threatened. He ran two meaty hands through his blond hair. "Or..."

"Or what? You'll teach me to respect my betters?" I clicked my tongue. "Yeah, I don't think so. Here's how this is gonna go down. You're gonna run back to your precious master and tell him you couldn't find me. *Or...* I'll kill you."

That sharp tongue of mine might've been spouting arrogance, but in my chest my heart beat hard against my ribcage. I was good, there was no question about that, but there were two of them and physically, I was outmatched. The tall man on my right had about a head on me and the stocky blond probably sported three times as much muscle. Zaina was somewhere securing our transport, Shade was back at his guild getting his assassins ready, and Elaran had gone back to the school to get his bow. I was on my own.

The two men laughed. It was a cocky derisive sound that made me want to kick their teeth in.

"You're gutsy, I'll give you that," the dark-haired man said. "But this is what will happen. You either fall in line. Or you die. Simple as that."

So, it seemed as though Marcellus had finally rescinded his do-not-kill order. I really shouldn't have been surprised given that he'd tried to kill us himself in that warehouse fire earlier. However, the Fahr brothers had dealt with the Rat King before, and talking to underworlders wasn't exactly something Marcellus enjoyed. That was probably why it had taken him so long to realize that he could also have someone else attack us or, well, attack *me*. Not having to worry about this Rat King dude had been a nice reprieve. Oh well, guess that was over.

I snatched a throwing knife from my shoulder and hurled it towards the muscled man. My instinct had been right. He wasn't as quick as his tall friend and only managed to partially evade the flying projectile. A sharp hiss sounded from his lips as the knife buried itself in his shoulder. I darted forward just as the tall brown-haired man drew his sword.

The blond man fumbled with his own weapon while I threw another knife at him. Metal clattered against stone as he managed to get his wicked-looking mace loose while also ducking the flying blade. Steel whizzed through the air behind me. *Shit.* I twisted down and to the side to avoid the tall man's sword. It cut through the space my chest had occupied only seconds before.

A moment too late I realized that my evasion tactic had put me straight in the path of the blond man's mace. I watched the muscles in his forearm tense as he got ready to lift and swing it. Damn. This was going to hurt.

My eardrums pounded as a sharp cry rang out. The mace slumped back by his side and he put a hand to his injured shoulder and the blade still buried in his flesh. Whatever my knife had hit, it must've been important because it seemed as though he could no longer lift his heavy weapon. While yanking a hunting knife from its sheath, I kicked at the large club in his hand.

Crashing metal rang out both above and below me as the tall man's sword slammed into my raised hunting knife while the blond man's dropped mace collided with the stones. Shoving the sword away, I slipped out from between them. This wasn't going to work. I couldn't keep fighting two people at the same time. One of them had to die within the next few seconds or I would lose.

Pain shot up my abdomen as the muscled man barreled straight into my chest. I took a quick step back to steady myself but wasn't fast enough and soon found myself falling. The hunting knife flew from my grip as I crashed back first into the street with the stocky man on top of me. Air rushed out of my lungs.

From under the weight of my attacker, I sucked in a desperate breath just before his meaty hands locked my throat in an iron grip. Malice shone in his eyes as he started to slowly squeeze, as if he wanted this moment to last.

Panic flashed through my body. I shoved my arms into his elbows, intending to break his grip, but I might as well have been hitting a tree trunk. He leaned forward and grinned at me. Somewhere above us, I could feel the dark-haired man standing there, watching his partner crush my windpipe.

Terror made my mind slow and unresponsive. I put my hands against his chest and pushed with all my might to get him off me. If my brain had been working properly, I would've known it was useless. I would never have been able to get his weight off me. But I kept at it anyway. My hands slipped along his shoulders while I let out a strained groan in an attempt to breathe. Something sharp grazed my left hand and hope shoved the intense panic aside.

I yanked it out and sliced. The strong hands around my throat lost their grip. Oxygen filled my starved lungs as I gasped in air. The man straddling my chest reached for his own throat as blood welled down his shirt. Gripping the knife I had taken from his shoulder tighter in my fist, I stabbed it in his chest. Once. Twice. Three times to make sure it really took.

Above me, a man's voice roared. Coughing violently in between deep breaths, I managed to regain my senses enough to see the tall man lift his sword. *He wouldn't.* The gleaming tip pointed straight down. *Crap. He would.*

The blond man gurgled his last words while I used all my strength to shove him upwards and roll out from underneath his dying weight. Steel pierced flesh until it hit stone as the tall man rammed his sword through his partner's body in an attempt to skewer me. Gravel scraped against my skin as I slid away and kicked one leg up.

Another howl sounded as my foot connected with the sword-wielding man's crotch. He staggered backwards. While he was busy recovering from my below-the-belt attack, I climbed to my feet. The world swayed around me. Forcing another deep breath through my hoarse throat, I tried to steady myself. My remaining attacker straightened too.

I threw another knife. His sword was still stuck in his partner's body but he whipped out a long dagger to deflect it. It hadn't been necessary. Since my head was still spinning from the assault and the choking, my aim was completely off and the blade sailed past uselessly. Damn.

The dark-haired man sprang forward. I was in no shape for a straight up fight, so I whirled around and made for the wall behind me. If I could just get up on the roof, I'd be alright. I had only begun to reach for the closest ledge when the whizzing of steel vibrated behind me. Twisting back around, I yanked my remaining hunting knife and barely managed to block the strike. My attacker drove his fist into my abdomen. Staggering back into the wall, I gasped for air while parrying another thrust. However, that time my grip and position had been so off balance that the blade flew from my hand.

Snapping my empty hand up, I managed to catch the tall man's wrist but I wasn't fast enough. The edge of his dagger pressed against the skin under my jaw. Blood trickled down my neck. My treacherous heart hammered in my chest. If he pushed the blade any further in, it would be over. Still gripping his wrist, I bent my hand backwards.

He leered at me. "You should've just fallen in line. But now you will die because you thought you were better than us. You're too arrogant."

The mechanism clicked into place. A raw shriek tore from his throat as the stiletto I'd shot out of my sleeve pierced his wrist. His dagger clattered to the ground. My other stiletto blade appeared in my left hand and I rammed it into his heart while he still stared in shock at the metal sticking out of his arm. He released a stunned gasp and his head fell forward until it came to a halt on my shoulder.

"You talk too much," I said into his ear.

Only strained gurgling answered me as I yanked both knives from his body and stepped back. His knees buckled and he crashed to the stones. I took in the scene. Knives, blood, and bodies littered the alley around me. Again.

Heaving a deep breath, I bent down and wiped the stiletto blades on his shirt before retracting them. While I retrieved the rest of my knives and wiped the blood from my face and body, I tried to count the number of times I'd been in a situation like this. The best I could come up with was: a lot. I shook my head as I left the dead bodies and the blood-soaked alley behind and made for the main gate. I really had to do something about that.

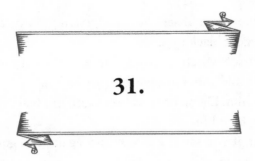

31.

"**Y**ou're late."

I blew out an exasperated breath and glared at the eternal grump that was Elaran. "Yes, thank you, I know."

Horses neighed and snorted behind the mob of twenty-odd assassins, three elves, and a pirate. Zaina was busy talking to a man close to the stables while the twins studied the large animals behind Elaran. Excitement seemed to bounce around inside Haela's body. I released a soft laugh as I came to a halt in front of the rows of silent assassins.

Shade ran his eyes up and down my body. "How many?"

"How many what?"

The Master Assassin just looked at me expectantly.

I rolled my eyes. "Two."

"And?"

"And now they're dead." I shrugged. "Whatever Marcellus had on the Rat King that made him leave me alone has been dropped. He's told him I'm fair game again. Nothing I can't handle, though. I mean, it wasn't even close."

Shade strode forward and placed a hand on my jaw. I jerked back a little in surprise but didn't stab him. Tilting my chin up, he drew two fingers along my neck. They came back red.

"You sure about that?" he asked, staring down at me with those intelligent black eyes.

"Of course." Mischief sparkled in my eyes as I met his gaze. "I've already told you, I'm a hard person to kill."

Behind him, Elaran opened his mouth but before any sound made it out, I cut him off.

"I swear, if you say *like a cockroach* again, I'm gonna throw something at you."

The self-satisfied archer smirked at me. "You're the one who said it this time, not me."

Shade chuckled and released my chin. A strange tingling sensation remained on my skin where his fingers had been. How odd. I shook my head and turned back to Elaran.

"I see you found more than your bow at the school." I nodded in the direction of the twins.

"Are you surprised?" Elaran muttered. "If there's anyone who can talk Haela out of something when she sets her mind to it, I haven't met them yet."

From across the courtyard, the stubborn twin flashed me a mischievous grin. I chuckled at her just as Zaina made her way back to the group.

"Alright, boys and girls, we're a go," she announced.

Turning my head, I glanced around the area. "A go? On what?"

"The horses of course, silly," Haela said, eyes sparkling.

"Wait, wait, wait." I held up my hands. "We're *riding*? That's the transportation you were getting?"

"Yeah." Zaina looked at me curiously. "Problem?"

"Yes! Who even knows how to ride a horse?"

Zaina, the three elves, and Shade all raised a hand. After a nod from their Master, every single assassin did as well. I stared at them in disbelief.

"How the hell does everyone know how to ride a horse?" I stabbed an arm in Shade's direction. "How do you know how to ride a horse? We live in a city, for Nemanan's sake! When have you *ever* had the need to ride a freaking horse?"

"It's not about having the need." Shade waved a lazy hand and all his assassins dropped their arms again. "It's about being prepared for every eventuality. Maybe if you learned that you wouldn't get into so many situations where you almost die."

Crossing my arms, I drew my eyebrows down. "Well, I'm still here, aren't I?"

The Master Assassin nodded at the cut on my neck. "Barely."

"As entertaining as this is, we've got work to do," Zaina interjected before I could retort. "We're riding. End of story. Let's go."

Haela practically jumped up on the dark brown horse next to her while her brother performed the action is a much calmer fashion. The rows of assassins remained standing until Shade nodded at them. Zaina was already up when the Assassins' Guild made for their horses. I stared at them. Yeah, this was so not happening.

Shade trotted up to me on a big horse with a coat made up of large black and white patches. He jerked his chin. "Get on."

I raised a hand and pointed at the humongous creature. "I'm not getting on that."

"Wanna bet?"

Reaching down, he grabbed my outstretched wrist and hauled me upwards. I let out a startled yelp but soon found my bearings and climbed up clumsily behind him. This was absolutely mortifying. Elaran and the twins rode past us with effortless grace and joined Zaina by the main gate.

"You should put your arms around me," Shade said.

"What?" I blurted.

"Otherwise you're going to fall off."

Since I sat behind him, I couldn't see the expression on his face but I was pretty sure he was smirking. After taking a deep breath to stave off the embarrassment, I wrapped my arms around his stomach. His muscles rippled under my hands. Damn, he was fit. Suddenly, I was very glad he couldn't see my face either. If he'd seen the ridiculous blush on my cheeks, he would never have let me live it down.

"Move out," Shade said to his assassins. "Stay in formation."

"Yes, Master," came the collective reply.

Man, these guys obeyed his every order without question. I guess that was the way of the Assassins' Guild. A sharp hiss escaped my teeth as our horse started forward as well. Involuntarily, I tightened my hold on the Master Assassin and pressed my body against his muscled back. Whatever happened, I was *not* going to fall off.

As Zaina took the lead and the rest of our cavalry followed her along the dirt road, I found myself thinking about what Shade had said that night we got drunk in the Silver Keep. He had talked about his old Master. That meant there had been a time when he was bowing his head and saying 'yes, Master' when someone else ordered him about. Man, I would've liked to see that.

"Is that how you became Guild Master?" I asked as another thought struck.

"Is what?" Shade said over his shoulder since he obviously couldn't follow the ever-changing stream of thought going through my head.

"You said your old Master groomed you for it. So, did you inherit it?"

A hearty laugh rippled through his chest. "No, not even close."

We continued riding in silence for a few moments.

"You're really not gonna tell me, are you?"

I could hear the grin in his voice when he replied. "Nope."

Clicking his mouth, Shade spurred the horse on and sped to catch up with Zaina and the elves. This mode of transportation definitely wasn't among my favorites. It was far too bouncy. Though, at least it beat sea travel since it didn't constantly make me want to empty the contents of my stomach. Yet, anyway.

"How are we going to be able to set anything on fire?" Haemir called to the group as we caught up.

"What do you mean?" his sister asked.

"It rained yesterday. We can't set fire to something that's wet."

He did have a point. Puddles still lingered on the dirt road we followed and the vast grasslands around us smelled of damp earth. Water droplets might no longer decorate the dark green leaves of the low bushes since the midday sun beat down on them, but they were bound to be soaked.

"Just because it rained where we were, doesn't mean it rained everywhere." Zaina let go of the reins with her left hand and raised it to tap her temple. "The weather is different in different places."

"I know that," the male half of the twins grumbled. "But does that mean it doesn't rain in these Salt Woods?"

"Correct. Not a lot anyway. There's a reason this is all grasslands." The Pernish smuggler swept an arm at the scenery around us. "And that there's a desert out by the Salt Woods. There's something odd with the landscape so it almost never rains there."

"Huh."

We continued riding in silence until the dirt road took a left turn while Zaina continued barreling straight ahead into the grass. Exclamations of surprise rose from our group but she assured us that this was the fastest way to our destination. I didn't talk much. Mostly, I just focused on trying not to bruise my tailbone as a result of all this bouncing up and down. Shade's muscles shifted against my body.

Before long, the lush green grass gave way to large stretches of sand broken up only by the odd brittle bush or two. At least until the towering gray giants that were the dead trees of the Salt Woods rose in the distance. Shade and the rest of our cavalry reined in their horses and came to a halt in front of it.

"It's so sad," Haela said as she gracefully slid down from her horse. "But I agree with Elaran, it's better that it becomes ash so that new things might grow instead of this... graveyard."

"Alright, we take a quick breather here and get organized," Zaina said.

I fell rather than climbed down from our black and white horse while Shade gave the order to his assassins. My whole body hurt as I strode across the sand before stopping next to Haela.

"When all this is over, you're gonna teach me how to ride a horse," I said to the energetic twin. "Because I'm never doing that again."

Haela glanced down at me, her face full of mirth and mischief. "Why is your face so red?"

I jerked back a little, startled, but then drew my eyebrows down. "It's hot."

"Yes, he is."

"I... wait, what?" I looked up to find a wide grin on Haela's face so I gave her arm a shove. "Shut up."

My teasing friend just laughed. From across the mass of horses, Elaran and Shade approached with Zaina and Haemir in tow. When they stopped in front of us, Elaran frowned at me.

"Your face is red," he stated.

I threw my arms up. "Because we're *in a desert*! Now can we move on from the state of my face and start focusing on what our plan is?"

Zaina gave me a knowing smile but didn't comment.

"Fine," Elaran said. "I would say it's a very simple plan. Seeing as you're the only one who doesn't know how to ride, we will all ride back and forth creating the dust cloud while you set the fire."

"That was my thinking as well," Shade said.

Seeing no reason to argue, I shrugged. "Sure, I'll set the fire."

Elaran unslung his pack and dropped to a knee. We all studied him while he dug around inside the backpack until he finally found what he was looking for. Straightening, he shoved two thick wooden sticks into my hands. I frowned at him.

The wood produced two thuds as I knocked the sticks against each other. "What am I supposed to do with these?"

"Light the fire."

"With what?"

Elaran heaved an irritated sigh and snatched the unlit torches back. "Give me that. Useless city dweller."

The twins laughed next to me and Haela nudged an elbow in my ribs.

"I'm adding how to make a fire to the list of things I'm gonna teach you when all this is over," she said.

I grumbled under my breath but I knew she was right. If my life continued down the same path it had been barreling down lately, knowing how to make a fire could definitely be a useful skill to have.

"There." Elaran pressed the now lit torches back into my hands.

"Alright, we'll come get you after our little joy ride," Zaina said. "It might be a while, though."

And with that, she strode back to her waiting horse. Elaran did the same without another word but Haela gave me a playful salute before leaving.

"Be careful," Haemir said and followed his sister.

Shade cocked his head to the right and studied me for a few seconds. "Don't screw this up."

I snorted. "When have I ever screwed anything up?" Regretting my comment, I held up a quick hand. "You know what, don't answer that. But come on, I'm just setting things on fire. How hard can it be?"

The Master Assassin sent me a lopsided smile before wandering back to his horse. When everyone was seated on those uncomfortable creatures again, he raised his voice.

"Move out."

Neighing and thundering hooves echoed across the sands as the party took off. While they disappeared in a cloud of dust, I turned to the graveyard of dead trees beside me. I flicked my eyes between the dry trunks and the two burning sticks in my hands. Now it was time to do what I did best: hurt and destroy and burn things to the ground. Oh, the Salt Woods never stood a chance.

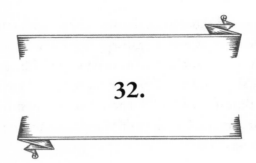

32.

Eerie. That was how I would describe the Salt Woods. Sand and grass long dead crunched under my feet as I moved through the hollow husks that had once been trees. Looking at this abandoned graveyard, I couldn't help agreeing with my elven friends. It was sad.

"This should be far enough," I said to myself as I stopped after what I judged to be an appropriate distance.

I had no idea how big this dead forest was, so it was impossible to know when I had reached the middle, but I figured that the fire would spread in every direction eventually. Light flickered from the torches in my hands. No time like the present.

A *whoosh* sounded as I put a torch to the closest tree. Flames devoured the dry wood while I moved to the trunk next to it and did the same. I had concluded that it was best to create a long wall of fire first and then just continue adding to it in a narrow line as I made my way out. That way, the risk of getting trapping in the fire should be slight. The wood popped in the heat as I made my way to my next victim.

Once I had burned a sufficiently long row of trees and returned to the middle of it, I spared a moment to study my handiwork. Flames licked the gray giants and reached for the heavens in an inferno of yellow and orange. Heat washed over me as the wind changed and fire leaped from one tree to another.

"So ends the Salt Woods," I said. "May new life grow."

With those final words to the forest previously trapped between life and death, I turned around and began my long walk out. Holding out the torches in my hands, I lit the trees on fire as I passed through the woods like a demon from hell burning the world to the ground. Whooshing, popping, and hissing echoed as a great wall of flames followed me on my path.

A roar reverberated through the air. I recoiled as a large animal crashed through the clearing and stopped in front of me. Its coat was yellow-gold and around its neck was a dark mane. Though I'd never seen an animal like this in Keutunan, I recognized it from the flag of Pernula. Norah had called it a lion.

The deadly-looking animal stared at me. My heart pattered in my chest. I would not win a close-up fight against this beast and I doubted that my throwing knives were large enough to kill it. Most likely, they would only anger it and make it attack me. Shit. I had to keep it away from me.

An explosion racked the forest as a large tree broke apart and fell to the ground. The lion jerked back and then crouched, ready to spring forward. It looked frightened. Nervous eyes flicked between me and the flames eating their way towards us as if it couldn't decide who the real threat was. I had no idea how to tell it that I wasn't the enemy, so I did the only thing I could think of: scare it with more fire.

Gripping the torches tightly, I swung them in a wide arc. The lion jumped back when the burning wood swished by its face. I waved the torches back and forth between us again so that the infernal animal would understand that it was time to run. At last, the beast seemed to take the hint and bolted in the opposite direction. Tipping my head up towards the sky, I heaved a deep sigh of relief.

That's when I noticed it. The fire. I snapped my head back down. Shit. How could I have been so stupid? My mad waving of the torches had caused sparks to fly and those had now caught the trees around me. Rage at my own incompetence flashed through me. And then the wind shifted and my anger was replaced by sheer panic. Flames leaped from tree to tree in front of me while the burning wall I had created earlier picked up speed and closed in behind. I was trapped.

Dropping the torches, I darted forward to escape the flames before it was too late. A loud *whoosh* erupted behind me. I whipped around to see the second mistake that might very well get me killed. Panic was not good for my decision-making skills.

Behind me, the whole forest floor was on fire. Dread welled up in my chest as I realized that the dropped torches of course set the dry grass aflame. Shit. I sprinted towards my exit. Oppressive heat pressed in on my body while bright orange flames clawed at me from every direction. I sucked in a deep breath of searing hot air.

A treacherous wind blew its forceful breath through the forest and the fire roared as it welled forward. The world around me was engulfed in flames. In front of me, a tree trunk snapped and crashed to the ground. Sparks sailed into the air as it connected with the grass and sand but there was no stopping now. If I stopped, I would die. Throwing up my arms to protect my face, I jumped over the fallen log.

Trees were on fire in every direction while the burning grass hunted me from behind. I sent a quick prayer to Nemanan. If the flaming forest floor caught up with me, I would have nowhere to run. Continuing my mad dash through the woods, I fervently hope I would make it out before it did.

My chest heaved, and drawing breath was getting increasingly difficult but I pressed on. The wind had died down which made the wall of fire slow down slightly, but I didn't trust it to stay that way, so I decided to take this chance to put even more distance between us. Pushing my body as far as it would let me, I picked up speed and sprinted towards the edge of the forest.

At long last, I spotted the horizon between the trees. My heart leaped in joy and my whole soul drew a deep breath of relief. I'd made it. Sand swirled in the air as I skidded to a halt outside the Salt Woods. Turning around, I watched the flames lick the trees further in so I backed away until I was a safe distance away from the fire. I flopped down on the dusty ground.

"Yep, definitely never doing that again either," I mumbled.

Resting my back against the warm sand, I draped an arm over my face and closed my eyes. For a long while, I just lay there and let my chest heave and my heartbeat slow. That had been close. Way too close. Again. Shade had been right. I did find myself in a lot of situations where I almost died. Maybe it was time to learn more about this outdoorsy stuff so that I didn't make these kinds of rookie mistakes again.

Minutes turned to hours as the flames consumed the Salt Woods. After a while, I sat back up and studied the horizon that Shade and the others had disappeared into. A huge cloud of dust had risen in the distance and mingled with the smoke from the fire. There was no way anyone in Pernula could miss it.

Movement flashed past in the corner of my eye. Jumping to my feet, I whipped my head around and scanned my surroundings. *Oh, crap.* A pack of, I didn't know what it was, approached from all sides. They looked kind of like dogs but with longer limbs and their fur was light brown and full of dark spots. Then, a sound made my blood turn to ice. One of the animals... laughed. I yanked the hunting knives from their sheaths.

"What the hell is wrong with this continent?" I said, fear lacing my words.

The pack of laughing predators closed in. Sweat trickled down my back as I gripped the blades tighter and turned around and around to keep them all in my sight. They continued circling me.

"Well, get on with it then!" I screamed at them and twirled the knives in my hands.

As one, the dog-like animals bolted. I stared after them. What had just happened? I mean, I was scary, but I wasn't *that* scary. Then I heard them. Thundering hooves in the distance. Releasing a soft laugh of relief, I stuck the blades back in their holsters. *Here comes the cavalry.*

After dusting myself off, I adopted a neutral look on my face just as twenty-odd horses came into view. The big one with large black and white patches that Shade rode aimed straight for me. Every instinct in my body told me to take cover but I stood my ground. The Master Assassin reined it in and the horse skidded to a halt an arm's length from me. Blood pounded in my ears but outwards, I was calm like a bucket of milk.

Shade pulled down the cloth covering his nose and mouth and glanced at the scene around us. "Any trouble?"

"Nope," I lied and gave him a nonchalant shrug. "Everything went without a hitch."

"Mm-hmm." He cracked a lopsided smile and then reached down towards me. "Come on, we have to get back to the city."

I grabbed his arm and, with all the grace of a slab of granite, climbed up behind him. Even though I couldn't see it, I knew he was smirking. However, instead of slapping that infuriating arrogance off his cheekbones, I had to settle for grumbling under my breath before wrapping my arms around his ripped stomach.

"We'll use the back gate to get in this time to avoid suspicion," Zaina called after she had removed the fabric tied over her face. "Follow me."

As she called encouragement to her horse, the pair sprang forward. The elves followed her and, after a brief nod from their Master, so did Shade's assassins. I tightened my grip on the athletic assassin as our horse moved out as well.

The ride back to Pernula was much slower than the one to get here, but given what the horses and riders had been doing for the past few hours, I didn't blame them for being tired. Eventually, the tall city walls became visible in the distance. I had no idea how we had managed it but we were approaching the city from the other side, the one we'd used when we'd arrived at Hidden Oaks Cove. The pirate apparently knew her way on land as well.

Tension clung to the guards at the back gate when we arrived but, with Zaina's help, we bribed our way through. Inside the walls, it was even worse. Panicked citizens ran up and down the streets and soldiers hurried past on their way to the main gate while still strapping on their armor. Mothers shoved their children indoors. Everywhere, shutters banged shut.

Zaina brought her horse closer. "I rented the horses 'til tomorrow since we can't return them right now. Not with the whole army there."

"Can we stable them at the school?" Elaran asked.

"Yeah. All the kids should be home by now so we can keep them there tonight. Tomorrow when everyone finds out it was just a trick by Marcellus and things have calmed down, we'll bring them back."

With our large animals, we plowed through the terrified crowd without much resistance. I watched them flatten themselves against the buildings as we rode past. Fear shone in their eyes. Norah had been right: this was an awful thing to do to all the innocent people living here, even if it was only for one night. Tearing my eyes from their faces, I let my brief and uncharacteristic flash of conscience drift back into oblivion. Oh, well. Whatever it took to win.

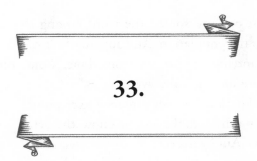

33.

A tall man with a large battle axe stepped onto the street. I drew up short. Next to him, a blond woman appeared. When they noticed me, a smile spread across the man's face.

"Storm!" he called. "Been a while, hasn't it?"

"Yngvild. Vania," I said and closed the distance in a few quick strides. "You alright?"

"Yeah, yeah, we're good." Yngvild held out a tattooed arm. "You?"

I clasped his forearm. "I'm still alive."

A horse-drawn carriage rattled towards us on the street so we took shelter under the colorful awning of a baker's shop. The scent of baking pies drifted through the afternoon air.

"Crazy thing, this star elf scare yesterday, right?" Yngvild said. "I heard General Marcellus made up the whole thing so that people would rally behind him. Heard it's because he's afraid he'll lose the election to your boy Shade."

It took great effort to stop a victorious grin from spreading across my face. "You did, huh? Yeah, I heard the same thing."

So, our rumormongering was working quite well. Liam and the twins were doing a fabulous job in the Upperworld and I was on my way to my third Underworld tavern for the day. Even though Shade could only socialize in legit circles right now, his guild helped me spread the word among the less refined members of the population. And apparently, it was working.

Vania's intelligent blue eyes studied me. "Something tells me that you were somehow involved in this."

I looked back at her, not sure how to respond.

"But I'm thinking, the less we know, the better." She peered down at me. "Am I correct?"

Blowing out an amused breath through my nose, I gave her an impressed nod. "Yeah, probably."

"Then I won't ask." The blond warrior gave me a rare smile. "Until next time."

"See you later, Storm," Yngvild called over his shoulder as he followed his partner down the street.

As far as people went, those two were alright. Leaving the shade of the awning behind, I stepped into the still bright fall sun and set course towards my next tavern. There were people to dupe and lies to spread. Business as usual, then.

GOLDEN LIGHT COVERED the pale stones as I stepped onto the street. Though my social skills still needed serious work, I had managed to plant the seeds of dissatisfaction in the minds of the underworlders I'd met. Not that it was overly difficult. Most of them already believed that Marcellus had orchestrated the fake attack to gain support because they had heard it from so many different sources now. Perfect.

Stretching my arms above my head, I let out a yawn. "Ah, a good day's work." I started back towards the school.

Heavy footfalls thudded behind me. Heaving a deep sigh, I shook my head. *Not again*. I picked up the pace. A cross street was coming up ahead so I veered onto it. Two men with swords blocked the way. Damn. I whirled around and took off at a sprint. The person hunting me from behind did the same.

Another side street presented an escape route. Darting onto it, I found two more men with weapons sealing it off. Gods damn it. I had to get up on the roof. Taking a few quick strides, I reached the nearest wall. A crossbow bolt whizzed past and hit the wall next to me. I snatched my hand back and cast a hurried glance over my shoulder. The lone hunter had now turned into four men with raised crossbows. Shit.

Boots smattered against stone as I dashed along the street with my pursuers behind me. Another pair of men stepped onto the road from a building up ahead. I skidded to a halt. There was a cross street a few paces away. The men behind me closed in. Praying to Nemanan that the adjacent alley would be empty, I put all my faith in it and sprang forward.

My hammering heart skipped a beat when I rounded the corner and found it deserted. Moving quickly, I scrambled to the nearest wall to make another attempt at getting up on the roof. Another crossbow bolt struck the wood next to my hand. That desperate gamble had lost me precious seconds so I had no other choice but to keep running.

Up ahead, another wall of men with weapons blocked the way. Gravel sprayed into the air as I veered into the alley on my left to escape them. Realization spread like cold poison through my chest when I found it empty. I was deliberately being forced in this direction. Unfortunately, I couldn't do much about that right now so I kept sprinting, hoping against hope that a way out would present itself.

The street ended in a large courtyard boxed in by tall buildings. My mad dash screeched to a halt as I took in the scene. Men and women were positioned all along the sides of the courtyard and an array of weapons gleamed in their hands. Blood pounded in my ears. Behind me, the men with crossbows closed in. After casting a quick look over my shoulder, I reluctantly moved into the open square. This was bad.

"The Oncoming Storm," a man's voice called.

Out of the rows of armed people, a slim man with graying hair and dark beady eyes appeared. My heart sank.

"The Rat King," I said, coming to a halt in the middle of the courtyard.

"This piece of foreign scum killed two of my men," the Rat King called and swept his arm in a dramatic arc until it pointed at me.

Behind the Rat King's weapon-wielding subjects, frightened-looking underworlders had appeared and were now watching the exchange with cautious eyes.

"Well, they tried to kill me." I raised my chin. "I was only returning the favor."

"Arrogance," the skinny king said before turning in a slow circle. "I have ordered you all here today so that you can see firsthand what happens to people who cross me."

Fantastic. Another person who wanted to make an example out of me in front of his people. Though I guessed that technically, the frightened-looking people at the back weren't part of the Rat King's gang. They were most likely independents that he wanted to scare into submission. Great. Just great.

"How have I crossed you exactly?" I demanded, impatience creeping into my voice.

"I told you to stop recruiting in my territory and yet you've been seen fraternizing with people like this."

He snapped his fingers and two men shoved a pair that I recognized very well into the courtyard. Swords gleamed at the neck of both Yngvild and Vania. Shit. I couldn't let them get caught up in this.

"Those two?" I scoffed. "I sure as hell haven't been *fraternizing* with them. They cornered me earlier today only to threaten me to stop encroaching on your territory, as they called it." I flicked a hand dismissively. "Cowards."

Surprise flashed over their faces but it was gone by the time the Rat King had turned towards them.

"Is this true?" he demanded.

Knowing that Vania was the most likely to play along, I locked steady eyes on her.

After an intense second, she broke my gaze and moved her eyes to the Rat King. "It is."

Disappointment washed over his face but he recovered quickly. After waving a hand to the two men with swords, he turned back to me. The relief flooding through my body at seeing Yngvild and Vania be released was hidden by the arrogant mask I presented to the Rat King when his beady eyes found mine.

"Regardless, there have still been lots of black-clad people running around lately, interfering in all kinds of matters," the graying king said.

"So?" I gave him a nonchalant shrug. "They're not mine. They're Shade's."

"The foreign guy who is running for General?"

"Yeah, he brought his Assassins' Guild back with him after his last trip to Keutunan." I frowned and flicked my arms to the side in an exasperated gesture. "Why are you even making a thing out of this? Shade's an assassin, for Nemanan's sake! If he wins, it would benefit the whole Underworld and *I* am working to make him General. Shouldn't that be in your best interest too?"

The Rat King was silent for a moment. Lifting a bony hand to his face, he stroked his chin. "That may be true... but I warned you about infringing on my territory. And the Rat King always keeps his promises."

Rage burned inside me. I was so sick of bullheaded men who were too insecure about their manhood to back down. Why couldn't they realize that sometimes it was best to just let the insane knife-throwing girl with the temper of a psychotic demon do whatever the hell she wanted?

I yanked the hunting knives from the small of my back as the darkness ripped from the deep pits of my soul. Black clouds swirled around me while lightning crackled over my skin.

"Ashaana," people whispered around me but I ignored them.

With eyes that had gone black as death, I stared at the Rat King. "You want my life?"

The suddenly nervous-looking king flinched. He opened his mouth but no sound came out.

A crazed laugh slipped from my lips while rage and insanity swirled in my eyes. I bared my teeth at him in a grin tinted with madness. "Come and claim it."

"A-attack!" the Rat King spluttered and pointed a shaking finger at me but his weapon-wielding subjects hesitated. "Now!"

Three men brandishing swords and axes stepped forward. Anger burned through my body and the black smoke grew until it swirled around me like storm clouds. Lightning danced and thunder boomed inside the mist.

"Yes, do attack." Another insane laugh bubbled out of my throat. Gripping the knives so tightly my knuckles turned white, I leveled mad eyes on the three men. "See how that works out for you."

"Shoot her!" the Rat King screamed as his three subjects backed away.

Four crossbow bolts whizzed past me but in the dark of the smoke, none of them hit. I squeezed my fists tighter. Lightning exploded around me and the black clouds swirled faster.

"Now," I called in a voice dripping with madness, "you either leave. Or you die."

Thunder punctuated my every word. Feet smattered against stone as the people around me fled. Across the courtyard, the Rat King yanked the shirt of the closest man and yelled something in his face, but to no avail. All his subjects followed the retreating underworlders and left the area in a hurry. After one last furious look in my direction, he whirled around and stalked away as well.

Tiredness washed over me like a tidal wave. The darkness shrank back into my soul while I staggered into the alley on the other side. I only made it halfway through it before I had to stop and put a hand to the rough wooden wall in order to steady myself. Gods damn it. I couldn't pass out now. If the Rat King came back, he could just slit my throat as I lay there helpless on the street. After sticking my hunting knives back in their sheaths, I stumbled forward with one hand still on the wall. Splinters lodged in my palm but I didn't care. I had to get out of there. Fast.

My knees buckled. I crashed into the stones with a force that jarred my bones. Footsteps echoed down the street but I couldn't muster enough energy to lift my head. After all that, I couldn't believe it would still end with someone shoving a sword through my heart. Darkness pressed in. Blinking repeatedly, I tried to force the oblivion away but it was hopeless. When the feet finally stopped around me, I was already gone.

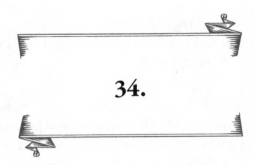

34.

Flames flickered around me. Of course there was going to be fire in hell. Anything else would've been odd. Something moved at the corner of my eye and I squinted at my surroundings. They had tables and chairs in hell? And a bed? I sat bolt upright.

"Easy," a woman's voice said.

Blinking, I tried to clear my vision. "Vania?"

The blond warrior woman gave me a small smile while a very muscular man lumbered over and peered down over her shoulder.

"You're kinda terrifying, you know that?" Yngvild said, grinning down at me.

I managed a strained chuckle. "So I've been told."

For a moment, I closed my eyes and just breathed. In and out. In and out. When I felt my senses return to normal, I opened them again to find both my rescuers studying me.

"You stood up to the Rat King," Vania said without preamble. "No one has ever done that and lived."

"Well, it was that or be killed." I gave her a wry smile. "So, not much to lose."

Her intelligent eyes never left mine. "You're an interesting person."

"And terrifying," Yngvild added.

"You already said that." Vania gave her partner a soft smack on the arm with the back of her hand. "Now give her some room."

Both blue-eyed warriors straightened and backed away. I swung my legs over the side. We were in a small bedroom. Only a set of drawers, a table with a chair, and the bed I sat on occupied the room. A candle illuminated the space because outside the window, the sky was dark.

"How long was I out?" I asked as I stood up.

"About two hours," Vania said.

Two hours. A lot could've happened in that time. Blacking out like this was dangerous. If they hadn't found me... I looked from Vania to Yngvild.

"Thank you," I said.

"It was the least we could do after what you did for us back there," Yngvild said with a broad smile.

Massaging the back of my neck, I returned the smile. "Yeah, but just so you know, I didn't mean the *cowards* part, though."

Yngvild's huge battle axe bounced on his back as a laugh rumbled in his chest. "We know."

After giving my body a good stretch, I glanced at the darkened outside. "I'm sorry, I appreciate everything you've done, but I have to go."

Vania nodded. "We understand." She held out her arm. "Until next time, Storm."

I clasped her forearm. "Until next time."

Once I had repeated the gesture with Yngvild, I surprised them both by climbing out the window instead of using the door. Baffled laughter followed me as I scrambled up the side of the building and onto the roof. Drawing a deep breath of cool night air cleared the rest of the fog from my mind.

There was something about tonight. I had a feeling that something bad was about to happen but I wasn't sure what. It was a ridiculous notion given that something bad had already happened but I couldn't shake it.

If I'd been out for two hours then the sun would've set about an hour ago. That meant Liam would've been back from his visit to the hatmakers a long time ago. Same with the twins. Their debate club ended early afternoon. Elaran hadn't left the school at all and Zaina was with her own gang while Norah, of course, was looking after her school. That left Shade. He was at a meeting with a group of merchants that should be finishing up any time now. Better sure than dead, or however the saying went.

Wind rushed in my ears as I sprinted across the rooftops. I had missed that. The Thieves' Highway, as we called it in Keutunan. The freedom of running unhindered and high up in the air was unparalleled. Besides, it was usually the quickest way to go.

Scattered conversations from people out for an evening stroll drifted up from the street and the scent of blooming night flowers blew past, but mostly it was just me, the wind, and my beating heart. Before long, however, I arrived at my intended destination. On the street below me, Shade was talking to a bespectacled man in a finely tailored vest.

"Thank you for coming to the meeting," Shade said. "And I'm also deeply shocked at General Marcellus' actions. Hopefully, he will explain himself as we give our closing statements the day after tomorrow."

"Ah, yes, indeed," the man said. "Goodnight."

While the vest-clad man wandered off, I climbed down the side of the building and dropped to the ground.

"Did something happen?" the assassin asked as I approached.

"No." I blew out a sigh. "Yes. I was attacked by the Rat King and his army again."

Shade whipped around to face me. "What?"

"Don't worry, I handled it."

"Uh-huh." He narrowed his eyes at me. "Then why are you here?"

Clicking my tongue, I glanced away. "Don't know. I just have a bad feeling, is all."

Instead of making fun of me as I thought he would, the Master Assassin just nodded and motioned for us to get going. We moved down the deserted street. For a moment, everything was silent as we stalked soundlessly through the tall buildings. Shade's eyes darted around.

"You're right," he whispered to me. "It's too quiet."

Something small whizzed through the air, disturbing the calm. We both noticed it a fraction of a second too late.

"Down!" Shade yelled just as the projectile struck his upper arm.

He keeled over and dropped like a stone at the same time as I drew four throwing knives. My mind tried desperately to process what had happened. His eyes, full of panic, kept darting around but the rest of his body didn't move at all. *A paralytic.* Something small hit my shoulder and I fell to the ground next to him.

"Told you we didn't need to hire any... what have they started calling themselves again?" a woman's musical voice said somewhere behind me.

"Underworlders, I believe," a man answered.

"Right," the woman continued. "Told you we didn't need any of them. This really wasn't all that hard. And now we have all night to make it look like an accident."

Oh, brilliant. They were going to kill us. This day just kept getting worse. What in Nemanan's name had I done to deserve this? Actually, I kind of knew. But still. It sucked.

I locked steady eyes on Shade. "Not hit. How many? Blink," I breathed.

His panicked eyes moved around the area behind me and then blinked five times.

Five. Damn it. I'd only drawn four throwing knives. That would leave one behind me and then the coat-clad man making his way towards us from the side I could see. I had to do it before he got too close. While drawing a soft breath, I readied the knives in my hands.

Whipping my body around, I sat up straight and in that split second of confusion I caused, I aimed and threw the blades. Our attackers were so close that I couldn't have missed even if I wanted to. All four knives buried themselves in my targets' throats.

Shocked cries rang out from the two survivors as I jumped up while their comrades crashed to the ground. The man in the coat recovered first and drew his sword. I flicked another throwing knife at him but he batted it away with the flat of his blade. Behind me, the surviving woman released a howl and charged at me. Damn. I had to keep them away from Shade.

After twitching the fingers on both my hands at them, I gave them a haughty smirk and bolted towards the opposite wall. My arrogance had the desired effect and both attackers ran straight for me. *Now what?* I had a nasty habit of falling unconscious after using the darkness and since I'd already done that once tonight, I was pretty sure trying it again would end with me dead as a doornail.

Yanking out my hunting knives, I whirled around to face them. When I noticed that they were both coming at me at the same time, I realized something very important. These people weren't used to fighting as a team. I could use that.

The man swung his sword at me. Ducking under the blade, I stepped out of his reach. When he tried to follow through, he bumped straight into the dagger-wielding woman.

"Move!" he yelled and shoved her aside.

While they were busy getting untangled, I twisted into position between them. Victory sparkled in the woman's eyes. She stabbed the dagger at my chest. Throwing myself to the side, I brace a hand on the ground just as she rammed the sharp point through flesh. The coat-wearing man's brown eyes widened. He stared down at the blade sticking out of his chest for a second before toppling backwards.

Another ear-splitting howl cut through the air as she drew another knife and rushed at me. Having straightened from my strategic dive, I readied my own blades. She slashed at me with all the speed and fury of a hurricane. Metal dinged against metal as I blocked her strikes and tried to get through her guard. She was fighting with more aggression than tactics but she was still good. And fast. To get through her flailing arms, I had to sacrifice something. This was going to hurt.

Pain flashed through me as her dagger sliced across on my forearm. *Now.* With my arm blocking her weapon for a second, I shoved the hunting knife in my other hand through her windpipe. She stopped dead and stared at me. The blade came back red as I withdrew it and watched her tumble to the ground in a mess of limbs.

Heaving a deep sigh of relief, I shook my head. This was getting exhausting. My eyes flicked to the still unmoving body of Shade against the other wall. I was pretty sure it was just a paralytic but I still needed to get him to his guild as soon as possible. Fortunately, we were still in the Inner Ring, which was where the new Assassins' Guild was located as well. After darting around the alley to retrieve all my missing knives, I approached the paralyzed assassin.

"They're all dead," I announced as I came to a halt next to him. "Come on, we've gotta get you to your guild."

His eyes became a bit calmer at the news but he still looked afraid. If I couldn't move, I probably would be too. I bent down and reached for him. One look at my arm stopped me in my tracks. Blood trickled from the cut caused by the woman's dagger but that wasn't what sent icy dread shooting up my spine. The skin at the edge of the wound was green.

"Oh, this isn't good, is it?" I said. "Wait here."

Wait here? I wanted to slap myself. Why yes, Storm, do tell the paralyzed man not to go anywhere. Idiot. I raced back to the dead woman and grabbed the dagger she had dropped. Ripping off a piece of her shirt, I wrapped the blade in it. While I was at it, I also removed the paralytic dart that had gotten stuck in the leather shoulder holster for my throwing knives, which had saved me from getting paralyzed too. After wrapping that as well, I stuffed both objects in my pockets and sprinted back to Shade.

I yanked the dart from his arm and put it in the same cloth cover as the other dart before hauling the tall assassin to his feet. Man, he was heavy. Draping his arm around my neck, I staggered forward. As attractive as all those muscles were, they were incredibly inconvenient right now. I drew strained breaths as we made slow but steady progress towards the Assassins' Guild.

"So, I might've been poisoned," I said as I dragged him along the next empty street on our way to the white mansion. The edges of my vision were tinged with a sparkling green color. "Alright, yeah, I'm actually pretty sure I've been poisoned."

Shade, of course, couldn't answer and I didn't want to see the look in his eye so I kept staring at the cross street ahead. Only two more and then we'd see that ridiculously conspicuous manor. The muscles in my legs and back shook under the weight of the unmoving assassin but I kept pushing forward.

If there had been such a thing as ice fire, that would've been closest thing to describing how my arm felt. It was on fire. But it was also freezing. A weird giggle bubbled up my throat as I tried to imagine what ice fire would look like. Blue flames? Or orange in spiky shards? Another giggle made it out while sparkling green haze covered my eyes.

Stumbling forward, I hauled us both onto the last street. Halfway down it, the white brick house that was the Assassins' Guild waited. Almost there. Every step jarred my soul and made my skull feel like it was about to crack open but the odd giddiness in my chest kept me from drowning in the pain.

Wasn't the mansion supposed to be white? I squinted at the green structure before me as I staggered onto the path leading to the carved wooden door. Those last few steps up to the porch might as well have been the city walls. My feet slipped and both

Shade and I crashed down outside the building. So close. And yet, so far.

The door was shoved open and a mob of black-clad people rushed out. They were saying stuff but I was too detached to hear them. Instead, I used the last of my strength to draw two bundles from my pockets.

"Paralyzed," I mumbled and waved the hand with the wrapped-up darts in the direction I thought Shade was in. "Poisoned." I pointed the covered dagger in my direction.

My arms slumped down by my sides. The bundles disappeared from my hands and for a moment I felt like I was flying. What an odd way to die. Again. I had survived a full-scale ambush by the most vicious man in the Pernulan Underworld and now I was going to die because that godsdamn windmill of a woman had turned out to be a bloody poisoner. Life. Wasn't it ironic?

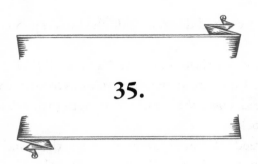

35.

I ntense brown eyes stared at me from the window.

"Gah!" I yelped and scrambled away.

My head hit a wooden headboard with a dull thud. I rubbed my scalp. The intense brown eyes belonged to a tall man with dark brown hair tied back in a bun. Now that the initial shock of finding someone studying me while I slept had faded, I recognized him as Shade's second-in-command. Man-bun. Or at least, that's what I called him in my head. One of these days I really needed to ask what his real name was.

"How do you feel?" Man-bun asked, gracefully pretending not to have noticed me scuttle away like a startled crab.

Untangling my limbs from the sheets, I studied the white bandage around my left forearm for a few seconds before flexing my fingers. "Good... I think?" I flicked my eyes back to his face. "Shade?"

"Alive. Thanks to you." He rose from the chair. "I'll let him know you're up."

The tall assassin strode through the room but then surprised me by halting halfway to the door. He started back up but then stopped again, as if he couldn't quite decide what to do. At last, he swung around and leveled those observant eyes on me again.

"The Master explained what happened."

Aw, shit. What has Shade told them now? Keeping my face carefully neutral, I just watched him.

"You went back for him," Man-bun continued. "You didn't need to but you did, just because you had a bad feeling. Then, you sacrificed precious minutes of your own life dragging him here even though you knew you were dying of a poison quickly spreading through your veins. You take care of your friends." He held my gaze steady. "So does the guild. We won't forget this."

Without waiting for a reply, he closed the distance to the door in a few long strides and disappeared into the hallway beyond. Huh. I had not seen that coming. It appeared as though the risk of me getting my throat slit because my smart mouth had ticked off the death guild one too many times was now considerably lower. Wasn't that an interesting development?

The door cracked open and another tall black-clad assassin stepped through. "You really are a hard person to kill."

"So are you," I observed.

Shade's mouth twitched upwards in a smile. He looked as healthy and arrogant as ever, but when he raked his fingers through his black hair, I swore I could see some tension leaving his body. Strange. I wondered what had put him on edge.

"Bringing the darts and the dagger was a smart move," he said, dropping into the empty chair and swinging his feet onto the windowsill. "Because of that, my people could give you the antidote straight away."

"You just happened to have the antidote lying around?"

Shade lifted his eyebrows, amusement evident on his face. "We're the Assassins' Guild. We have the antidote to every known poison in here. For obvious reasons."

"Oh. Right." I cleared my throat and glanced out the window instead.

It was still dark outside so the candles flickering around the room was the only source of light. Wait. *Still* dark? Was I sure about that? I moved my eyes back to the assassin in the chair.

"I'm getting a bit sick of asking this question but... how long was I out?"

"About one full day. The attack was last night."

"And you? How long were you out for?"

"Because you brought in the darts, they could give me something to counter the paralytic. It wore off after an hour or so."

I studied him. "Are you okay?"

A soft laugh escaped his lips as he shook his head at me. "Am I okay? You're the one who got poisoned."

"Yeah, I guess so."

He swung his feet off the windowsill and pushed out of the chair. "Speaking of, Liam's here. He refused to leave until you woke up, and now I'm pretty sure he's started making friends with my assassins."

I managed a hoarse chuckle. "That sounds like Liam."

"I'll go let him know you're awake."

"Yeah."

Only the bed and the chair by the window furnished the room so his footsteps echoed against the bare walls as he made his way to the door. When he reached it, he paused a second with his hand on the handle and looked back at me.

"I, uhm..." the Master Assassin trailed off.

The look on his face was one I knew very well. Gestures of gratitude and appreciation weren't exactly my strong suit either, so I recognized the struggle in others.

"Yeah, me too," I assured him.

Cracking another smile, he gave me a nod before disappearing out the door. Outside the window, the night was quiet. If I'd been unconscious for an entire day, that meant Shade and the other candidates were giving their closing statements tomorrow. Then after that, there was only one more day of grace before the city of Pernula went out to vote. Weeks and weeks of plotting and scheming, fighting and almost dying was coming to an end. In three days' time, it would all be over.

Feet thundered up the stairs and the door was flung open. Sparkling blue eyes and a mop of curly brown hair appeared in the doorway.

"I was so worried," Liam said as he flew across the room and drew me into a sheet-tangled hug.

"I'm alright," I mumbled into his shoulder. "I'm alright."

He drew back and, with his hands still on my shoulders, stared into my eyes until he was satisfied that I was telling the truth. After giving me a brief nod, he dragged the chair over from the window and plopped down on it next to my bed. He rubbed his hands up and down his face.

"I'm sorry," he said.

"For what?" Reaching out, I pulled his hands from his face. "It's not your fault that Marcellus tried to assassinate Shade, and I got caught in the middle." I let out a soft chuckle. "Though, you've gotta appreciate the irony in someone trying to assassinate the Master of the Assassins' Guild."

I thought Liam would laugh at my stupid joke but when he looked at me, his eyes only held sadness. And shame.

"Not that," he said. "I'm sorry for how I've been behaving lately."

"What do you mean?"

"You're a violent person."

A surprised laugh made it out of my throat. "Thanks?"

Liam gave me an apologetic smile. "Wait, just let me finish. I've told you this before and you know it's true. You're the kind of person who fights and kills without hesitation or remorse. And I know why. After Rain died, you didn't want to watch anyone else you care about get hurt."

Pain and sorrow bled from my heart at the mention of Rain. The girl I had put into harm's way because I wanted to help some random strangers and the girl who had died because I hesitated to kill someone.

"What I'm trying to say is that you're fiercely protective of the people you love and that's not a bad thing." Liam reached out and put a hand on my bandaged arm. "But I've been making you feel bad about who you are because I was confused about who *I am*... and because I was ashamed."

I squeezed his hand. "What could you possibly have to be ashamed of?"

His sad eyes met mine. "Do you remember what I said when you told me you had killed Rogue last year?"

"No?"

"Good, I'm glad he's dead. That's what I said." My friend closed his eyes for a moment. "What kind of person says something like that?" He met my gaze again. "I've been ashamed of that and I've been blaming you for it and making you feel like a bad person just because I didn't want to face it."

"Liam, it's okay."

He shot up from the chair and started pacing back and forth in front of the bed. "No, it's not. I'm not an all good person. I know you think that but I was also the kid who got his whole family killed because I was out making trouble." He ran his hands through his hair. "And not being that person while living in the Underworld is hard because... it's the Underworld. So that messed-up kid has been popping up again."

Not sure what to say, I just stared at him. I knew that Liam had been struggling with the meaning of life but I had no idea that he had also been struggling with who he was.

"But being here in Pernula, away from the Underworld, I've once and for all realized that I'm not that troubled kid anymore. And I don't want to be. He will always be a part of me, which is why I sometimes say things like *I'm glad he's dead*. But that's okay because it's not who I am. *This* is who I am. And I'm just sorry that I made you feel bad while I figured that out."

Silence reigned as Liam stopped pacing and instead watched me, apprehension mingling with determination in his dark blue eyes. He was afraid that *I* was mad at *him*. If he only knew the terrible dread I'd been carrying around lately because I thought he was angry with me for being who I was.

"You have nothing to apologize for, my friend," I said. "Nothing at all."

Liam edged back to the bed and gave me another hug. "I'm glad we met."

"Me too."

He looked me up and down. "I'll let you get some rest."

After he had slipped out the door again, I slumped back against the pillows. My heart felt loads lighter now that I knew he wasn't ashamed of me but some of the things he had said these past few weeks still lingered in my mind.

He might not believe that he was an all good person, but I knew he was. With all that charm, he would've survived the Underworld perfectly well without me. The only reason he had needed protecting was because of *my* enemies. If I hadn't been in his life, people wouldn't have been kidnapping him and trying to kill him as much as they had. And then he wouldn't have had any reason to say things like *I'm glad he's dead.* I was pretty sure I was the reason his life had been so full of blood and violence this last decade.

Turning around, I pressed the pillow into my cheek to stave off the ache in my heart. A real fine friend, wasn't I?

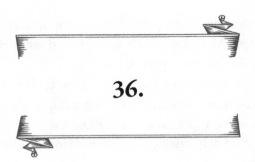

36.

The crowd buzzed around me. It was odd sitting on a chair with the audience like a normal person instead of skulking around on the beams above. This was probably my first time attending an important meeting as a civilian. Or as much of a civilian as a thief hiding two stilettos in her sleeves, one blade between her breasts, and one in her boot could be.

"Ladies and gentlemen," a man's voice boomed.

It was the same man who had led the debate some weeks ago, and all the other public events Shade had participated in since, for that matter. He straightened his well-tailored garments before holding up his hands to quiet the audience.

"Tonight, you will hear the closing statements of all the candidates before you make your final decision for the vote the day after tomorrow," he called. "Please welcome the candidates for General."

Six men strode onto the platform. Before the election, everyone had assumed that Marcellus was the only real candidate and the other five were just there for the sake of appearances, but after the dents we'd put in Marcellus' campaign, the outcome was no longer certain. Tonight, we would put the last nails in his coffin.

Shade, wearing his crisp black suit, took up position by the lectern next to Marcellus. Both men exuded authority as they locked eyes. This was going to be fun.

While the other four candidates gave their speeches, the Master Assassin just continued staring straight ahead with an impassive look on his face. Marcellus, on the other hand, couldn't seem to help casting murderous glares at his dark-haired competition.

The General must have somehow maneuvered his way into being the last speaker because when candidate number four ended his address, the moderator called up Shade.

"Esteemed citizens," Shade began. "It is an honor to be here today. Though, I very nearly couldn't make it. As I'm sure you have all noticed, General Marcellus has been staring at me all evening. I can understand that he is surprised to see me, given that he tried to assassinate me two days ago."

A shocked murmur rippled through the crowd. Next to me, Haela and Zaina grinned at the growing commotion and even Elaran almost smiled.

"Outrageous!" Marcellus called and slammed a fist into his lectern.

"Yes, it quite is, General," Shade continued. "But the most outrageous part of all is that it is not the first time." He paused and swept his gaze through the audience. "I'm sure you all remember that awful warehouse fire. Some of you already know this but it bears repeating: the fire was meant for me."

Shocked gasps mixed with nods of recognition. On the row in front of our group of seven, several ladies raised a hand to their mouths.

"My associates and I were in that warehouse when General Marcellus set an explosion to kill us and make it look like an accident." The Master Assassin shook his head while the mask on his face transformed into one of sadness. "That is why I had to leave for a while afterwards. I feared for my life and the lives of my associates." He raised a fist in the air. "But I decided that I would not let a bully scare me into giving up!"

Enthusiastic nods could be seen throughout the audience while comments of support and outrage rose. By Nemanan, he was good. Behind the lectern next to the well-dressed assassin, General Marcellus was fuming.

"This is absolutely–" the furious General began.

"Please, wait for your turn, General," the moderator interrupted.

When Marcellus only muttered under his breath in response, Shade continued.

"Do you really want a man like that to lead this great city?" He swept his arms to the sides. "A man who frightens and bullies people into doing what he wants? A man who tries to kill his competition?"

I had to bite my tongue to keep from laughing out loud. Yeah, because what kind of man would do something like that? Certainly not the Master of the Assassins' Guild who threatened and blackmailed people into doing his bidding and assassinated those who crossed him. A low chuckle made it past my lips. How he managed to say stuff like that with a straight face was beyond me.

"A man who orchestrated a fake attack by the star elves just to make you all rally behind him!" Shade boomed across the stage. "Would you really trust someone like that to lead you?"

Gripping the sides of the lectern, he swept a steady gaze through the room. "Would you not instead trust the man who dared stand up to such injustice and trickery? Me." He executed a quick bow of his head. "Thank you."

Clapping and cheering rose from the gathered crowd. Liam and I exchanged a look. We might actually win this.

"General Marcellus, the floor is yours," the moderator announced as the noise died down.

The General took a deep breath and plastered a smile on his face. "Good people of Pernula. After all the years we've known each other, it saddens me that you would believe the word of this man over mine. I feel it my duty to point out that this man is a foreigner and an *assassin*."

A ripple went through the audience and uncertain whispers spread across the sea of chairs.

"You cannot trust anything he says," Marcellus continued. "Everything he has accused me of this night is false. In fact, *he* is the one responsible for them. The warehouse fire, the fake attack. All of it."

"Oh please, General," Shade interrupted. "Stop this childish finger pointing and no-he-did-it and take responsibility for your actions. The evidence against you is overwhelming."

"Shade, you have had your say," the moderator warned.

The black-eyed assassin fell silent but the mood of the crowd shifted again. Being reminded of the evidence found after the explosion at the docks helped fuel the dissatisfaction again.

Marcellus snarled at the assassin. "That's it! I have had enough of this!" He turned back to the packed hall. "I came here to give you a speech about everything good I have done and will continue doing for our nation but my honor is constantly, and unjustly, being attacked. I will not stand for it."

As one, the spectators held their breaths. I glanced at the twins, who shrugged, but next to them, Zaina suddenly looked very worried.

"In order to restore my honor and once and for all cast off these ridiculous accusations, I challenge you to a duel."

A great collective gasp reverberated through the room. I whipped my head towards Zaina. She closed her eyes. On my other side, Norah squeezed Liam's hand while concern marred her face.

Up on the podium, Shade looked unfazed. "I accept."

"Tomorrow at midday," Marcellus said. "In front of Blackspire."

The Master Assassin nodded while a commotion broke out in the audience. Arguments mixed with excited cheering.

"Why's everyone reacting like this?" I hissed to Elaran. "This is good for us, isn't it? I mean, Shade's the bloody Master of the Assassins' Guild. We've got nothing to worry about, right?"

"Maybe the crowd is worried that Marcellus will lose?" The auburn-haired elf furrowed his brows as he watched the anxious expression on Zaina's face. "I don't know."

"Ladies and gentlemen, we will take a short break before we bring in the candidates for High Priest," the smartly dressed moderator called while holding up his hands. "Please remain calm."

As Shade and the other five candidates made their way to the stairs leading down from the podium, our group of seven exchanged glances. At last, Elaran jerked his head in the direction of the assassin.

We all rose and started pushing our way through the packed room of chairs and murmuring people. It was time to find out what those anxious expressions on Zaina's and Norah's faces were for.

LEAVES RUSTLED ABOVE us in the soft evening breeze. Despite the late hour, the Lemon Tree Café was open for business and guests dotted the chairs on the stone courtyard. Music drifted from the far wall. Our party of eight occupied the large table in the corner but the mirthful chatter present at the other tables shone with its absence at ours.

Zaina had suggested we move away from the debate hall and to an area more suited for private discussions. Since none of us had the patience to walk all the way back to the school, we had settled for the café we had visited when we first arrived. An attractive girl with golden hair placed the last of the lemonade mugs on the table before weaving back through the waiting patrons. I took a sip of the sour yet refreshing liquid.

"Okay, now can someone please tell me why the two of you are so freaked out?" Haela said.

I backed her up with a nod. "Yeah, this is a good thing, right? A lot of the soldiers are already on board after our rumor about them being used as cannon fodder but when Shade wins this, they'll all definitely vote for him."

Zaina released a long sigh and turned to Shade. "You won't win."

The Master Assassin frowned at her. "You've seen me fight. Are you seriously telling me I'll lose?"

"Yes, I've seen you fight. And I'm telling you, Marcellus is gonna beat you." She leaned back and ran her fingers through her curly black hair. "He didn't become General without merit."

"It's true," Norah said. "He's the best swordsman I've ever seen."

"And that's saying something," her sister picked up again. "This is a military state, you've noticed that, right? There are *a lot* of soldiers in this city and Marcellus... he's the best of them all."

Elaran swept grave eyes around the table. "If Marcellus wins this fight, we're screwed."

"Correct," Zaina confirmed. "None of the soldiers will respect the one who loses. They value combat skills and military tactics above all else. We probably have none of the elite classes, we might have some of the merchants, but right now, we have a lot of the soldiers and there just might be enough of them voting for us to win this election. If we lose the soldiers, we lose it all."

Our table fell silent as we all pondered this depressing news. Oblivious to our quandary, the band struck up a joyous tune. I took another sip of lemonade.

"We could always cheat," I said with a light shrug.

"No." Zaina shook her head. "Then we'd lose everyone. In this city, no one outside of us underworlders would ever respect someone who fought dirty."

I drummed my fingers on the table. "They won't know we cheated if we don't get caught."

"It's too much of a risk." Norah looked from face to face. "Isn't it? And besides, if you win by cheating, have you really won at all?"

Elaran pushed the mug away and crossed his arms. "I agree. Fighting with honor is important."

Of course he would think that. I had noticed early on that honor was a big thing with him. Though, I had to say, since meeting me and especially since he became friends with Shade, the grumpy elf had become a bit more open to the Underworld way. However, now he'd made his position crystal clear. I didn't understand it at all because to me, winning was winning regardless of how you did it. But I appeared to be outvoted so I raised my hands.

"Fine," I said. "No cheating. So, what do we do?"

We all looked from face to face but since no one spoke up, I assumed our scheming gang was fresh out of ideas. Tipping the mug back, I downed the rest of my drink. How did normal people get anything done if they couldn't cheat, lie, or steal to do it? Watching the Master Assassin from the corner of my eye, I wondered if he knew. I guess we were about to find out.

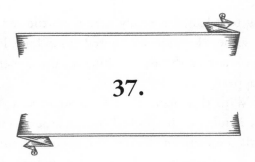

37.

People. There were people everywhere. Anticipation hung over the whole square as men and women pressed as close to the stage as they could get. Faces popped out of every window and even the lower roofs nearby were being used as vantage points. Eager voices chatted everywhere. It seemed as though the shock from yesterday had been replaced by exhilaration as the crowd looked forward to the impending duel.

I slid through the crowd like a snake. Two tents had been erected on either side of the large platform in the middle of the square and inside, the two fighters waited. Weaving through a group of cheerful young women, I made for the one to the left. Marcellus' tent.

Yes, yes, I know. They did say not to cheat. But see, cheating is only a crime if you get caught.

Dark red fabric flapped in the warm breeze as I closed in. It was no more than a small rectangle of cloth and poles holding it up, but it was enough to give the contestants somewhere private to get ready for the battle. I skirted around the structure. The main opening at the front was the intended door but as I reached the back of the tent, I noticed that the fabric overlapped there as well. It might not have been meant as an entrance, but it could most certainly be used as one.

Coming to a halt, I tore my gaze from the red cloth and took in the scene. The audience buzzed around me. Everywhere I looked, eyes roamed the area, waiting for the General and the assassin to appear.

Damn. With this many eyes, I would need a distraction. Placing soft hands on the packed bodies around me, I edged back towards the front of the tent. This would require careful scheming. I cast an impatient glance at the sun high above me in the sky. Or some brute force. Or maybe a bit of both.

While gliding between two groups of young men, I lowered a deft hand into an unguarded pocket. My fingers wrapped around a pouch. Drawing it out, I set my sights on the unattended pocket of a man from the other squad.

He turned around and stared straight at me. However, I was too much of a professional to stop dead in my tracks. Instead, I simply continued forward with a vaguely disinterested look on my face. Twisting my body as I passed him, I stuck my fingers in his pocket.

The stage was set. Now, all I had to do was tip the pieces in the right direction. I slunk through the crowd until I arrived next to a plump lady talking loudly to her friend at the edge of the two gangs.

"Did you see that?" I whispered to the woman.

She jerked back slightly at the sudden comment. "Did I see what?"

"That guy in the blue shirt, he took a pouch from that man's pocket when he wasn't looking."

"He did?"

I nodded. "Yeah."

"Youngsters these days," she muttered and crossed her arms. "Hey! You in the blue shirt, give back what you stole."

When the talkative lady raised her voice to call him out, I was already slipping away. The man I had pickpocketed soon discovered his money missing and an argument broke out as the accused man defended himself after finding the stolen pouch in his pocket. Safe on the other side of the two groups of young men, I decided it was time for some brute force. Just as I passed on the edge of the two squads, I threw an elbow into the side of the closest man.

"Ey!" he called and whipped around.

Since I had already ducked away, he only found the confused face of a completely innocent man from the other group who had just turned around.

"Watch it!" the guy I'd hit warned, and gave the other man a hard shove.

That'll do it. The crowd cried out in alarm as the two groups of young men broke into a brawl. I rolled my eyes as I stalked around the side of the tent. Amateurs. With all eyes currently focused on the commotion at the front, I slid unseen through the gap in the fabric at the back and into Marcellus' tent.

I dropped to the ground. Rolling in behind a chest, I tried to slow my hammering heart. Marcellus stood in the middle of the cloth-covered structure, stretching his muscled arms. Fortunately for me, he had his back to me.

Moving with deliberate care, I edged my head up. Apart from the chest I used as cover, only a table and a chair furnished the space. Not much to hide behind. My eyes continued darting around the room. The table was completely empty, as was the floor. I would bet my whole fortune that whatever weapons he was going to use were stored in the wooden trunk.

General Marcellus dropped his arms to his sides and turned around. I jerked my head back down. *Oh, shit.* The weapons. In the chest. The one behind which a very shady member of his opponent's team currently hid. If he found me in here, he could just kill me on the spot and claim I'd been there to assassinate him.

Blood pounded in my ears. If I didn't move before he got to the chest, he would see me. On the other hand, if I did move, he would also see me. Damn. Regardless of what I did, I would get caught. My heart beat against my ribcage. Reaching behind my back, I let my fingers snake around the handle of a hunting knife. If I was to be framed as an assassin, I might as well do the job.

"General!" someone called from outside the front of the tent.

"What?"

Clothes rustled faintly above me as I assumed Marcellus turned around. I was not about to let this brief opportunity slip by. Before the man calling had a chance to enter the tent and before Marcellus could turn back around, I darted from my cover.

"There's a disturbance outside," the man said. "Two groups are fighting over something."

"So? What do I pay you for? Deal with it," Marcellus muttered as the tent cloth fell back into place behind me. "And then get me my sword and shield!"

I didn't dare stop moving until I was past the stage on the other side. Leaning my back against the large platform, I closed my eyes. That had been close. What was that thing I'd said?

Cheating was only a crime if you got caught. I blew out a soft chuckle. Good thing I hadn't been. After sending a quick prayer of thanks to Nemanan, I pushed off the tall stage and moved towards the other tent covered in dark red fabric.

This one was much easier to get into. I simply walked through the front door. Slim eyed me as I passed but didn't make a move to stop me, so I assumed Shade had instructed him to let members of our scheming group pass. When the soft cloth rustled shut behind me, I drew up short.

The athletic assassin was in the middle of getting changed. I stared at the lean muscles covering his chest and stomach while his toned arms were busy pulling off a shirt. By Nemanan, he really was fit.

"Enjoying the view?" Shade said as he finally got the shirt past his head and away from his eyes.

Oh, I was. As much as I hate to say it, I was enjoying the view. A lot. But I would die before admitting it to that arrogant bastard, so instead I let a smirk settle on my face.

"Actually, I was admiring my own strength. Hauling all that through the streets while dying from some weird poison was no small feat, you know."

Amusement flashed past on his face. "That right?"

"Mm-hmm."

Shade folded up the shirt in his hand and placed it on the neat pile next to him. When he turned around, I got a full view of his body. I ran my eyes over it. Not only his arms but also his chest, abdomen, and back sported evidence of fights. Pale scars, some faint and some prominent, decorated his skin. There was no question that he, too, had lived a life full of violence and bloodshed.

"Did you want something?" he asked while lifting another black shirt from the pile.

Crossing my arms, I strode forward until I reached the large center pole. I leaned my shoulder against it. "So, I snuck into Marcellus' tent."

"I thought you were told not to cheat."

"Yeah, well, doing as I'm told isn't exactly my forte."

After putting on the tight-fitting black shirt he'd picked up, he advanced on me. I rolled my eyes. *Oh, here we go again.* A knife appeared in his right hand while he planted his left on the support beam next to my head. Putting the blade under my chin, he used it to tilt my head up to meet his eyes.

"I can't have people going rogue on me and disobeying my orders."

"First, I don't take orders from you."

Shade pushed the knife higher up under my chin, his black eyes glittering. "Wanna bet?"

I shot a stiletto blade into my palm. Putting the cold metal to the inside of his wrist, I moved his knife hand out of my face. "And second, that thing about not cheating..." I narrowed my eyes and gave him a knowing smirk. "They weren't exactly *your* orders, now were they?"

While twirling the knife in his hand, he let out a short chuckle. "No."

"Exactly. The others said not to cheat but they aren't underworlders. We are. And we do whatever it takes to win."

"We do indeed." His intelligent eyes peered down at me. "But?"

"But... there was nothing I could tamper with. No food or drink to drug. Even his weapons were stored away safely. He's careful, I'll give him that. Short of slitting his throat, there wasn't anything I could do."

Shade removed his hand from the wooden pole next to my head. "Yeah, and killing the General of Pernula the day before the election wouldn't have ended well for us."

"Probably not." I lifted my free shoulder in a one-sided shrug. "I overheard his choice of weapon, though. A sword and shield."

The wheels were already turning behind the assassin's black eyes. "Sword and shield, huh?"

I peeled my shoulder off the support beam and made for the door. "Don't lose."

"I don't lose."

Stopping, I twisted around and repeated his own words to me from so many months ago. "Humility isn't your strong suit, is it?"

"Neither is it yours."

He remembered. I blew out a soft chuckle before turning back to the opening in the tent. Holding the flap open, I cast one last look back at the Master of the Assassins' Guild.

"Whatever it takes."

His mouth drew into a lopsided smile. "Whatever it takes."

Outside the tent, the crowd had gotten even more excited. It seemed as though members of every faction were there. Lords and ladies were mixed in with bakers in stained aprons, sailors smelling of seaweed, and soldiers in full armor. Perched on the roofs around the stage, I even recognized some underworlders I'd met in different taverns while I'd been out spreading rumors. This duel was definitely a spectator sport.

Drawing a deep breath, I started weaving towards the spot where the rest of my companions waited. We were about to find out if the muscled General really was more skilled in the art of swordplay than the cunning assassin. For all our sakes, I hoped to Nemanan that Zaina and Norah were wrong. Otherwise, we were all dead.

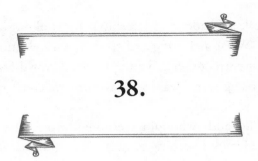

38.

A roar rose from the audience. Shade and Marcellus climbed the steps at the back of the stage and moved towards the middle of the large rectangle. No fence lined the platform so the crowd's view was uninterrupted. I placed my hands on the warm tiles while dangling my legs over the side of the roof.

Getting Norah to scale a building had been entirely impossible. Apparently, winning an argument against a determined teacher was about as easy as persuading a three-story building to move out of the way. I'd soon abandoned my efforts and decided to let the bossy girl do what she wanted.

She had found a spot on the ground together with Liam and Zaina but I wanted to see every single thing that happened on that stage so I'd climbed onto a flat roof near the platform. The couple who had previously occupied the space kindly moved further down when they saw three tall elves and a well-armed thief make their way towards them.

"He will win, right?" Haemir said and cast a glance at the three of us.

Elaran crossed his arms but kept his gaze on the platform. "He has to."

"Welcome, ladies and gentlemen," an excited-looking man called across the square in a surprisingly strong voice. He placed himself between Shade and Marcellus before holding up his arms in the air. "What a riveting end to this year's election! A duel between our current General and predicted crowd favorite, and this year's rising star. Please give a warm welcome to General Marcellus and Shade!"

Cheering and whooping erupted from the gathered spectators. Heat did nothing to quell their enthusiasm, it would seem. Since it was midday and the sun was at its highest, the gleaming towers of Blackspire provided no respite from the scorching sun. I wiped a hand along my temple.

"Gentlemen," the fight supervisor continued and looked at both combatants. "Declare your weapons."

Even though they were now speaking in more conversational tones, this close to the stage, we could still hear them perfectly.

"A sword and a shield," General Marcellus said.

"Two swords," Shade said.

The excited-looking man raised his voice again. "General Marcellus has declared a sword and shield and Shade has declared two swords."

A ripple of anticipation spread through the crowd. Drawing up my legs, I crossed them under me and leaned my elbows on my knees. My heart pattered in my chest.

"There will be no fatalities and no maiming!" the supervisor called and moved eyes that had turned as hard as steel between the two fighters. "Is that clear?" When both contestants nodded, he continued. "The duel ends when first blood is drawn or when one of you surrenders."

Up on the roof, I scoffed. *As if that would happen.* Shade and Marcellus nodded once more before retreating to opposite sides of the rectangular stage. I released a long exhale to steady my nerves. This was it. This was the moment the election was either won or lost.

"Begin!"

The fight supervisor hurried down the steps just as Marcellus hoisted his broad shield. Shade spun his twin swords in his hands and flashed the General an arrogant grin. Marcellus shot across the stage.

Sparks flew as his large sword slammed into the assassin's blades and scraped along the steel. Shade shoved it aside and aimed a strike at his other side. A loud crash reverberated as Marcellus brought his shield up to deflect the blow. Putting his shoulder behind it, the General used his shield to shove Shade backwards.

The Master Assassin staggered at the sheer force of the push but recovered quickly and spun to the other side to deliver another blow. Marcellus slammed his sword down and blocked the swipe aimed for his ribs while throwing his shield in a wide arc. With not a second to spare, Shade twisted out of reach. The painted steel shield produced a *whoosh* as it flew past.

Not letting the moment go to waste, Shade kicked at Marcellus' exposed hip. Since his shield was out of position, he took the hit straight on and stumbled back. The assassin darted forward but the muscular General flung his sword out, forcing him to dodge. In those precious few seconds of respite, Marcellus found his footing again.

Raising his sword and shield once more, he advanced on the assassin. Shade feigned a strike to the left but when Marcellus readied his defense, he changed direction and launched himself into the air. Metal clashed as the assassin slammed his twin swords at Marcellus' head only to be blocked by the General's own blade, thrown up at the last second. Having missed his strike, Shade's side was completely open.

A collective gasp rang out from the crowd as General Marcellus slammed the heavy metal shield into the assassin. Shade flew to the side. Dull thuds echoed as his body crashed down on the wooden planks of the platform. I winced.

Shade was good. There was no question about that. He was all speed, agility, lightning strikes, and quick direction changes. Marcellus, on the other hand, fought like a block of stone with tight defense and powerful blows. They were almost matched in fighting skills but Zaina had been right. The muscled General was better. Not by much, but it was still enough. My heart sank. Shade was going to lose.

Down on the stage, the Master Assassin sucked in a deep breath and rolled away from the blade coming for his throat. Splinters sailed through the air as Marcellus' sword struck the wooden planks Shade had occupied only seconds before. The dark-haired assassin swung his right-hand sword at Marcellus' ankles, forcing the General to jump back. Using the added space to his advantage, Shade pulled his legs up towards his chest. After rolling back on his shoulders, he kicked his legs upwards while pushing off with his fists. Launching himself from the ground, he landed in a crouch and spun his swords in his hands.

Metal vibrated as Marcellus pounded his sword on his shield, telling the assassin to get on with it. Shade sprang forward. His blades flashed like lightning as he delivered one strike after another, forcing Marcellus back towards the edge of the stage. Cries of surprise and encouragement rose from the crowd. I stared at the flurry of blades trying to get through Marcellus' defense. *He might actually win.*

I jinxed it. The assault came to a screeching halt as Marcellus twisted his shield and trapped Shade's right-hand sword against it. When the General threw his shield out, the assassin was forced to release his weapon to avoid being flung away with it. Metal clattered against stone as Marcellus tossed the sword over the side of the stage.

Jumping backwards, Shade switched his remaining blade to his right hand. Victory shone in the General's eyes as he advanced on the retreating assassin. Shade paused. His calculating gazed roamed over the approaching warrior and he shifted the sword back to his left hand. What was he doing?

He darted forward. Marcellus crouched and braced himself for the impact as Shade barreled straight for him. At the last moment, the Master Assassin danced away and twisted inside Marcellus' guard. Shade whipped his sword towards the General's throat but it was all for nothing when Marcellus threw his own sword up and blocked the strike.

My chest tightened. Trapped inside Marcellus' shield like that, and with his sword locked outside, it was over. Shade's desperate gamble was the one that would lose him the fight.

Down on the stage, no one moved. Trying to shove the hopelessness aside, I squinted at the two contestants. Shade hissed something in Marcellus' ear. The General looked furious but then spread his arms wide.

Shocked gasps of utter disbelief echoed through the whole square as General Marcellus dropped his sword and shield. They clattered to the floor next to him. My eyes widened as the proud General raised his hands, palms out. What the hell was going on?

That's when I saw it. The knife. A dark chuckle slipped from my lips. There on the middle of the platform, Shade pressed the edge of a short knife into the skin below Marcellus' jaw. I was both impressed and unsurprised at the same time.

"The winner is Shade!" the duel supervisor called while climbing the stairs back up to the stage. Just as the crowd was about to break into cheers, he saw the unauthorized blade in the assassin's hand. "Stop!"

The Assassins' Guild Master drew a shallow cut along Marcellus' neck to drive the point home. Blood trickled down the General's throat. After one last arrogant smirk, Shade removed the knife and stepped back.

"Ladies and gentlemen," the supervisor called. "It appears as though an undeclared weapon has been used in this fight."

"He fought dishonorably," Elaran said, his face blank.

I cast him a quick look before turning my gaze back to the assassin on the stage. "No, he fought to win."

The gathered audience was dead quiet as General Marcellus dropped his arms and took a step forward.

"You cheated," he growled before raising his voice to a shout. "He cheated! This disgraceful assassin used a hidden knife to win this fight. That goes against the rules."

"Rules?" Shade scoffed before raising his own voice to carry across the square. "You keep talking about cheating but there's no cheating in war. When you fight, you fight to win."

"When you fight, you fight with honor!" the furious general bellowed.

"The enemy won't stop to fight honorably." Shade threw his arms to his sides and turned in a slow circle. "When the star elves come here and attack our city, do you think they will hesitate? No. They will kill your families to take this city. And when someone is trying to kill your family, you do whatever it takes to win. Honor and rules be damned."

The crowd stared at the assassin in stunned silence.

Shade swung his arm and stabbed a finger in Marcellus' direction. "Would you really trust someone like him to protect your families? Someone who wouldn't do everything in his power to keep you safe, just because it might not be honorable. Or would you trust me, who will use whatever means necessary to keep your enemies from laying as much as a finger on your loved ones?"

For a few moments, no one said anything. Even General Marcellus appeared to be too flabbergasted to come up with some kind of retort. Then, a shout cut through the square.

All around us, soldiers lifted fists and weapons in the air while releasing long cheers. While the cries of support grew in strength as more armor-clad men joined in the rhythmic chanting, the rest of the spectators looked undecided. Marcellus' feelings, however, were not difficult to interpret. Rage painted his face red.

"You scheming little..." the General growled and snatched up his sword.

Shade gave him a quick rise and fall of his eyebrows while a smirk decorated his face but before it could turn into another fight, the supervisor planted himself in the middle.

"Gentlemen, the duel is over," he said in a low voice before calling across the square. "Ladies and gentlemen, since Shade cheated in order to win, this duel ends without a winner. Thank you for coming and despite the upsetting end, I hope you enjoyed the excellent display of fighting skills. Please disperse quickly and calmly so that we can get the stage ready for the election result announcements tomorrow evening."

As the crowd starting moving, Haela and I exchanged a look. She gave me a shrug.

"Tent?"

I nodded. "Tent."

Without another word, the four of us climbed down the side of the building and pushed our way through the exiting citizens. I only caught bits of many different conversations but the general consensus seemed to be that they weren't sure what to think of the events that had transpired on that stage today. As it stood, it might go either way.

When we entered the dark red tent to the right of the stage, Liam, Zaina, and Norah were already there. I'd seen Shade through the crowd. He'd been retrieving his sword and was right behind us. We squeezed into the tent and waited for the last member of our group to arrive.

"Why?" Elaran demanded as soon as the fabric had swung closed behind the assassin.

Shade strode through the room and placed his swords on the table. "It was that or lose."

"When we crossed blades you fought well." Elaran locked eyes with him. "That's when I saw that you have honor. But now, I don't know what to make of you anymore."

"Maybe you don't know me as well as you think." Shade's face was an unreadable mask. "I'm the Master of the Assassins' Guild. There's nothing I won't do, no lines I won't cross, to get what I want."

Silence hung heavy inside the dark red drapes. Norah flicked nervous eyes between the two men but relaxed a little when Liam took her hand.

"After everything we've done to screw with Marcellus these past weeks, why's this such a big deal?" I asked.

"I don't care about the other illegal things we've done because we did them to stop a war." Elaran crossed his arms. "But cheating in a prearranged one-on-one? In our culture, doing that is... You don't do it. You just don't."

I knew we had our cultural differences with the elves, and with Elaran in particular, but to me, cheating was an everyday staple so I had a hard time understanding his point of view.

"He did this to stop a war too, remember?" I said. "If Marcellus wins the election tomorrow, he's free to declare war on our island."

The auburn-haired elf opened his mouth but then closed it again. The tent walls flapped in the breeze. When Elaran only drew his eyebrows down and made no further attempt to speak, I turned to Zaina.

"So, how are we doing with that?"

She shrugged. "Your guess is as good as mine. We seem to have the soldiers on our side at least." She nodded at Shade. "Thanks to your rather impressive speech there at the end. But everyone else? No idea."

"So, it can go either way?" Haela asked.

"Yeah, basically."

I tapped my jaw. "Can we rig the election?"

Elaran scowled at me. "What do you think we've been doing for the past months?"

"I mean the actual votes." I glanced around the room. "Can we rig the actual votes tomorrow so Shade gets the majority?"

All the foreigners fell silent and looked to the pair of natives in the room. The two dark-haired sisters exchanged a look before shaking their heads in unison.

"No, it's impossible," Norah said. "Especially on this short notice."

Zaina scratched the back of her neck. "Actually, it was impossible from the start." She lifted her shoulders in an apologetic shrug directed at her sister. "I did consider it."

"So, this is it?" Liam said.

Grave faces met him but no one wanted to voice the words.

"What happens if we lose?" Haemir asked.

"If we lose, we'll have to fight our way out." Shade swept hard eyes through our group. "That's why none of you will be up there on that stage with me. If push comes to shove, you get out and don't look back. Is that clear? I'll have my guild on standby to back me up so don't worry about me."

Haemir opened his mouth to protest but before he could get a word out, the Master Assassin cut him off with a hand.

"This isn't up for debate," he said.

"Alright," Haela joined in. "But then we're gonna grab our bows and back you up from a distance. You know we got range in our shots."

Shade looked like he was about to argue but then he just heaved a long sigh. "Fine."

The energetic twin grinned. "See? He's learning you can't argue with reason."

"He's learning you can't argue with crazy," her brother corrected.

"Oh, shush," she muttered and gave him a playful shove.

Despite the heavy atmosphere, we all laughed at the constant sibling rivalry between those two.

"I have to get my guild ready." Shade picked up his swords and made for the opening but right before he got there, he stopped. For a moment, he just stood there with his back to us. Then he turned around. "Given that this might be the last time I see you, I just wanted to say thank you." His eyes held strange emotions. "Thank you for staying." Whirling back around, he flung open the tent flap. "Don't be here tomorrow."

And with that, he was gone. I glanced at the rest of my companions left in the room. These past weeks had been intense. Mischief had been managed, battles had been fought, secrets had been outed, and new friendships had been made. We had done what we could. Whatever else happened tomorrow, we at least knew that. Now, it was out of our hands. Tomorrow we would either win. Or we would die.

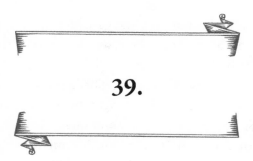

39.

Shocked black eyes met me as I climbed onto the platform. I smirked at him. Shade waited in the row at the back of the stage with the rest of the candidates and their attendants. Crossing my arms, I took up position next to him.

"I thought I told you to say away," he said in a low and deadly voice.

"And I thought I told you that following orders isn't exactly my specialty."

He barked a short laugh and shook his head. "If this goes sideways, we'll have to fight our way out but there are no weapons allowed on stage."

"You mean, there are no *visible* weapons allowed on stage."

His mouth curved into a smile as he glanced at me from the corner of his eye. "Correct."

I flicked a discreet hand in the direction of a building across the square. "The twins are waiting on that roof."

Blackspire cast long shadows in the setting sun, making it too dark for human eyes to see them from this distance, but Haela and Haemir had said they'd be there so I knew they were. Shade stared across the sea of murmuring people.

"Elaran?" he asked.

"Don't know. I haven't seen him since yesterday. Haemir said he often disappears when he's not sure where he stands. He likes to think alone, apparently."

The Master Assassin nodded. "The others?"

"Out there in the crowd somewhere. They wanted to see how it ends but promised to stay away from any fights."

"Unlike some."

I snorted and was just about to retort when the large man with the double chin who had been moderating all the speeches and debates stepped up on stage. All around us, the audience fell silent. He ran both hands down the front of his shirt to smoothen it before making his way to the front of the stage. I drew a deep breath. This was it.

"Ladies and gentlemen," he boomed across the area. "The votes are in."

My heart hammered against my ribcage. Zaina had explained that they would announce the exact number of votes each candidate had received from the different social classes. Since we already knew we were screwed with the nobles, the only votes that really mattered were the ones that would be announced after that. The workers. That included everyone. Merchants, sailors, laborers. Soldiers.

I had no idea how large a percentage of the citizens actually voted. All of them? Half? Ten percent? Estimating great numbers wasn't something I'd done often so I didn't even know how many people lived in this city. Therefore, when they announced the votes for one candidate, it was impossible to know how many had already voted and how many votes remained in each class.

"As usual, we will start with the position of High Priest," the heavyset man continued.

It took all my self-control not to pace back and forth across the stage while the votes were announced. The audience clapped and cheered enthusiastically when High Priest Sorah was announced as the winner. Sorah? I recognized that name. Wasn't he the current High Priest?

When the votes for Master of Knowledge were announced and Herodotos was named winner, my stomach twisted. They had both been the current holders of their position. Maybe this really was how all Pernula's elections went. The same three people were voted in again and again until they died. If that was the case, what chance had we ever really had to win?

"And now, for the position of General," the election supervisor called. "From the nobles we have the following votes. For Marcellus, nine thousand six hundred and fifty-three."

It's over nine thousand? Given that the number of nobles living in this city couldn't be all that many, I shook my head. I might not be able to accurately estimate population numbers but even I could figure out that we would get next to no votes from the elite class.

"For Konstantin, zero," he continued. "For Gregory, zero. For Suleiman, one hundred and sixty-three. For Jeremiah, zero. For Shade, forty-two."

Man, wasn't that depressing? Marcellus had gotten over nine thousand and Shade had only received forty-two. But the nobles had never been our target anyway, so I wasn't too discouraged.

"And now, to the votes from the workers. For Marcellus, one hundred and twenty-three thousand five hundred and twelve."

My eyes widened. That was a lot of people. I wondered if that was only people living in the actual city of Pernula or if that included people who lived out in the country. Why had I never asked Norah or Zaina about how many people lived inside the city walls and how many lived out on the land surrounding it?

"For Konstantin, zero. For Gregory, six hundred and seventy-two. For Suleiman, sixteen thousand eight hundred and six. For Jeremiah, two hundred and ten."

That treacherous heart of mine beat so hard I thought it would rip from my chest. I drummed my fingers against my thigh. If my calculations were correct, we needed one hundred and thirty-three thousand, one hundred and twenty-four votes to win. Was that even doable? How many soldiers were there in this city? How many of them voted? Had any merchants voted for us? I swore I could hear the blood rushing in my ears. Gods damn it. We had to win.

"For Shade..."

I held my breath.

"Eighty-six thousand nine hundred and seventy-eight."

Everything, the noise, the people, the stage, seemed to fade away as the whole world crashed down around me. We had lost. I forced short breaths in and out of my lungs. After everything we had done, after all the fights and assassination attempts we had survived, we had still lost the election. And now we would die.

"Arrest the terrorists!" General Marcellus bellowed across the stage.

I whipped my head towards Shade. He looked as stunned as I was but he recovered quickly and magicked two long daggers out of his clothes.

"Now we fight," he whispered to me.

Armed guards barreled onto the stage, heading straight for us, while the rest of their comrades formed a ring around the tall wooden platform. Shade's assassins would have a hard time getting here. I shot two stiletto blades into my palms and twisted around until I was back to back with Shade.

"General Marcellus!" the election official cried. "General Marcellus, what are you–"

Victory mixed with vengeance in the General's eyes as he raised his voice to carry through the evening air. "I didn't want to disrupt the election but now that the people of Pernula have chosen wisely, this terrorist will answer for his crimes before he can disappear back into the shadows he crawled out of. You see, I have come across incontrovertible proof that this assassin and his accomplices were behind both the warehouse explosion and the false star elf attack. But fear not, justice will be served."

"General Marcellus!" The announcer of the votes looked distraught as he tried to make himself heard over the clamor. "The–"

"Take them!" Marcellus screamed and stabbed a finger at us.

As the guards closed in, I gripped my knives tightly and crouched into an attack position. On the streets below us, black-clad men fought the ring of guards. Shocked gasps and cries of outrage floated up from the gathered audience.

"Why aren't the twins firing?" Shade hissed.

"I don't know."

Back to back, we moved in a slow circle while the guards and the General advanced. Malice gleamed in Marcellus' eyes as he enjoyed the moment for another few seconds before he spoke up again.

"Before you do anything stupid, I suggest you look at that roof over there." He pointed to the flat one close by that we had watched the duel from yesterday.

"General Marcellus!" the moderator tried again.

"Quiet!" the General boomed.

Since I had my back to the indicated roof, I trusted Shade to find whatever it was Marcellus wanted us to see. When the assassin just came to a screeching halt without saying anything, I twisted around as well. *Oh no.*

On top of the roof were three armed humans. In front of them, on his knees, was Elaran. Two men held swords to his throat while the third pressed the bolt of a crossbow into the back of his head. Now I knew why the twins hadn't fired any arrows. One wrong move and Elaran died.

"You have three seconds to drop your weapons and get down on your knees or your friend over there dies," Marcellus said.

Shit. I knew what I was going to do. That damn elf might be the grumpiest and rudest person I'd ever met but for some weird reason that only the gods knew, I considered him my friend. And I take care of my friends. There was no question about it. I was going to surrender.

"One..." Marcellus began. "Two..."

The problem was Shade. He was always a wild card since I never knew what his endgame was. If Shade refused, even if I surrendered, Elaran would die. I opened my mouth.

"Back!" Shade called over the ring of guards.

Just as I snapped my head towards him, two things happened. The commotion down on the ground stopped as the black-clad men withdrew and two daggers clattered to the floor.

It took half a second to realize that they hadn't been mine. Quick as a snake, I dropped mine as well.

"Good," General Marcellus said. "Now, on your knees."

Still holding our hands in the air, Shade and I got down on our knees. I glanced at the Master Assassin. He had actually surrendered to save Elaran. Shade's words from yesterday drifted through my mind. *There's nothing I won't do, no lines I won't cross, to get what I want.* It seemed as though there were lines he wouldn't cross. I wasn't sure if I was surprised or not.

Cold steel kissed my neck. Without turning my head, I watched another guard place a sword against Shade's throat as well. My heart slammed against my ribs. As long as he didn't plan on executing us right here, we would have a chance. The Assassins' Guild could rescue us from a dungeon but not if we were already dead. I closed my eyes. It couldn't end here.

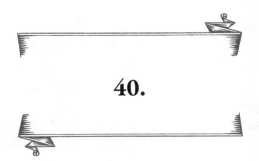

40.

A metallic boom echoed through the air. We all whirled towards it. Across the stage, the election official stood holding a heavy mace and in front of him lay a metal shield. He looked thoroughly out of breath as he let the large weapon fall to his side.

"General Marcellus," he panted. "All the votes have not been announced yet."

Marcellus scrunched up his eyebrows. "What are you talking about? The votes from both the nobles and the workers have already been announced."

"Yes, but for the position of General, the third class have voted as well."

"The third class?"

"Yes, I believe they call themselves *underworlders* now."

The General flicked a hand dismissively. "They don't vote."

"They have now."

"Fine." Marcellus blew out a frustrated sigh. "Announce their votes. But unless you can scrape together over forty-six *thousand* so-called underworlders, it won't matter. And I can tell you right now that an Underworld barely exists in this city."

The election official cleared his throat. "These are the votes from the Underworld. For Marcellus, zero. For Konstantin, zero.

For Gregory, zero. For Suleiman, zero. For Jeremiah, zero. For Shade, ninety-eight thousand four hundred and forty-four."

Deafening silence followed the announcement. I worked my tongue around inside my parched mouth. By all the gods, what had just happened?

"That can't be true." Marcellus ripped the paper from the moderator's hand and stared at it. "Are you seriously telling me that there are almost a hundred thousand people in this city who can't provide documents of employment? It's absurd! What would all those people be doing for a living? This has to be some kind of trick."

"I don't know," he replied. "But you know as well as I that you can't cheat the election. It appears as though the portion of the population that you... and I... and everyone else have been pretending doesn't exist, is far larger than we thought."

Marcellus stared unblinking at the piece of paper. My heart continued thumping in my chest. One hundred thousand underworlders? I had so not seen that coming. And what in the world had made them all vote?

"Ladies and gentlemen, let me introduce the new General of Pernula: Shade!" the votes announcer called across the square.

For a few seconds, nothing happened. Then, a cheer rose. It grew in volume until the whole area echoed with excitement. Shade rose from his knees and snapped his fingers at the closest guard.

"You," he said. "Make sure the elf on that roof is released unharmed. Right now."

The man snapped to attention. "Yes, General."

After climbing to my feet as well, I just continued staring dumbfounded at the people around me. How had this happened? I jerked back as I recognized a bunch of people standing in the mouth of an alley some distance away from the stage.

Vania stood with her arms crossed and a satisfied look on her face while Kildor and other people I recognized from their local tavern waited behind. Yngvild raised a large hand to his brow in a salute. A surprised smile spread across my face as I replicated the gesture.

Moving my eyes closer to the stage, I noticed another figure I recognized. At the mouth of a side street nearby, a woman with red hair had appeared. Her green eyes twinkled as she winked at me. I let out a stunned laugh.

While I moved towards the stairs at the back of the stage, Shade approached the detained former General. Hatred burned in his eyes but since his own former guards held him captive, he could do nothing more than glare.

"Marcellus," Shade said, his voice quiet and deadly. "If you're still here when the sun has set, you're a dead man." An evil grin flashed over the assassin's lips as he motioned for the guards to release their prisoner. "You'd better run."

For a moment, it looked like Marcellus was about to fight but then he thought better of it and thundered down the steps next to me. Sunset was only an hour out so the fallen General was in an understandable hurry.

"I'll be back," I said to Shade. "I just gotta talk to someone."

The new General of Pernula nodded. "We'll meet at the walls above the main gate in an hour and watch Marcellus hightail it out of here."

I snorted. "Good plan."

While Shade made his way back to the election official, I wove through the crowd until I reached my intended target. The copper-haired woman I had saved in that warehouse fire so many weeks ago stood at the front with her arms crossed while a mass of people filled the whole road behind her. Watching her warily, I stopped in front of her.

She held out her hand. "I'm Rowan."

Reaching out, I took it. "I'm–"

"The Oncoming Storm." She let out a brief chuckle. "Yeah, I know. After that stunt you pulled, standing up to the Rat King like that, there's probably not an underworlder in the whole city who doesn't know who you are by now."

"Oh, uhm, I see." I cleared my throat. "So, how's it going being the leader?" I nodded at the crowd behind her.

"Still sucks. But I don't trust any of the others to lead so I'm stuck with it."

I chuckled in recognition before turning serious again. "So, you got your whole gang to vote for Shade, then?"

"Figured I kinda owed you after you saved my life and all." Her eyes sparkled as she narrowed them at me. "Though I still remember the slaps."

"Yeah..." I scratched my jaw. "Sorry about that."

Rowan waved her hand as if to say that she'd been joking. "Besides, an assassin for General? Who would pass that up?" Before I had a chance to reply, she pressed on. "Alright, the Oncoming Storm. I've gotta go."

I watched her in silence for a second before making a decision. "My friends call me Storm."

"Storm." She cracked a smile and looked me up and down. "Well then, Storm, if you ever decide to set up shop in this city, come find me, won't you?"

"Will do."

After one last nod, she turned around and disappeared into the mass of people behind her. A few moments later, her whole crew moved out as well. I tore my eyes from their retreating backs and made for the next alley.

The scent of warm stones and spices filled my nose as I drew in a deep breath of air. All around me, the square was alive with excitement. People were chatting and gossiping about tonight's events while trying to push their way out of the packed space. Some had given up and remained rooted in their spots until the outer streets were clear but they were all engaged in intense discussions.

With basically none of the nobles to help him and mostly soldiers backing him from the working class, Shade would sure have an interesting start to his reign. But knowing what I knew about him, he would make it work regardless.

"Do you know who that was?" Yngvild said as soon as I was within earshot.

"Who?" I threw a look over my shoulder. "That woman over there? Yeah, her name is Rowan."

"That's Red Demon Rowan," the tattooed warrior said. When I just looked back at him with a blank face, he elaborated. "She took over the second biggest gang in the city after their leader died in the warehouse explosion. It's the only gang even close to rivaling the Rat King for power."

"Huh."

"How do you even know her?"

"I sorta saved her life back in that warehouse."

Both Yngvild and Vania looked at me with raised eyebrows. The blond warrior woman leveled her piercing eyes on me.

"Interesting things happen around you, don't they?" she said.

I let out a short chuckle. "I guess. Speaking of interesting things, what the hell happened tonight? I thought underworlders didn't vote."

Yngvild lifted his broad shoulders. "We haven't had anyone to vote for. Until now." He spread his hands. "Look, word of what you've been doing during this election has kind of spread. The ruined dinner, the drugged debate, the angry mob and the riot. All that. People talk." He shrugged again. "We're underworlders. We appreciate good shady skills when we see them."

"Precisely," Vania picked up. "And then when word was out that there was an assassin running for General, people actually started talking about voting. How often do you think an assassin and a thief run a political campaign in this city?"

Moving aside, I stepped out of the way as a group of well-fed gentlemen bustled past us on their way out.

"Not often?" I supplied while Yngvild and Vania joined me by the wall.

"You're right about that," the muscled warrior said and adjusted the battle axe on his back. "Then that night in the square with the Rat King, what you said about having an assassin General being good for us, it really resonated with a lot of people. The Rat King still hates your guts but even he understood the advantage of it and told his gang to vote for Shade. And after that, I think most crews decided to vote. Didn't know there were this many of us, though."

Wow. How about that? By sending the Rat King after me, Marcellus had actually started the process of his own demise. Though, I suppose I couldn't fault him too much. Not even the underworlders themselves had known how many they numbered. But now we knew. And the future looked bright for Pernula.

Casting a glance over my shoulder, I watched the sun edge towards the horizon. If I was going to make it to the city wall in time, I had to leave.

"I'm sorry, I've gotta..." I hiked a thumb over my shoulder.

"Same." Yngvild reached out and clasped my forearm. "Don't be a stranger."

After nodding and doing the same with Vania, I took off towards the main gate. This incredibly intense day was almost over. Almost. I grinned as I jogged through the streets still packed with people. First, I had a fleeing General to watch.

THE LONE FIGURE THAT was Marcellus tore out of the gate with not a minute to spare. His fast horse kicked up a cloud of dust as it disappeared into the grasslands. Leaning against the still warm stones, I watched him being swallowed by darkness.

"You let him go," I said to Shade.

"Had to," the assassin replied next to me. "Killing or imprisoning the previous General on my first day in power would've made a bad impression."

"True."

Shade was quiet for a moment before turning to face me again. His arm brushed against mine, sending a pulse through my body. "Thanks. For... uhm... you know, backing me up today."

"Yeah." Trying to ignore the strange sensation that had coursed through me, I scratched the back of my neck while my mouth drew into smile. "Anytime."

We watched the darkness fall around us in comfortable silence until our resident grumpy elf stalked over. He crossed his toned arms over his chest and leaned back against the wall next to Shade.

"You're incredibly arrogant and have an infuriating habit of ordering people about," he said to the assassin.

Shade lifted his eyebrows while I was completely unsuccessful at stifling a surprised snort. Elaran turned to scowl at me.

"And what are you laughing about? You're rude, violent, and the most disagreeable person I've ever met." He drew his eyebrows down. "But..."

We both watched him with amused expressions on our faces while a struggle raged behind Elaran's eyes. It seemed as though he had decided what to say earlier but was now suddenly unsure of whether he actually wanted to say it.

"You're underworlders," he finally pressed out. "You do things that I'll never understand and never approve of and I thought that meant you had no honor." He moved his eyes to Shade. "But then you fought me honorably and so well it ended in a tie. But then you fought dishonorably against Marcellus. *But then* you were ready to sacrifice your own damn life to save mine!"

No one said anything as the elf ran a hand over his tight side-braid and blew out a forceful breath.

"How was I supposed to make up my mind about what kind of person you are?" Elaran cleared his throat and shook his head as if to get himself back on track. "What I'm trying to say is, you do have honor. Maybe I don't always see it or understand it but you have your own kind of honor."

A memory from the under the ash trees of Tkeideru drifted past in my mind. *Honor?* I had scoffed at Elaran. *I have my own kind of honor.* He had used my own words from the summer we met. Turning away for a second, I wiped the wistful smile from my face before he could see it.

The tall elf straightened and held out his arm to the assassin. "Besides, anyone willing to risk his own life for me is a brother of mine."

Shade clasped his forearm. "Likewise."

I rolled my eyes and blew out a sigh. "Yep, this is officially a bromance."

"Shut up," both fighters said in unison.

However, before I had a chance to retort, Liam approached. Shade and Elaran exchanged a look, apparently taking the hint, and slid further away to give us privacy. Liam placed his arms on the gray stones next to me and leaned against the wall.

"Remember that couple I talked about who sell hats? The ones I made friends with?" he said.

Sand lodged under my nails as I picked at the stones. "Yeah?"

"They're opening up a new shop and they think I'd be the perfect salesman for it so they offered me a job." He paused for a few seconds. "I said yes."

Uncontrollable laughter bubbled inside me but I didn't let it out. Sell hats? After everything we'd been through, everything we'd done, he was going to sell hats? The sheer ridiculousness of it all threatened to have me break down so I used all my self-control to shove it aside.

"That's wonderful," I said instead. "Congratulations."

His face was caught somewhere between a happy grin and a sad smile. "But that means I'm staying. Here in Pernula." Putting a hand on my arm, he turned me towards him. "Storm, I finally know. This is what I was meant to do, where I was meant to be. With the money I make I can help Norah keep the school open and we can let even more poor kids go to school. And living here, I don't have to be that person I don't want to be. I can just be me."

"I'm really happy for you," I said and truly meant it. "I'm glad you've figured out what you want from life. And Norah is a lucky woman."

My friend blushed. "I really like her."

"I know. If staying here with her makes you happy, then I'm happy."

I gave his arm a short squeeze and showed him a bright smile but inside, my heart was shattering into a million pieces. My best friend was leaving me.

Liam drew me into a tight hug. "Thank you for saying that."

When he released me, it was only by sheer force of will that no trace of the heartbreak was visible in my face.

"Are you coming?" he asked and moved towards the stairs.

I shook my head. "I think I'm gonna stay for a while."

"Okay, I'll see you back at the school."

One by one, my friends climbed the steps back down to the ground while I watched the darkness. What an adventure it had been. We had actually won an election in a foreign country, despite Elaran's previous pessimistic predictions, and now Shade was the new General of Pernula. No war would be brought to our island as long as he held that position. And given everything I'd found out about that power-hungry assassin who also happened to be the real heir to the throne of Keutunan, I had a feeling that he was going to stay in power for quite some time. The war against Pernula had been won. By deceit and trickery. I cracked a grin. As most things in my life were.

"The others have left," Zaina said as she paused behind me. "I'm heading back too."

"Alright," I said before a sudden thought struck me. "Wait. I have a question."

"About?"

Turning around, I met her eyes. "What's Ashaana?"

Laughter erupted from her throat. "Funny." When I just stared at her, she drew back. "You're serious?"

"Yeah."

"You don't actually know? What you are? All this time..." She ran her hands through her curly black hair. "Wow."

"Well, to be fair, it was the only thing keeping you from slitting our throats there in that alley so I figured it was best to play along."

Zaina let out a hearty chuckle. "Good point."

"So, what is it?"

"Ashaana is another name for your people."

In my chest, my heart thumped against my ribs. This was it. I was finally going to find out what I was. "My people?"

"You're a Storm Caster."

Air rushed out of my lungs. A Storm Caster? What did that even mean? As if she had heard my thoughts, Zaina continued.

"I don't know much about it, no one does, because your people are very rare and very secretive. They exist, but I'm afraid that's about as much as I can tell you." She rubbed her hands up and down her arms. After clapping a hand to my shoulder, she moved towards the stairs. "I'll leave you to it."

The darkness inside me lay quiet, oblivious to the monumental truth I had, at long last, learned about myself. I still didn't know how it worked or how to control it, but now I had a lead. Excitement built in my chest as I stared out into the darkened wilderness. There were others like me. Out there. Somewhere.

Finding them would probably not be easy. It might take years and require lots of threats, bribery, and intimidation. But I was good at that. And when I wanted something, I made sure I got it. A great challenge awaited me but at least now I knew what I was. I was a Storm Caster.

Acknowledgements

Thank you for accompanying Storm on another adventure. Writing a book and sharing it with the world can be terrifying but with support from wonderful readers like you, it's also an amazing experience. Thank you for your kindness and generosity.

I would also like to say a huge thank you to my family and loved ones. Mom, Dad, Mark, thank you for everything you do for me. I love you and I don't know what I would do without you. Lasse, Ann, Karolina, Axel, Martina, thank you for all your support and encouragement. It truly brightens my day.

Another group of people I would like to express my gratitude to is my wonderful team of beta readers: Deshaun Hershel, Jennifer Nicholls, Luna Lucia Lawson, Orsika Péter, and Stephanie Good. Thank you for the time and effort you put into reading the book and providing helpful feedback. Your suggestions and encouragement truly makes the book better.

To my extraordinary copy editor and proofreader Julia Gibbs, thank you for going out of your way to help me when disaster struck. It means the world. After you have gone through my books, I always feel much more confident about publishing them.

I am also very grateful to Dane Low, the amazingly talented designer from ebooklaunch.com who made the absolutely stunning cover for this book. Dane, thank you for this gorgeous cover. You knocked it so far out of the park with this one that we're not even in the same city anymore.

Another person I would like to express my gratitude to is Ariel, the owner of the book box company called No Shelf Control. Ariel, thank you for everything you have done for me. I am truly lucky to have met you.

I am also very fortunate to have friends both close by and from all around the world. My friends, thank you for everything you've shared with me. Thank you for the laughs, the tears, the deep discussions, and the unforgettable memories. My life is a lot richer with you in it.

Before I go back to writing the next book, I would like to once again say thank you to you, the reader. Thank you for being so invested in the world of the Oncoming Storm that you continued the series. If you have any questions or comments about the book, I would love to hear from you. You can find all the different ways of contacting me on my website, www.marionblackwood.com. There you can also sign up for my newsletter to receive updates about coming novels. Lastly, if you liked this book and want to help me out so that I can continue writing books, please consider leaving a review. It really does help tremendously. I hope you enjoyed the adventure!